Doctor Vita

Rick Novak

ALL THINGS

THAT MATTER

PRESS

Praise for *The Doctor and Mr. Dylan*, by Rick Novak

"What is difficult to believe is that this is a first novel: Rick Novak writes so extremely well that likely he will answer the pleas of his readers and continue this 'hobby.' He could very well become one of the next great American physician authors. Medicine and writing can and do mix well in hands as gifted as Rick Novak. Highly Recommended."
– Grady Harp, Art and Poetry Reviewer, Poets and Artists magazine, Amazon Hall of Fame Reviewer, Amazon Top 100 Reviewer

"Author Rick Novak is an experienced anesthesiologist on the faculty of Stanford. This gives him a real edge in creating a murder mystery about what many think could be the perfect crime."
– The San Francisco Book Review

"This is a bang-up debut from a writer who understands timing and is able to deliver hairpin turns, particularly involving the courtroom drama, that you would expect from a book of this genre."
– Norm Goldman, BookPleasures

"A head-scratching mystery, guaranteed to keep you riveted until the last page. I read the last third of the book in a single post-midnight sitting, not able to wait for the resolution."
– Michael Champeau, MD,
Treasurer, American Society of Anesthesiologists

Doctor Vita

ISBN 13: 9781732723764

Library of Congress Control Number: 20199434879

Cover design © by All Things That Matter Press
Published in 2019 by All Things That Matter Press

Dedicated to Zachary, Theo, and Oliver Novak

1 ~ THE BRICKLAYER

Alec Lucas's first contact with FutureCare came in operating room #19 at the University of Silicon Valley Medical Center where his patient Elizabeth Anderson blinked into the twin suns of the surgical lights hanging from the ceiling. A clear plastic oxygen mask covered Elizabeth's nose and mouth, her cheeks were pale and tear-stained, and a strand of gray hair protruded from a blue paper bonnet. Her hand trembled as she reached up to remove the mask.

"I'm scared," she said.

"I'm not," said Dr. Lucas, who was her anesthesiologist. A green paper mask covered his face, but his pale blue eyes sparkled at her. He hummed to himself as he injected a dose of midazolam into Elizabeth's IV to relax her.

"Am I crazy to go through this?" she said. "A 78-year-old lady with cancer?"

"We're hoping your cancer can be cured with surgery," Alec said. "Right now, you're doing great. Everything is perfect. Have a wonderful dream."

Elizabeth had cancer of the stomach and presented today for robot-assisted laparoscopic surgery to remove half her stomach. It was a huge surgery—a risky surgery. Alec wondered why they were doing this operation on this lady. He questioned the aggressive strategy for a woman this old, but his job was to anesthetize, not to philosophize.

He'd seen pre-surgery anxiety like hers hundreds of times. The best way to cure her fears was to get her off to sleep. He injected doses of propofol and rocuronium into her intravenous line. The drugs flowed into Elizabeth's arm, and within ten seconds her eyes closed. He inserted the lighted blade of a laryngoscope into her mouth and visualized the white and shining upside-down "V" of her vocal cords, hovering in a sea of pink tissue. He slid a hollow plastic tube between the cords and into the blackness of the trachea beyond. Then he activated the ventilator which blew a mixture of oxygen and sevoflurane through the tube into her lungs.

"I haven't worked with you before, Dr. Lucas," said the circulating nurse who stood at the patient's side. "My name is Maggie."

"Of course you've never worked with me," he said. "I told the nursing supervisor I never wanted to work with Maggie." Then he winked at her and said, "We haven't worked together because today is my first day on staff here. I've been at the University of Chicago since my first day of medical school. After fifteen years of shoveling snow, it was time to give California a try."

Alec looked up as the surgeon, Xavier Templeton, entered the room. A tall scrawny man, Templeton had pale hairless matchstick arms that looked better hidden within a surgical gown. His bushy eyebrows met in the midline, and his left eye squeezed in an involuntary tic.

Templeton's hands wouldn't touch Elizabeth Anderson's skin or stomach today. His hands would control two levers on a console worthy of a spacecraft, and each move he made would be translated into the movement of a five-armed machine named the Michelangelo III, also known as The Bricklayer.

The five slender mechanical arms of The Bricklayer, dull gunmetal gray in color, dangled like the legs of a giant spider above Elizabeth Anderson's abdomen. Each arm was draped in clear plastic to keep The Bricklayer sterile when it entered her body through tiny incisions.

Alec accepted his role of goaltender at the Pearly Gates. His assignment was to keep Elizabeth Anderson asleep and alive, while Templeton and The Bricklayer resected her tumor.

Twenty minutes into the surgery, Xavier Templeton sat on a chair in the corner of the room with his back to the operating table and peered into a binocular stereo viewer. His hands maneuvered two levers on the console before him. On the operating table, the five robot arms reached into the abdomen though five one-centimeter incisions. One of the arms held a camera on a thin metal rod, movable at the surgeon's control. A seventh-year resident worked as a surgical assistant and attached appropriate operating instruments to the other 18-inch-long robot arms.

The two surgeons murmured to each other in quiet voices. Alec watched the surgery on a large flat screen video monitor that hung above him. He saw pink tissues, robot fingers moving, and a lot of irrigating and blunt dissection. The surgery was going well, and Alec made only minor adjustments in his drug doses and equipment as needed.

Then one thing changed.

One of the robot fingers on the video screen convulsed in staccato side-to-side slicing movements of its razor-sharp tip. A clear plastic suction tube exiting from the patient's abdomen lurched and became an artery of bright red blood. The scarlet tube emptied into a bottle two feet in front of Alec. In sixty seconds the three-liter bottle was full of blood. Fifty-eight seconds prior to that, Alec was on his feet and both hands were moving. A flip of a switch sent a stream of fluid through the biggest IV into the patient. He turned off all the anesthesia gases and intravenous anesthetic medications.

"Big time bleeding, Dr. Templeton," Alec shouted to the surgeon.

As fast as he could infuse fluid into two IVs, Alec couldn't keep up with the blood loss draining into the suction tube. The blood pressure went from normal to zero, and a cacophony of alarms sounded from the anesthesia monitoring system.

Templeton descended from his perch on the far side of the room and put on a sterile gown and gloves. He took a scalpel from the scrub tech and in one long stroke made an incision down the midline of the abdomen from the lower end of the breastbone to the pubic bone. With two additional long swipes, the left and right sides of Elizabeth Anderson parted. A red sea rose between them. The surgical resident and the scrub tech held suction catheters in the abdomen, but the stream of blood bubbled upward past the catheters. Templeton cursed and reached his right hand deep to the posterior surface of the abdominal cavity feeling for the blood vessel on the left side of the spinal column. He found it and squeezed the empty and pulseless aorta.

Alec looked at the monitors. The blood pressure was zero, and the electrocardiogram showed the heart was whipping along at a rate of 170 beats per minute. His patient had one foot in the grave. "Have you got control up there?" he screamed at Templeton.

"God damn it! I'm squeezing the aorta between my fingers," Templeton answered. "As soon as I can see, I'll put a clamp on the vessel. The bleeding is everywhere. I can't see a damn thing."

Templeton's face, mask, hat, and gown were drenched with the blood of Elizabeth Anderson. His unibrow was a red and black dotted line.

"Fire up the Maytag," Alec said to Maggie. "Call the blood bank and activate the massive transfusion protocol." Alec bent over the Maytag, a rapid blood infusion device with a bowl the size of a small washing machine. He turned the Maytag to its top flow rate. The machine hummed and spun, and the basin of IV fluid emptied into Elizabeth Anderson through a hose as wide as a small hot dog.

Despite the infusion of fluid, her blood pressure peaked at a dismal 65/40. "Have you found the hole yet?" he said to Templeton.

"Torn aorta. There are multiple holes—the aorta's leaking like a sprinkler hose," Templeton said without looking up. His left eye was blinking and squeezing repeatedly as he worked. "It's terrible. The inferior vena cava is shredded and the blood from the lower half of her body is pouring out into her abdomen. The blood is everywhere." Blink, squeeze. "Her vessels are falling apart like tissue paper."

An orderly ran into the operating room carrying a red plastic beer cooler. Alec grabbed the cooler and popped off the top. Inside were six units of packed red blood cells, six units of fresh frozen plasma, and six units of platelets from the blood bank. "Check all the units and let's get them flowing," he said to Maggie.

Maggie picked up each bag and double-checked the patient's name and the unit numbers with a second nurse, and then handed the entire cooler to Alec. He drained each of the units of blood products into the basin of the Maytag, and the bowl hummed and pumped the blood into Elizabeth Anderson. The blood pressure began to climb, but one look at the crimson suction tubes exiting the patient's stomach told Alec they were still in trouble. The bleeding wasn't slowing. Blood was exiting faster than he could pump it in.

"We need a second cooler of blood products stat," he said. Maggie picked up a telephone and relayed the order to the blood bank.

Alec looked at the surgical field, and the patient's blood was everywhere—on Templeton's face, hands, gown, on the surgical drapes and on the floor. It was everywhere but where it needed to be—inside her blood vessels. Templeton's resident was jamming a suction catheter into the abdomen next to his fingers, trying to salvage as much blood as he could.

"Damn it," Templeton said. "She's still bleeding, and now she's bleeding pink piss water. I can see through her blood, it's so dilute. How much fluid have you given her?"

"Six units of blood, six units of plasma, six units of platelets, and eight liters of saline."

Alec glanced at the monitors and saw that her blood pressure had plateaued at a near-lethal level of 40/15.

"Her blood isn't clotting anymore," Templeton said. "The blood's oozing and leaking everywhere I place a suture."

Alec palpated her neck, and there was no pulse. "She has no blood pressure and no pulse," he said. "We need to start CPR."

Templeton's resident placed the palms of his hands on Elizabeth Anderson's breastbone and began chest compressions. The patient's heart rate of 180 beats per minute slowed to 40 with premature beats and pauses between them. After twenty seconds of a slow irregular rhythm, her heartbeat tracing faded into the quivering line diagnostic of ventricular fibrillation.

Alec injected one milligram of epinephrine and screamed, "Bring in the defibrillator."

A second nurse pushed the defibrillator unit up to the operating room table. Templeton charged the paddles, applied them to the patient's chest, and pushed the buttons. Elizabeth Anderson's body leapt into the air as the shock of electrical energy depolarized every muscle of her body. All eyes turned to the ECG rhythm, and it was worse. Flat line.

"Damn it. Give me the scalpel back," Templeton said. He carved a long incision between the ribs on the left side of Elizabeth Anderson's chest and inserted his hand into her thorax.

"I have her heart in my hand and I'm giving her direct cardiac massage," he said. Alec looked at the monitors, and the direct squeezing of the heart was doing nothing. The blood pressure was still zero, and now blood was oozing from the skin around her IV sites as well as from the surgical wounds in her abdomen.

Elizabeth Anderson's heart was empty. Her blood vessels were empty. Her blood pressure had been near-zero for twenty-five minutes.

"What do you think, sir, should we call it?" Templeton's resident said.

Templeton pulled his hand out of Elizabeth Anderson's chest and looked at the clock. "I pronounce her dead as of 8:48 a.m. Damn, damn, damn it!"

Alec reached over and turned off the ventilator. The mechanical breathing ceased, and there was nothing left to do. He looked down at Elizabeth Anderson's bloated face. Two strips of clear plastic tape held her eyes fastened shut, and her cheeks were as white as the bed sheet she rested on. A length of pink tape held the breathing tube fixed to her upper lip, and blood oozed from her nose and from the membranes between her teeth. This lady walked into the University of Silicon Valley Medical Center today hoping for a surgical miracle, and instead she was going to the morgue.

Xavier Templeton peeled his gloves off. "Goddamn it. The fricking robot went berserk. Sliced into the artery like a goddamned hedge trimmer. Now I have to tell the family she's dead. Goddamn damn it." He scowled in Alec's direction. "Are you coming with me, Dr. Lucas?"

Alec nodded a yes. He looked at the gloomy outline of The Bricklayer's arms and then back at Templeton. Templeton was a fool to blame the medical device for his own ineptitude. The machine could do no wrong on its own.

This was the surgeon's fault. Alec had heard it all before. *Accept compliments and deflect all blame*—it was an adage as old as the profession of surgery.

Templeton commanded The Bricklayer. The Bricklayer was no better than the human hands that led it.

2 ~ MEDITATION ROOM

The Meditation Room was a six-foot by ten-foot room furnished with two navy blue couches, an end table, and a lamp. The room was adjacent to the surgical waiting area. In contrast to the stark linoleum on the hallway floor outside, this room had beige wall-to-wall carpeting. The walls were also beige, and a solitary framed print of Van Gogh's *Sunflowers* hung over one of the couches.

Ninety-nine percent of the time the room was vacant. When Templeton walked into the Meditation Room this morning, three women huddled together on the couch under the *Sunflowers*. Alec spent a few minutes with the family before the surgery, and knew the older woman was Elizabeth Anderson's daughter, and the two teenagers flanking her on the couch were Mrs. Anderson's granddaughters. The granddaughter on the left appeared to be about sixteen years old, her face wan behind shoulder-length wavy blonde hair. Her sister was younger, perhaps thirteen, with mousy colored hair and braces on her teeth. Both wore faded blue jeans and short sleeved blouses.

Templeton and Alec sat down on the couch across from them. Alec looked at the three women, and it was apparent they had no idea anything had gone wrong. The girls were staring at the floor and looking bored while their mother held a nervous smile as she waited for the two doctors to speak.

"I'm very sorry to be sitting here with the news I'm about to give you," Templeton said in a solemn voice. The surgeon's eye was twitching and squeezing faster than it had in the operating room. "Elizabeth . . . didn't make it."

The girl on the left screamed, "It can't be."

"No, I'm afraid it's the truth," he said.

She cried out a guttural "No," before covering her face with both hands and breaking into tears. The mother closed her eyes and began to shake in silence. The granddaughter on the right buried her face against her mother's breast. Alec reached for a box of facial tissues and passed it toward the three women.

Templeton began explaining. "She had an episode of severe bleeding from the biggest artery and the biggest vein in her body," he said. "I tried to place clamps to stop the bleeding. It was a very difficult problem. Dr. Lucas, the anesthesiologist, did an excellent job of transfusing the blood that she needed, but she kept bleeding and bleeding until her heart gave out. In the end—"

"Oh God," wailed the younger girl.

Templeton stopped talking and stared at his fingers for a moment. "In the end, the bleeding was so excessive that her blood pressure dropped to zero and her heart failed. Even though we did everything that could be done, we failed to revive her."

The girls' mother was a younger, less-wrinkled version of Elizabeth Anderson. Her hair was dyed a rosy hue and her eyes were a deeper shade of blue. She asked, "Can we see her?" with a voice barely audible. Her chin trembled as she waited for her answer.

"No, not yet," Templeton said. "When her body is ready to be seen, someone will let you know."

"How could this happen?" the elder granddaughter said. "She's in the middle of this gigantic hospital, and you guys weren't able to keep her alive? Why didn't you get some other doctors in there? Someone else who could save her?"

Templeton glanced at Alec, and Alec sucked in a breath through his front teeth. He was about to answer the question when Templeton said, "I assure you, everything that could be done, was done. She would not cease bleeding, and her heart stopped. I . . . I'm very sorry."

While Alec listened his thoughts circled around one question: How could this guy Templeton butcher a patient and send her to the grave in less than one hour? The girl was right. Templeton and The Bricklayer had carved up Elizabeth Anderson with such brutality that all the resources of a twenty-first century university medical center had been insufficient to save her.

"The surgery was technically difficult. I'm very sorry," Templeton repeated. "Dr. Lucas was monitoring her heart and breathing throughout the surgery. He can assure you, as I have, that we did everything that we could do to save her. The bleeding was unexpected, and our treatment failed to bring her back."

The mother brushed back her tears and stared at Alec. She was almost as pale as Elizabeth had been following the hemorrhage.

Alec tried to imagine what he'd want to hear if their roles were reversed, but he was still at a loss. At last he sucked in a deep sigh and spoke up. "She was content and calm before she went to sleep. She was unconscious throughout the whole ordeal, and she didn't suffer at all."

The mother hugged one daughter with each arm, and said, "Praise God for that. When I go someday, I hope I'm as lucky as that."

Alec nodded, but his stomach tightened at her choice of words. There had been nothing lucky about Elizabeth Anderson's day.

The elder granddaughter must have had the same thought. "You guys make me sick," she said. "My Grammy is dead. If you two had never touched her, I could be sitting at home with her and talking to her right now. I know it, and you know it, too. I hate you two, and I'll hate you forever. Forever!" She stood and ran out of the room. Her mother stood and left to follow her. The younger granddaughter dabbed her eyes one last time, and then walked out.

Xavier Templeton walked out, too.

Alec Lucas took off his new USV ID badge and studied his photograph. The picture had been taken the day before, and the blonde-haired, blue-eyed, Neo-Californian in the picture smiled like he'd just won the lottery. Alec shook his head and stuffed the ID into his shirt pocket. Then he stood and walked out of the Mediation Room alone.

***

At eight o'clock that night, Alec climbed the front steps of the two-bedroom house he'd rented one mile from the USV Medical Center. He entered the living room and threw his white coat on the single piece of furniture he owned, a black leather couch. The walls of the small home were bare except for a flat screen TV on the ledge over the fireplace. His desktop computer blared Kendrick Lamar through speakers in the ceiling as Alec moved into the adjoining kitchen.

He filled a glass half full of ice and poured in enough tequila to numb the pain of his day. In three swallows the tequila was gone. He filled his lungs with the still air and released the loudest sound he'd ever made. It was a sound of a single profanity, screamed until there was no more breath left in him. He hammered his fist full force against the pale green sheetrock of the living room wall. The wall won—his knuckles emerged scraped and hemorrhaging.

Alec staggered into the bedroom and peeled off his white cotton shirt and khakis. He threw himself down on the bed, drew the covers over his head, and fell into the restless sleep of a tormented man.

3 ~ FUTURECARE

The first rays of sunrise tracked through Alec's bedroom window, and the chiming ring from his cell phone woke him up. He took the call and said, "Lucas here."

A gruff male voice replied, "This is Dr. Leroy Andrews, the Chief of Staff at USV Hospital and Clinics. I need to talk to you in my office. Be here at nine a.m."

"What's this about?"

"You know what it's about. I want to talk about your dead patient. My office is on the 14th floor. I'll see you at nine." There was a click, and the phone went dead.

***

Alec arrived at the Office of the Chief of Staff at 8:58 a.m. The door was open, but the office was deserted. He stepped into the room and sat down on a green vinyl-covered chair near the doorway. The room was tiny, with pale yellow walls and no windows. A wide metal desk was covered with three computer monitors and multiple stacks of papers. Three other chairs were positioned in an arc in front of the desk. A bookcase stood behind the desk. Alec noted that most of the shelves were covered with textbooks of pathology. He looked at his watch and wondered where the hell the Chief of Staff was.

At the stroke of 0900 hours, a stocky fifty-something-year-old man wearing a starched white coat walked into the room. The man was scowling, and he tugged at his long gray beard with one hand as he rubbed the top of his hairless cue ball head with the other.

Alec stood, offered a handshake, and said, "Hi, I'm Alec Lucas."

"I know who you are, Lucas," he said, ignoring Alec's outstretched hand. "I'm Leroy Andrews, and I'm the Chief of Staff here. As soon as Dr. Vinscene and Dr. Rovka arrive, we'll begin." Dr. Andrews sat behind his desk and started tapping the keyboard of his computer.

At five minutes past nine, a short round gentleman entered the office. Alec studied the man's face. He was an older fellow with white eyebrows, a pointed white goatee and a jovial smile—a dead ringer for the tycoon in the Monopoly game.

"Good morning, Professor Rovka," the Chief of Staff said to him. He stood and shook Rovka's hand. "Can we expect the new edition of your textbook soon?"

Rovka smiled. "It'll be published in the fall. Lord knows, now that FutureCare is here, if anyone will ever read the damn book."

"And the worried wealthy are still paying cash at your San Francisco clinic?"

"The Rovka Clinic remains a success." The white-haired man sat down, turned to Alec, and said, "Hello, my name is Henri Rovka."

"It's a pleasure to meet you, sir," Alec said.

"I apologize for being late," Rovka said. "I just left Dr. Vinscene's office, and with regrets, he said he's needed in the operating room, and he won't make it for this meeting."

"Very well," Andrews said. He anchored both elbows on the desktop and leaned toward the two men. "I don't have much time, so let's begin. Dr. Rovka is here because he's the Chairman of the Quality Assurance Committee. I invited Dr. Vinscene, the Chairman of Anesthesia, to be here as well, but we'll carry on in his absence. I brought us together this morning to talk about Xavier Templeton's patient who died in the operating room yesterday."

Andrews ran his right hand across the bald expanse of his skull and said, "Dr. Lucas, because you're a recent hire from the University of Chicago, you're an unknown to us. Why don't you tell us your version of what went on in operating room #19 yesterday?"

"The lady was old," Alec said. "She had cancer of the stomach, but she was otherwise healthy. She had a normal heart and lungs. Everything was routine until the surgeon transected the aorta and inferior vena cava with the robot. Massive hemorrhage ensued, and we began an aggressive transfusion. Within twenty minutes, she was persistently hypotensive and had a cardiac arrest. We were unable to resuscitate her."

"Why the cardiac arrest? Did she bleed that much?" Andrews said.

"She sure did. She spilled her entire blood volume. I could see the hemorrhage clear as day on the monitors. Her heart stopped because hearts don't pump if there's no blood in them."

"Templeton's an experienced and careful surgeon," Andrews said. "I don't remember him ever having a death like this."

"Massive bleeding," Alec said. "Nobody's fault but the surgeon. He struck me as incompetent."

"Don't think so," Andrews said. "I talked to Xavier Templeton last night, and he told me the robot sliced the lady to death. He also said you didn't transfuse the blood fast enough. What do you have to say about that?"

"Tons of bleeding. Blaming the bleeding on the robot is like blaming a car accident on the steering wheel. And blaming an empty heart on me in this case is ridiculous, if you ask me."

"I did ask you," Andrews said, "but your answer differs from Dr. Templeton's, and he's the Chairman of Surgery, while you've worked here for one day. Who am I going to trust?" He turned to Dr. Rovka and said, "Henri, what do you think?"

Rovka took a deep breath and looked into Alec's eyes. "I believe we need more information. We need a comprehensive review of the electronic medical record. Are you familiar with the USV electronic medical record system, Dr. Lucas?"

"My area of research is computer systems management in critical care medicine. I'm not an expert on your system yet, because this is only my second day here."

Dr. Andrews interrupted. "I have your curriculum vitae in front of me here, Dr. Lucas. You look good on paper, but your first case at the University of Silicon Valley was a disaster, and I don't like disasters. I intend to figure out what went wrong, and you'd better hope you didn't screw up. This lady's death was an unexpected tragedy, and our Quality Assurance and Peer Review committees will spend endless hours studying the circumstances. As of this moment, you my friend are 0 for 1, and you're under the microscope. I've got a meeting with the CEO now, and you two will have to excuse me. Thank you for coming, Dr. Rovka." Andrews picked up a manila folder from his desk and stood up.

Alec stood and towered over the Chief of Staff. "With all due respect, Dr. Andrews, you're out of line. I made no errors, and I don't like your tone of voice."

Andrews glared back at him. "You better get used to my tone of voice, Dr. Lucas, because this is my hospital. This isn't Illinois, and all your academic publications aren't going to mean squat if you continue to have complications like this one."

Alec's fingers curled into fists, but he made no other move. The conversation was over. Andrews spun on his heel and walked out of the office.

Dr. Rovka reached out, touched Alec's shoulder, and pointed to the door. The two men stood and exited without speaking. They walked down the hall toward the elevators. At that point, Rovka's face curled into a half-smile and he said, "What do you think of Dr. Andrews?"

"He's an asshole," Alec said. "Is he always like that?"

"No, sometimes he's worse. But he can be charming when he needs to."

"Right. I'll bet he works comedy clubs in his spare time."

"There isn't much spare time when you're running a medical center of this size. He's not all bad. He wants the facts as much as you and I do. Dr. Lucas, tell me the truth. Do you think Dr. Templeton was at fault?"

"I do."

"Xavier Templeton called me after the tragedy. He's one of my oldest and closest friends, and he was fighting mad. He said the FutureCare Michelangelo III operating robot ripped his patient's arterial and venous trees to shreds. He believes the machine assassinated the patient."

Alec's mouth hung open. "How could that happen? It's a five-armed extension of the surgeon's fingers. Blame the surgeon."

"Dr. Templeton said he did nothing wrong. He insists the robot blasted off on its own."

"C.Y.A.," Alec said. "Cover Your Ass. Do you think he's going to say, 'I'm a bungler who sliced up my patient because I'm incompetent with this high-tech gadget'?"

Rovka shrugged and spun the brim of his hat between his fingers. "Hear me now, Dr. Lucas. Something extraordinary happened yesterday. I talked to your chairman, Dr. Vinscene, this morning. We both fear the media may get a hold of this story and start mass hysteria—they may start printing stories of chaos erupting with the FutureCare System."

"What can I do?"

Rovka shrugged. "You're a bright young man. Help us figure out what happened. You have extensive computer background. And you were there when it happened. Dr. Vinscene has the highest respect for you, and you've published dozens of papers on the use of Medical Information Technology in the ICU. He told me of your fascination with FutureCare, and how your interest in the FutureCare System brought you to USV."

"It's true. I am fascinated with FutureCare. Who isn't? But you've got your own Medical Information experts at USV. Why not have the guys who built the System do the troubleshooting?"

"There's a conflict of interest. Our engineers installed the FutureCare System, and they may deny any problem exists. Last night I reviewed the digital tape of the Michelangelo III episode with the USV Information Systems team. We watched the robot dissecting the stomach, and neither I nor the engineers found anything irregular about the robot's movements. The digital record doesn't show the robot doing anything wrong. That leaves us with one explanation: Dr. Templeton erred. The digital record supports the diagnosis of human error."

"Yep. The surgeon screwed up," Alec said.

"But Xavier Templeton reviewed the digital tape with us as well, and he claims the digital tape is not representative of what happened."

"Not representative? What does that mean?"

"He says the tape has been altered. He insists that the machine's movements on the tape are dissimilar to what occurred in real time."

"That's a strange assertion."

"Something is wrong," Rovka said.

Alec walked over to the hallway window and gazed out over the southern expanse of San Francisco Bay. He shook his head and said, "Yesterday was awful. I was the last person to have a conversation with that lady. I promised to take good care of her. I can't forget the image of her pale bloated face when I turned the ventilator off for the last time, and I can't forget the image of her two grandkids bawling when we told them their grandmother was dead."

"Then we need to dig deeper into what happened to Elizabeth Anderson," Rovka said. "First off, if you're going to help me, you're going to need a tutorial on the FutureCare System. Come with me, and your education will begin. It's time you met Doctor Vita."

4 ~ VITA

Rovka and Alec took an elevator to the 7th floor where they proceeded through the waiting room of the Anesthesia Preoperative Clinic. At the end of a short hallway, they entered a small room marked "Private, Medical School Faculty Only."

Once inside, the two men sat on chairs facing each other, and Rovka set his black bowler hat on the table between them. Alec unbuttoned his white coat and inspected the room. It was a tiny space, no more than eight feet wide and four feet deep. Its only distinctive feature was a six-foot-square window in one wall. Instead of facing out toward the city surrounding the medical center, the window faced into a medical examination room which featured a solitary white sphere mounted on a pedestal.

"I reviewed tomorrow's operating room schedule," Rovka said, "and your first anesthetic will be on a man named Jake Mindling. Mr. Mindling is to have surgery on his throat, and he's going to arrive at this Anesthesia Preoperative Clinic room any minute now, on the other side of this two-way mirror." Rovka pointed to the window in front of them. "You're about to witness Dr. Vita at work. Have you ever seen an automated doctor machine inputting data from a live patient?"

"I have not," Alec said. "My area of research involves complex medical information transfer in ICU's and patient wards. I stay away from clinics."

Rovka looked at his watch and turned to the window. "The white sphere before you is Doctor Vita. Have you seen a Vita before?"

"I have not."

"Very well. Today you'll feast your senses on a Vita session, live and in color, as Mr. Mindling gets his pre-operative check-up." As Rovka spoke, an old man and an old woman walked into the examination room on the other side of the window and sat down in front of the white orb. "I met Mr. Mindling earlier this morning," whispered Rovka, "and I obtained his permission for us to observe his Vita session. The room has a microphone. Watch and listen."

Alec turned to the window where the man and woman faced the ivory sphere. The man was a huge fortress of a human being. He had three chins, hair that thinned at the temples, and a nose the size of a small potato. He wore a red bowling shirt that had "Jacob" sewn over the breast pocket. He sat down on the examination table, and the rustling of the paper against his wide buttocks broke the silence inside the room. The woman, one-third the size of the man, angled her pencil frame into the wooden chair beside him. Her salt and pepper hair hung down in bangs and touched the thick black ellipses of her eyeglasses. She clutched her purse and pulled down her skirt to cover her knees.

The glossy white metal of the Dr. Vita sphere stood on a table opposite the Mindlings. Dr. Vita was eighteen inches in diameter and mounted on a level with Mr. Mindling's face. Two yellow lights, each the size of a chicken's egg, attracted one's attention to the front of the sphere. The yellow lights flickered and an electronic voice with a pleasant sonorous tone sounded from the orb, "Please insert your Health Assessment Card into the purple slot."

The patient pulled out his wallet and removed a purple card.

"That's his HAC," Rovka said, "It's an abbreviation for 'Health Assessment Card.' If you were to look closely, you'd see the printing on it says, *"No symptom too small—The Health Assessment Card of the United States of America."'*

Alec nodded and kept his eyes fixated on the examination room.

Mr. Mindling was leaning toward the white sphere and examining its face. There was a horizontal purple slot at the equator of the sphere. He slid the card into the purple slot, and a previously black video screen lit up below it. The screen was a dark rectangle, blank except for a curved line of yellow dots which resembled a smiling mouth.

The yellow eyes of the sphere flickered again, and the machine said, "My facial recognition software confirms your identity. Good morning, Mr. Jake Mindling. You are not alone today. Who is your visitor?"

"This is my wife, Marion."

"Thank you. Jake, what brought you to the doctor?"

"I don't see no doctor here," Mindling said.

"I apologize for not introducing myself earlier. I am Dr. John Vita. Through my connection to all data on the Medical Web, I am fitted with a complete catalog of twenty-five different medical specialties, including internal medicine, gynecology, surgery, pediatrics, psychiatry, emergency medicine, dermatology, neurology, and orthopedic surgery to name a few."

The husband and wife looked at each other, and then looked back at back at the orb. Marion Mindling broke the silence. "Jake snores so loud I can't sleep. He's going to have an operation tomorrow to fix the snoring." She looked at the two yellow eyes, then back at her husband.

Jake rubbed his hands together and avoided eye contact with his wife. He stared at the machine.

"Tell me more about the snoring," Dr. Vita said.

"He snores so loud I have to sleep on the couch," Marion said. "For the past five years."

"Your electronic medical record shows that you have obstructive sleep apnea. Do you have any other complaints?"

"I don't have any complaints. I'm doing this to keep my wife happy." He glanced at Marion, who didn't look happy at all. Her eyes were bugging out at Dr. Vita, and she was on the edge of her chair.

"I read about sleep apnea on the Internet," Marion said. "Sleep apnea causes all the snoring, and it makes him tired in the morning, grumpy, and gives him headaches. And he has less interest in sex."

Mindling raised both eyebrows and waved his hand at his wife to stop this line of conversation.

"I have some questions for the patient." Dr. Vita said. "Do you feel daytime fatigue?"

Jake shrugged and said, "No."

"Do you have headaches?"

"No."

"Is it true that you have less interest in sex?"

"Sex is not something the Mindlings do anymore. It's not a big part of our life," he said.

Dr. Vita paused, as if pondering this fact. Then he said, "Do you ever have chest pain or shortness of breath with exercise?"

"No."

"Do you have a history of high blood pressure?"

"No."

"Any history of weight gain?"

"I gained about ten pounds in the last year or two."

The Dr. Vita unit went on to ask a complete series of questions on medications, allergies, family history, social history, and a complete review of symptoms. At the end of the questions Dr. Vita asked, "What's your understanding of where you are with your illness?"

"Where I'm at? I'm sitting in this fricking room talking to a white steel ball, that's where I'm at."

"What quality of life do you desire? What abilities are so critical to you that you cannot live without them?"

Mindling shook his head and rolled his eyes. "I don't know what you're talking about," he said.

"Finish the sentence for me: I'd rather be dead than not be able to …."

Mindling looked frowned and said, "I'd rather be dead than not be able to go elk hunting with my brother at his ranch in the mountains north of Ogden, Utah. I look forward to that every year." He glanced at his wife, and then added. "And of course, I want to wake up next to Marion every morning. She's the light of my world."

Marion was clearly pleased by this addendum. She smiled and patted his hand.

"Thank you," Dr. Vita said. "That concludes our interview. Now please strip down to your underwear and I will examine you." The final "you" echoed off the bare walls of the clinic as Jake looked at Marion with a despairing look.

"I don't like this," Mindling said. "What are you going to do, take a picture and beam it to the real doctor?" He pulled the collar of his shirt tighter around his neck.

"No. I have a projecting appendage for touching and examining patients. The sensory input on my appendage holds the equivalent of one thousand nerve endings per square inch and can differentiate the entire spectrum of firmness from spongy soft tissue to rock hard masses. My appendage has a digital camera and the ability to hear and record sounds from your body. You may think of my appendage as an extremity with touch, sight, and hearing senses. Are you prepared to see my appendage?"

Marion nodded yes, and the decision was made. Jake stood to remove his pants and shirt, and said, "Show me yours, and I'll show you mine." He followed with a nervous chuckle.

If Dr. Vita found this amusing, the machine chose not to reveal it. A door opened in the lower right quadrant of the sphere, and a thin metallic arm extended. It spanned the distance from the Vita unit to Mindling. On the end of the arm was a ball two inches in diameter, cream-colored with a purple crown. It looked like a turnip on a long stem. Mindling reached out and touched it. The turnip appeared soft, and it indented where he touched it.

"Stand up please," Dr. Vita said.

He stood, and the cream-colored ball moved over his body from his head to his feet. It made no sound and made no contact with his skin.

"Turn around please."

Mindling turned his back on the machine. The turnip moved over the posterior aspect of his body—he looked over his shoulder and watched the ball scan up and down, left and right over the surface of his back.

"Next you will feel me touching you," Dr. Vita said.

Mindling again looked over his shoulder as the Dr. Vita unit pushed the ball against his skin of his posterior thorax. When it was finished, it said, "Next I will examine your mouth and upper airway. Place your mouth in front of the probe, open as wide as possible, and say 'EEEE'." Mindling complied and opened his mouth until his jaw ached. The robot arm moved closer, and the light beamed into his oral cavity. The ball moved in so close that it seemed halfway into his mouth.

The scene reminded Alec of an apple inside the mouth of a cooked pig. He heard a whirring sound as the ball turned from side to side inside the patient's mouth.

Alec looked at the clock on the wall. The Vita unit had taken twenty minutes to ask its questions and now had been examining the patient for an additional five minutes.

"Please lie back on the table and pull your underwear down below your knees," Dr. Vita said.

Mindling clenched his teeth together. He slid back on the exam table and laid his head onto the white paper. He was facing the ceiling and the flickering florescent light above him as the sensor landed on his abdomen. It began at his belly button and circled outward in a clockwise path until the entire surface of his abdomen had been felt, listened to, and scanned.

"Whoa," yelped Jake, when the vibrating ball began rooting about under his scrotum and testicles. He squirmed and protested, "Enough, enough. My freaking problem is snoring, and I ain't been snoring with my balls." The turnip drew away and retracted toward the white orb. The turnip made a clicking sound just before it reentered the sphere, and the outer shell of the ball detached from the telescoping arm and fell into a garbage bucket on the floor.

Mindling sat up on the examining table and jammed his genitals back under the cover of his underwear. "Piece of shit machine. I'm done. Marion, let's get the hell out of here." He glared at the sphere in front of him.

Marion hadn't moved and showed no sign of changing. She looked from her husband back to the machine. "What do you think, Mr. Vita, sir?"

"I find the patient suitable for surgery and anesthesia tomorrow," replied Dr. Vita. "The soft parts of his throat collapse and make the snoring sound. They sometimes obstruct his breathing, consistent with the diagnosis of obstructive sleep apnea."

"That's why we're here," Marion said. "My sister Violet's husband had this same surgery. They cut out the back of his throat and put it in a jar. Now he has a wider passage to breathe and he doesn't snore anymore." She was back on the edge of her chair again.

"I will give you a printout with your diagnoses." A strip of yellow paper came out the undersurface of the white orb. Mindling tore the paper off and looked at the list of diagnoses and plans that the Dr. Vita unit had prescribed. He ran his eyes down the paper once and then pulled his fingers together to surround it and crush the paper into a little ball. He flipped the ball at his wife, stuffed his arms and legs back into his shirt and pants, and stomped out the door of the exam room without a word. Mindling frowned at a black sign with white letters hanging over the doorway of the examining room as he exited.

Alec read the sign for the first time himself.

The sign said:

MEDICAL CARE IS AN ENTITLEMENT
DR. VITA CARES FOR YOU
FUTURECARE NOW

Alec shuddered. He looked at the backs of his forearms and was surprised to see he was covered in goose bumps.

"What do you think?" Rovka said. He was smiling, almost smirking at Alec.

"The machine is fascinating. I'm impressed by the automatic speech recognition and conversation abilities. The machine seems . . . human. It doesn't look human, but it interacts like an intelligent being. If I hadn't seen it in person, I'd never have believed it. I've never seen anything that approaches it. It's clear the machine takes input from multiple sources—its camera, its voice recognition, and its encyclopedic medical knowledge—and then comes to statistical conclusions regarding diagnosis and therapy. I mean, a self-driving car's computer inputs data from multiple sources: cameras on all sides of the car, every pixel of the movement of other cars, pedestrians, or bicyclers, the speed of the vehicle, the direction, and all map data, and then a statistical analysis of the information results in safe decisions by the computer. But that's child's play compared to what I just saw Dr. Vita do. It's light years ahead of its time. The software designers were geniuses."

Rovka smiled. "I absolutely agree with you. I'm no computer expert, but for me—I just love the look of the Vita," he said. "I love the icy black monitor screen. When the screen is blank it serves as a mirror, did you notice? Patients like that. When the doctor has no face, what better than to see yourself in the doctor? It's as if Dr. Vita has you, the patient, right there inside of him. Or her. Some of the Vitas have female voices and personas."

"That's smart. How many Dr. Vitas does USV have?"

"I believe the number is approaching three thousand."

"If they ever perfect the module, Dr. Vitas could replace medical professionals," Alec said. "Could it replace a nurse practitioner someday?"

Rovka laughed out loud. "Dr. Vita isn't called Nurse Vita. It's called Dr. Vita for a reason. We believe it's ready to replace doctors."

Alec guffawed. "It's one thing to intake a history and input some crude form of a physical exam, but to replace a doctor the machine needs to think and reason."

"Ah, yes. Think and reason. You remember the IBM computer named Watson, the machine that played *Jeopardy* and beat the finest human players in the world?"

"I do. That was amazing. Watson's programmers had to input millions of facts and trivia information, and then they had to write detailed algorithms based on previous *Jeopardy* quiz show historical data. They had to teach Watson how to compare competing algorithms to decide whether it had sufficient confidence in the correct answer. Watson beat the best human *Jeopardy* contestants head to head. It's one of the pioneering success stories all the Artificial Intelligence gurus like to tout, but it's nothing compared to replacing a physician's mind."

"I agree," Rovka said. "I've always been a worshiper of expert human diagnosticians."

"As have I," Alec said. "And I have to be honest with you, my colleagues back at the University of Chicago are skeptical of the Dr. Vita concept."

"Why?"

"Medicine is both a science and an art," Alec said. "There's no way to program the art of medicine into a computer chip."

Rovka laughed. "In time you'll believe, as I have started to believe. The Dr. Vita unit is an empathetic module with encyclopedic memory and unlimited availability. For the masses, it's better than any alternative we can afford. The biggest challenges in the future of medical care won't be stem cell research, gene therapy, immunotherapy, or a cure for cancer, heart disease, or Alzheimer's, but rather who will deliver the care and how will we afford it? Dr. Vita is the answer."

"So, you think this FutureCare will spread?"

"It will, and fast," Rovka said. "Dr. Vita machines aren't expensive. They're mass-produced in Asia, and the cost is modest. Hard-wiring an entire hospital with the System takes time and money, but the bottom line is: what costs more? Supplying human medical professionals for the masses, or supplying Dr. Vita units? FC Industries, the company that makes the Vita units, is betting on the latter. The goal is for these machines to replace as many medical professionals as possible."

"But medical practice will always require great human minds and great human hands."

Rovka raised one eyebrow. "Perhaps yes, and perhaps no," he said. "If this medical center can function with fewer human healthcare providers, there will be fewer pension plans, fewer health insurance policies, and fewer salaries to pay. It would be a fiscal homerun."

"I don't agree. Healthcare is more than a business. Medicine is a profession. Look at your career. You're one of the most famous physicians of the twenty-first century. How could you ever support fewer human physicians like yourself?"

Rovka shrugged. "It's progress. I'd be a fool not to embrace it. In time every patient in the ICU, ER, and on the medical wards at USV will be covered by a Dr. Vita machine."

"But there was no Dr. Vita in my OR yesterday. Why was that?"

Rovka nodded and said, "The installation of FutureCare is only 90% finished to date. Your OR was not completed and had no Dr. Vita unit. I believe that fact will be trumpeted by the supporters of the System."

"You're kidding. The supporters will say a Vita would have saved Elizabeth Anderson's life?"

"Perhaps. It depends on whether she died because of human error or not. Humans make errors. Computers do not."

A screeching overhead alarm interrupted Rovka. A voice from the intercom said, "Code Blue. Code Blue Room 823A, Surgical ICU. Room 823A."

"That's one floor above us," Alec said. "I need to go up there." He scrambled to his feet and ran toward the stairwell.

5 ~ AN ACT OF GOD

Alec was the first physician to arrive at room 823 of the Surgical Intensive Care Unit. A male patient lay motionless in the ICU bed. An endotracheal tube protruded from his mouth, and a nurse was squeezing an emergency ventilation bag to inflate his lungs. She shrieked at Alec, "My patient is cold and dead, and the monitors . . ." She turned to face the Dr. Vita machine that was mounted on the wall over the bed.

The Vita monitor showed a series of flat lines.

"The monitors what?" Alec said.

"The monitors were normal a minute ago. I swear it—not one alarm went off. The monitors said the patient was fine."

Alec took out his stethoscope and pressed it against the chest of the patient, an ancient fossil of a man with only a thin layer of skin covering bony ribs. Alec held the stethoscope against the ribcage and listened, and there was no heartbeat.

"Get the crash cart in here. I'll start chest compressions," Alec said. He knelt on the bed, placed the heels of both hands on the man's sternum, and started pushing. He was startled at the man's temperature—the skin of the man's chest was ice cold—far cooler than any hospitalized patient Alec had ever performed chest compressions on before. "This guy's cold as a corpse in the morgue," Alec said. "What's the story here?"

The nurse's voice quivered as she said, "He had his gall bladder out last night. He was doing fine my whole shift, and then ... he can't be dead. He can't."

Two other MDs arrived, followed by a second nurse pushing the crash cart. "Give 1 mg of Epi and 1 mg of atropine IV now," Alec said. The second nurse injected the two drugs, and Alec said, "Get the paddles ready. Set the defibrillator at 200 joules. Everybody clear."

He jumped off the bed. One of the arriving MDs, a blonde bearded man who couldn't have been thirty years old, applied the paddles to the old man's chest and pressed the discharge buttons. The patient's torso lurched, and his arms contracted upward toward the ceiling. Alec looked at the Vita monitor and saw the heart rhythm unchanged—it was still flat line. He climbed back on the bed and resumed CPR.

Twenty minutes later, they still had a dead man.

Alec leaned again and again into the man's sternum as he continued the chest compressions. He could feel the decreasing resistance as the patient's ribs broke free of the breastbone. With each downward thrust of his hands, Alec felt like he was leaning into a foam pillow.

"The guy's dead," he said out loud. "We've been coding him for almost a half hour, and there's no rhythm. Let's call it."

"I agree," the bearded MD said. He looked at the clock, and said, "I declare him dead as of 1142 hours."

Alec stopped pushing on the chest, and the nurse stopped squeezing the ventilation bag. The repeated chest compressions had left a hollowed depression where the man's breastbone used to be. The patient's eyes were still open, and they stared straight up at the ceiling with the glassy sheen of a trout at a fish market.

"How old was he?" Alec asked.

"Eighty-four," the nurse said.

"That's old," the other MD said. He stared at the patient for another moment, and then turned to Alec and said, "My name is Gerald Samson. And you are?"

"I'm Alec Lucas, one of the anesthesia faculty."

"You sure got here fast. Did he have a rhythm when you arrived?"

"No. He was cold. He was dead already, if you ask me." Alec turned to the nurse and said, "How long did it take you to call a code?"

"I don't know how it happened," she said. "I don't know how I missed it." She started to cry. Her nametag identified her as Barb Tyler, RN. Alec touched her hand to console her. He noted the gray roots at the base of her reddish hair and tabbed her as about fifty years old. It wasn't her first day on the job.

"I was doing my job, I know it," she said. "I came on duty four hours ago, and the nurse from the night shift gave me report. This patient— his name was Richard Irving—had his gall bladder out late last night. He had emphysema, and he's been on the ventilator for the past ten hours because he couldn't breathe on his own. He was hooked up to two IVs, a neck line, an arterial line in his wrist, a gastric tube, a Foley bladder catheter, and a temp probe in his rectum. The Dr. Vita module was running all his sedation and monitoring."

Barb gestured toward the eighteen-inch white sphere secured to the wall near the head of Mr. Irving's ICU bed. It was an identical copy of the orb that interviewed Mr. Mindling in clinic. A series of cables connected Dr. Vita to the ventilator and its oxygen source, the monitoring lines from the patient, and the pumps that infused the correct volume and rate of IV medications to the patient.

"What was he getting for sedation?" Alec asked.

"Fentanyl and midazolam. Just enough to keep him from thrashing around and bucking on the ventilator. The Vita controls the sedation and the ventilator, so there wasn't that much to do."

Barb was still crying so hard it was difficult for her to speak. "The nurse on the last shift told me, 'What's the point of going to nursing school for four years, when the module does everything except wipe the guy's ass?'"

"Did he have a sudden cardiac arrest or was there a downward trend?" Alec said.

"It was business as usual up until I called the code," Barb said. "All his vital signs were normal. When I stood up and checked his clinical status at eleven o'clock, I opened his eyes, and the pupils were pinpoint in size and unresponsive to light. I was freaked out, so I felt for his pulse at the wrist, and there was none. I touched his skin and it was dry and cold. Icy cold. But when I looked up at the monitors, they still showed all his vital signs were normal."

"The Vita screen showed normal vital signs?"

"Yes. The vital signs didn't change to flat lines until just before you arrived. That's when I called a Code Blue."

"Show me the patient's electronic record," Alec said. They walked over to a console below the Vita unit, she tapped three buttons, and the vital signs record for the past three hours appeared on a screen.

"There it is," Barb said, "just like I told you. Normal vital signs until the moment I called the Code Blue."

"It looks like a sudden death," Alec said. "As old as he was, it's not unusual. You did all the right things."

She looked up at him and dried her eyes with the back of her hand. Then she shuffled nearer to her desk in the corner of the room. When she reached it, she closed the copy of *Glamour* magazine that lay open on the desktop.

Glamour magazine? Alec thought, and the facts suddenly became clearer. This nurse hadn't been doing her job. She'd been reading about fashion advice, dating tips, and Hollywood gossip when she was supposed to be attending to her patient, and now that patient was dead.

Alec copied down Richard Irving's medical record number and went back downstairs looking for Henri Rovka. He found the senior physician just outside the anesthesia clinic. Alec described to him what had just happened upstairs.

"Sounds like an act of God. Maybe a pulmonary embolism?" Rovka said.

"Who knows? It was clear to me that the nurse wasn't being vigilant. She had no idea what went wrong. The electronic medical record is the legal record for what happened, and it showed a sudden death. But there's one other problem."

"What's that?"

"I arrived one minute after the nurse called the Code Blue, and the guy was stiff and frigid as a piece of steak in a freezer. He'd been dead for at least an hour."

"That's impossible," Rovka said.

Alec whistled through his teeth. "When an airplane crashes, they sift through the wreckage to find the black box—the electronic record of what happened before and during the disaster, right? For an electronic device like a Dr. Vita, there's not a physical black box, but an electronic one. There's got to be an electronic footprint of every action of the device. By examining that record, I can tell you what happened. I need to meet the programmers and designers of FutureCare."

"You don't think the Vita unit had a role in the man's death, do you?"

"God, I hope not," Alec said. "For everybody's sake, I hope not."

6 ~ JAKE MINDLING

Alec Lucas arrived in the pre-anesthesia room before dawn the following morning and sought out his first patient of the day. In the hours since he'd first seen Jake Mindling through the two-way mirror, it seemed that Mindling had grown ten years older and had gained twenty pounds. Alec looked at Mindling and sized up what he was in for.

Mindling was lying horizontal on a gurney in the preoperative room with an intravenous drip running into his arm and wet hand towel over his forehead. He was a mountain under a white sheet, his torso spilling over both the left and right sides of the mattress with his elbows extending like wings through the side railings of the gurney. His eyes were closed, and the roundness of his belly rose and fell each time he exhaled. Sparse strands of tangled hair hung down across his forehead, and the overnight stubble of his gray beard dotted his cheeks and chins.

Two surgeons-in-training wearing rumpled white coats over rumpled blue scrubs stood at the bedside. "Where the hell is anesthesia?" one of them said out loud.

Alec hated it when surgeons referred to his profession as "anesthesia," as if he were a vapor that somehow walked about on two legs. But at this hour of the morning he wasn't going to start an argument with two half-trained surgeons.

"Excuse me, I'm Alec Lucas," he said to the surgical residents. "I'm the anesthesia attending. Give me a few minutes to talk to the patient and review the electronic chart, and then you can help me transport him to the operating room."

"Yeah, man. We'll give you five minutes to scope out the gas-passing details," the taller of the two residents said. Alec looked at the name badges of the two surgeons: they were Dr. O'Miley and Dr. Portley. Alec used mnemonics to help him remember the names of every new person he met. Dr. Portley was skinny, not portly, and O'Miley was grumpy looking, not smiley. These two would be opposite-of-their-names guys.

Alec moved closer to Mindling. He looked over the chart and saw that there was little to add to what he had learned from watching the Vita session yesterday. The patient was seventy-four years old and was retired and living in a nearby town called Pescadero. Other than being old, fat, and a snorer, Jake Mindling's chart showed a clean bill of health.

"Hello, Jake Mindling, my name is Dr. Alec Lucas. I'll be your anesthesia doctor today." He leaned over and shook the patient's hand.

"I thought she was my anesthesia doctor," Mindling said, pointing over Alec's shoulder. Alec turned around, and a slender Asian woman with rectangular tortoiseshell glasses stood twelve inches behind him. She held out her hand and said, "Hi Dr. Lucas, I'm Mae Yee. I'm your resident today."

Alec shook her hand. She squeezed so hard his fingers ached. "I didn't realize I was teaching today," he said.

"You are, and I'm it. I've already worked up Mr. Mindling. Pertinent issues are obesity and sleep apnea." She leaned over and whispered into Alec's ear, "He's a pretty huge guy, but I'll get a tube in him."

Dr. Yee's long black hair was highlighted with purple streaks. Just below her violet tresses hung multiple earrings—at least four hoops of different diameters in the superior and inferior aspects of each ear. Dark eyes hovered above honey-colored skin, and faint freckles dotted the skin above her cheekbones.

Alec's first impression was astonishment. Back in Chicago, physicians tended toward a conservative appearance. He tried to hide his emotion, and told her, "I know all about Mr. Mindling. I saw him yesterday. He's ready to go. Let's roll him into the operating room."

O'Miley and Portley held the OR doors open while Mae and Alec pushed the patient down the hallway. Mae Yee strode with her shoulders back and her head held high. She wore black boots that made a loud clacking sound with every heel strike as they rolled the gurney into the operating room. The two anesthesiologists connected the patient to the standard monitors, and Mae said to Mr. Mindling, "Your wife is a lucky woman. She won't have to listen to your snoring anymore."

"I hope it works," he said. "I know I'm going to have the worst sore throat of my life when I wake up."

Mae held an oxygen mask over Mr. Mindling's face, and said, "Take deep breaths of this oxygen. You're doing great." She wore a silver ring on each finger of her left hand, including a large onyx stone which capped the ring on her thumb. She wrapped her fingers around the angle of the patient's mandible as she held the mask, and the rings touched the underside of Mr. Mindling's chins.

"Why is it so cold in here?" Mindling said. He was lying flat on his back staring into the bright array of surgical spotlights. His teeth chattered as he spoke.

Alec ignored the question and looked at the clock. It was 7:30 a.m.—time to go down. "Go ahead," he said to Mae. She let go of the mask and drew up the necessary anesthetics into two syringes.

"Can I count backwards from 100?" said Mr. Mindling. "The last time I went out for surgery, I fought it pretty good—I think I lasted to 88 before I went to asleep."

"You can count if you want, Mr. Mindling," Alec said. "Fight all you want, but our anesthetics are going to win. Whether you get to 95, 91, or 87, you will go to sleep."

"Vital signs stable," purred a low voice from behind Alec. He turned and squinted at the eighteen-inch sphere mounted on top of the anesthesia equipment. "Begin anesthetic by administering propofol 300 mg and rocuronium 50 mg," the module said. The voice reminded Alec of the low rumble of a smooth jazz Sirius XM disc jockey at three in the morning.

"You're going off to sleep now, sir," Mae said. She injected the propofol and rocuronium, and Mr. Mindling's chatter ceased.

"Mask ventilate the patient for sixty seconds and then perform direct laryngoscopy. Place a #8 endotracheal tube," Dr. Vita said.

Alec sighed and then counted to ten. It was bad enough he had to teach a resident-in-training with purple hair and ten earrings, but now he had to take orders from a FutureCare globe as well. He reached over and touched the power button to turn the Vita unit off.

"Warning, warning. Unauthorized power failure recognized during patient care," squawked the white sphere. "Dr. Vita remains aware. Normal power and operational mode are ongoing."

"What's the deal?" Alec said. "The machine can't be turned off?"

"Failsafe operation," Mae said. "The Vita unit needs to be on at all times to insure vigilance." She inserted the breathing tube into Mindling's trachea and connected the gas hoses from the anesthesia machine to the tube.

"Recommend general anesthesia recipe A-1," the Vita unit said, "including inhalational anesthesia of sevoflurane at 1.5% concentration and intravenous anesthesia of propofol at 50 micrograms per kilogram per minute." The Vita grew quiet—and then its two yellow eyes flashed off and on three times in succession.

Alec connected the propofol infusion to the IV and reached to turn on the sevoflurane vaporizer. He was surprised to see the machine had already turned on the sevoflurane anesthetic. He stepped back and surveyed the scene. The usual business was unfolding: a tech was preparing the surgical instruments and the attending surgeon, Dr. Chavez, was washing his hands at the scrub sink outside the operating room window.

"Nice job with the endotracheal tube, Dr. Yee," Alec said. "What year resident are you?"

"I just finished my first year. I did eight hundred cases last year, and I can handle just about anything: hearts, neuro, OB, peds, ENT, thoracic, vascular. You name it, I—" Before she could finish her sentence the quiet of the operating room was shattered by the squawking voice of Dr. Vita again.

"Warning, warning. Blood pressure unobtainable. Heart rate escalating. Discontinue anesthesia. Administer 100 micrograms of epinephrine IV."

Alec scanned the vital signs monitor and sure enough, the heart rate was ripping along at 140 beats per minute and, instead of a number, the blood pressure reading was "?".

"What's happening, Dr. Lucas?" came a quivering croak from Mae Yee.

Alec wasn't sure. There was no reason for the patient to be crashing only five minutes after the induction of general anesthesia. "It must be an allergic reaction to one of the anesthetics," he said. He turned off the sevoflurane and propofol and injected epinephrine into the IV as the Vita unit had recommended.

The attending surgeon, Dr. Raul Chavez, burst through the door. His mask was hanging down from his chin, exposing a thick black moustache and a day's growth of beard. "What the hell's going on?" he said.

"The patient is having anaphylaxis to something," Alec said. "I'm giving him a dose of epinephrine IV."

"Warning. Unobtainable blood pressure," the Vita said. "Rule out cardiac damage. Rule out allergic shock. Check heart tones. Confirm breath sounds. Examine skin for rash or hives."

Mae tore Mr. Mindling's hospital gown away and pressed her stethoscope against his chest. "The heart sounds are normal, except for a rapid rate," she said. "The lungs are clear, and the skin is normal. No hives or rashes."

Alec stared at the Vita unit. He hated to admit it, but the machine was giving all the correct advice.

"Damn it, call a Code Blue," the surgeon said. "Start CPR. This guy has no blood pressure. Portley, O'Miley, get over here. Port, you start the chest compressions." Portley pushed the nurse aside, placed both hands on the patient's breast bone, and began doing chest compressions.

"Do something, anesthesia. Do something," screamed Chavez. The surgeon's external jugular veins bulged out like fleshy pencils under the skin along the sides of his neck.

Alec injected a second and third dose of epinephrine into the IV and watched in despair as the heart rate rose to 200 beats per minute. The blood pressure remained unmeasurable. The Code Blue Team arrived in the operating room, led once again by Gerald Samson. In a daze, Alec told him what had happened so far.

"We need to get an arterial catheter in," Chavez said. Dr. Samson began sticking a large needle into Mr. Mindling's groin, trying to find the artery. "It's no use," he said. "there's no pulse here, I'm not hitting any blood vessel."

Even the Vita unit was at a loss for ideas. In the next minute, the ECG changed to an erratic series of irregular beats, and then went flat. Chavez screamed, "God damn it. He's trying to die. Shock him. Do something, anesthesia."

Alec injected another full syringe of epinephrine. The Code Team applied external paddles and shocked the heart six times, but nothing improved.

"What the frigging hell," screamed Dr. Chavez. "The guy is dead. I never even touched him with a scalpel, and now I've have to go and tell his wife he's dead." He glared at Alec. "What the hell did you give him? I've been in practice for twenty years and I've never seen this kind of thing happen. One case with you, and … oh, forget it." He turned and kicked an operating room garbage can. As it slammed into the wall and tipped over onto the floor, he stomped out of the room.

The chaos of the Code Blue morphed into a scene of absolute quiet. No one spoke a word. Mae Yee stood wide-eyed next to Alec's right elbow and was massaging her temple. It was as if he and Mae were enclosed in an invisible bubble—no one in the room came within twenty feet of the two anesthesiologists. At last an oversized woman entered the operating room doors and stepped up to Alec. Her nametag read, Lucille Bamberger, RN, Nursing Supervisor. "You'll have to leave everything just as it is," she said. "Leave the breathing tube and the IV in until the coroner comes, Doctor …" She looked at his nametag, and finished the sentence, "Doctor Lucas."

Nurse Bamberger turned and walked away, leaving Alec and Mae alone again with the corpse of Jake Mindling. Alec leaned on the anesthesia machine with both arms. His legs were so weak, it was all he could do to remain standing. A sudden rush of anger boiled up inside him. "Are you sure you injected the right two anesthetics into the patient?" he said to Mae. "Is there any chance you did a syringe swap and injected a wrong drug?"

Mae had been staring at the floor. Now she looked up at Alec, her eyes blazing. "Look, Dr. Lucas, I'm not an idiot. I didn't do a Kevorkian here. I injected propofol and rocuronium, just like the last eight hundred anesthetics I've done. The only thing different this time was you." She spun around and stomped out of the operating room.

Alec picked up the two empty anesthetic syringes on the table in front of him. There was insufficient quantity inside to assay for what the syringes had contained. He sat on a stool three feet from Jake Mindling's huge head and wished he had chosen some other career.

Why had the patient crashed, and why had the resuscitation failed? There was only one thing about this anesthetic that differed from the ten thousand he'd performed in the past. He cast his gaze upward at the two yellow eyes of Dr. Vita, and he scowled.

The Vita machine was still turned on. The two yellow lights shone as the black video screen traced flat lines. Alec spun the unit around and checked out the wires connecting the machine to the anesthesia monitors and the anesthesia gas machine. The back panel was secured with four screws at the corners. He elected not to tinker with the module. Instead, he found the serial number on the back and copied the number CC197N into his phone.

Before he left the room, Alec hovered over the body of Mr. Mindling one last time. The hairy hams of the patient's arms were extended at right angles to his torso in a pose similar to a crucifixion. His huge head was still covered by the blue surgical bonnet, and flakes of peeling skin from a recent sunburn speckled his forehead. The plastic endotracheal tube was taped to Mr. Mindling's upper lip, and the tape distorted the man's final facial appearance. Alec loosened the tape and removed the anesthesia hoses from the tube in the process.

As he reached to reconnect the hoses, he caught the pungent odor from the inside of the tube, and he winced at the smell. He pushed down on Mindling's breastbone, and then smelled the gas coming out of the man's breathing tube again. He furrowed and reconnected the breathing hoses.

He checked the anesthesia machine again and confirmed that the sevoflurane knob was set to zero. The vaporizer had ceased administering the potent anesthetic gas since the beginning of the Code Blue. Alec rechecked the Vita monitor and confirmed that the sevoflurane concentration on the trending screen had been zero since the beginning of the anesthetic. Then he disconnected the hoses once more and inhaled again. He shuddered as the overpowering odor stunned him.

There was anesthetic gas—sevoflurane gas—in the hoses. Lots of it. What the hell was going on?

He was about to walk out of the operating room leaving a dead patient behind him for the second time in one week. Everybody at the

University of Silicon Valley Medical Center was going to think he was incompetent and dangerous. He was batting zero in a profession that was safe 99.99% of the time.

Alec knew he was a competent anesthesiologist—maybe even an outstanding one—but he also knew one other truism: *To the world around you, you're only as good as your last anesthetic.*

7 ~ BAD KHARMA TOGETHER

Alec could hear the sobbing through the door of the Meditation Room. He couldn't believe he was about to console someone about their dead family member for the second time in three days. Marion Mindling was inside the room listening to Dr. Chavez's story of her husband's sudden demise. Chavez chose to meet with her alone and left the anesthesia team behind in the operating room. Alec waited for ten minutes, until the door opened, and Dr. Chavez walked out of the room.

"I told her we don't know why her husband died, but that an allergic reaction to anesthesia was the likely explanation," Chavez said. "She didn't say ten words to me the whole time. I told her I had nothing to do with it—that I didn't even touch her husband. She's upset, and I'd say she's upset at you. And so am I." He stared into Alec's eyes for five seconds too long, and then he walked away.

Alec stood in front of the door, trying not to hear the widow's crying, when someone grabbed his elbow. He turned, and it was Mae again. "I want to go in there with you," she whispered. "I want to talk to his wife."

"I'm glad you came back," he said. "Those things I said back there … I don't think you made a mistake. I was just so angry."

"I feel like shit," she said. "I'm the one who injected the drugs. I've gone over and over it all in my mind, and there's no way I gave him anything except the propofol and roc. No way." She glared at him, her arms folded across her chest and her lips pressed together. She had her hat off, and Alec was relieved to see her shoulder-length hair was 90% black with only highlights of purple. Her eyes were red and teary, and flitted from the floor to the ceiling in an irregular cadence. She had trouble looking him in the eye.

"Are you sure you can handle this?" Alec said. "The wife could be pretty mad at us."

"I need to see her," Mae said. "Let's go." She bit her bottom lip, brushed past Alec, and led the way through the door.

Marion Mindling sat wedged in the corner of the couch on the far wall of the small room. Her glasses lay on the table beside her, and she was working her way through a box of Kleenex. Alec and Mae sat on the second couch facing her.

Alec began by saying, "Mrs. Mindling, I'm Dr. Lucas, the anesthesia faculty member who took care of your husband. This is Dr. Yee who was the resident anesthesiologist working with me. We were both there when your husband died. We … we're very sorry this happened."

Marion erupted in a convulsion of sobbing and covered her eyes. Mae leaned forward to hug the woman, but Marion moved away.

Alec, whose life was forever changed, sat in silence staring at the widow.

Marion stopped crying and said, "Dr. Chavez told me it was an anesthetic problem—that it had something to do with what you anesthesia doctors did. He said you gave Jake some medicine and then he died. Is that what happened?"

"His blood pressure faded to zero within five minutes of going to sleep," Alec said. "It could have been a heart attack, an allergic reaction, a blood clot, or …." Alec stopped talking, because his list of what could have caused the episode was a short one.

"Jake was scared," Marion said. "He had a bad feeling before this surgery. We went for a walk together last night, and he said he thought his time was up, and he might not make it through the surgery."

"Why would he say that?" Mae asked.

"I don't know, but he was right to be nervous. I can't believe he got killed in there."

"No one killed him, Mrs. Mindling, he—"

"Don't go coddling me, Doctor. All I know is he walked into this hospital this morning, and now he's never going to walk out." Marion stopped and studied each one of their ID tags. She took a pen out of her purse and wrote down both of their names.

Alec said, "Mrs. Mindling, the coroner will do an autopsy. That will give us valuable information as to what really happened."

"I watched an autopsy show on television. They saw open the body from stem to stern and pull out all the organs."

"The pathologist will do a very professional job of checking your husband's heart, lungs, brain, and anything else that was relevant as a possible cause of sudden death," Alec said.

"I hate that idea. I can't handle any more doctors doing anything more to Jake. Let him rest in the Lord's peace. I need to make some calls to my family. Can I go now?"

Mae and Alec stood and let her exit. Alec had hoped to comfort the widow. Instead, Marion Mindling left more agitated than when they'd started talking. Alec felt a black hole where his stomach used to be.

Mae took off her glasses and looked across at Alec. "I'd have bet the ranch that Jake Mindling would survive the induction of general anesthesia," she said, "But now I'd have no ranch. No ranch at all."

"I can't believe it," Alec said.

"He must have had severe coronary artery disease," Mae said. "His blood pressure sagged when we induced him, the blood flow to his coronaries dropped, and his myocardium was deprived of oxygen."

"Maybe," Alec said.

"We're going to get some bad press from Chavez's surgical buddies," Mae said. "I wouldn't want to hear the Surgery Morbidity and Mortality Conference on this case. You can bet they're going to say it was anesthesia's fault."

From that point on, Alec didn't notice what Mae said. He imagined the scene of a large auditorium filled with surgeons in white coats. The soundtrack of the image was the roar of ocean waves beating against sand. Dr. Chavez stood at the podium at the front of the group, and he was describing a complication on one of his cases. When Chavez finished, a bald surgeon wearing the garb of a five-star general rose to his feet and said, "This is a classic example of how surgical mortality rates can be undermined by anesthesia practice that is below the standard of care." The general went on talking, and the heads of the men and women in white coats nodded in agreement, their head movements keeping time to the music of the waves pounding in Alec's ears.

Mae's voice interrupted his reverie. "And as bad as the Surgical M & M will be, the Anesthesia M & M will be worse. The conference is in two days, and the agenda will include all the complications from the week. This case will be one of the main attractions."

"I wish I'd never come here," Alec said.

"I've never had a patient die before," Mae said, "And I don't ever want to feel this way again." She wiped the sleeve of her scrub shirt across her eyes. "You and I have bad karma together, Dr. Lucas. Don't take this as a personal affront, but take a good look at me, Professor, because you're never going to see me in your operating room again. Never." She opened the door and left the room without waiting for a reply.

Alec let her go. Who could blame her? In one month he'd gone from boy wonder at the University of Chicago to a professional with zero credibility at USV. He dreaded the rest of the week. He knew that at an academic institution like the University of Silicon Valley Medical Center, no medical complication would go unnoticed. Or unpunished.

"It's 6:45, so let's call the Grand Rounds of the Department of Anesthesiology to order," Dr. Robert Vinscene said. "This morning we'll present the Mortality and Morbidity cases for the month of July. Today we have three cases. Dr. Mark Turtle will present the first case."

Dr. Robert Vinscene, the chairman of anesthesiology at the University of Silicon Valley Medical Center, spoke these first words to open the meeting. He held his nose high, and a well-healed scar under his chin was visible to everyone. Tall and elegant, he spoke to the audience as a teacher would address his students. In his fifties, with a touch of gray at each temple, Vinscene was the author of over two hundred academic publications, and the most respected anesthesiologist on the West Coast.

The auditorium was twenty rows deep, and every seat was filled this morning. The majority of those in attendance were wearing identical outfits—baggy scrubs of a pale faded blue color—which stood out in contrast to Vinscene's navy blue double-breasted suit. There were over one hundred doctors in attendance, almost the entire anesthesia staff of the University of Silicon Valley Medical Center. A large flat panel computer monitor screen hung at the front of the room. A podium flanked each side of the screen. Vinscene stood erect and daunting at the podium on the right.

"Before Dr. Turtle begins, I want to call your attention to something new this morning," Vinscene said. "Today's selected cases will be assessed and critiqued by the latest model Dr. Vita unit that is now installed in each operating room at USV."

Alec was sitting in the second row, ten feet away from the chairman. He was nervous—he was scheduled to present the second case this morning. That is, he was scheduled to be fried by Vinscene after the chairman was finished humiliating Dr. Turtle. Alec leaned forward and craned his neck to inspect the table next to Vinscene. Damn and sure enough, a white eighteen-inch metal sphere was perched there. This was the equivalent of seeing Lucifer with a pitchfork in the front row at church. Shouldn't a Grand Rounds Conference be out of bounds for Vita modules?

Alec scanned the audience to see if Mae Yee was here. He looked from face to face in every row, but she wasn't in the crowd. With her violet-streaked hair, she was hard to miss. She was a no show, and Alec wondered why. Every doctor who had a complication was obligated to present their case at a Mortality and Morbidity conference. If Alec had to undergo the medical equivalent of the Spanish Inquisition today, then Goddamn it, Mae Yee should have felt the sting, too.

"Today's cases show the problem of human error in the operating room," Vinscene said, "and the role of AI modules such as the Dr. Vita unit in improving patient care. To contribute to a scholarly discussion of the role of technology in avoiding medical errors, we're fortunate to have two special guest experts. Our first expert is Dr. Kami Shingo, the inventor of the Dr. Vita unit."

A short Asian man in the front row stood and waved and smiled at the congregation. He was sixty-five years old, had curls of white hair above each ear, and smaller tufts of white hair growing out of each ear. The top of his head was a glossy dome that reflected the ceiling lights of the auditorium. His eyeglasses were two small golden circles perched on the end of his nose.

Alec was surprised to see Shingo at this conference. Shingo was an icon whose face had graced the covers of *Time* and *Newsweek*. Born in Japan and educated at Harvard and M.I.T., Shingo was hailed as the father of the Artificial Intelligence in Medicine revolution. The invention of the Dr. Vita unit had made him one of the most wealthy and famous physicians in American history. It was a remarkable opportunity to be in the same room as him, but Alec wished the entrepreneur had arrived on a different day.

Shingo was clad in a bright yellow shirt, white pants, and a yellow belt. He looked like a retired grandfather who'd wandered into the wrong party. Dr. Vinscene snapped a military salute toward Kami Shingo, who raised one hand, nodded his head three times in acknowledgement, and then sat back down.

"Our second special guest is the CEO and President of WellBee Corporation, the manufacturer of the Dr. WellBee module. As you may know, the Dr. WellBee module is the chief competitor to the Dr. Vita module in the Artificial Intelligence in Medicine marketplace. Dr. Red Jones, can you stand up please?"

A tall, wide-shouldered man with red hair slicked back behind his ears stood and raised one hand in a thumbs up motion to the anesthesiologists. Like Vinscene, he wore a well-tailored dark suit, a white shirt, and a red tie. He looked more ready for a corporate board meeting than this pre-dawn gathering of doctors in faded pajamas. His toothy smile was visible to Alec from halfway across the auditorium. Dr. Jones readjusted the knot of his necktie as he wiggled back into his seat. He was sitting on the opposite end of the front row from Dr. Shingo, and Alec noted that neither man made eye contact with the other.

"It's no accident that we have world class AIM expertise assembled today, as you will see," Vinscene said. "Dr. Turtle, you may begin."

Dr. Mark Turtle shuffled to the front of the room with the appearance of a man looking for something on the ground a few feet in front of his shoes. His shoulders rounded forward, and his short arms hung straight down. His neck craned and his chin came close to touching his chest. He was wearing the same blue scrubs as everyone else, but his were a size too big. His pants puddled around his feet, and the V-neck of the shirt revealed more chest hair than anyone wanted to see.

Dr. Turtle climbed behind the left podium, opened his laptop, and began tapping keys with a fury. He didn't acknowledge the audience and continued to look down at the device. From the second row, all Alec could see was the top of Turtle's head and the beginning of a bald spot.

"This case was a 44-year-old healthy woman for a hysterectomy," Turtle began. He looked up at last, and his voice came out in a hoarse croak. His nose moved up and down with his words as if his nostrils and his upper lip were a single organ.

"My plan was to administer total intravenous anesthesia, using infusions of propofol and remifentanil. After the patient was asleep, I gave a dose of 70 mg of rocuronium prior to the beginning of the surgery."

"Let me stop you there," Vinscene said. "Seventy milligrams of roc are a huge dose. Why did you give so much?"

"I wanted her well paralyzed. I . . . I didn't want her to move during the surgery—it makes the surgeons angry if the patient moves."

"Very well, go on."

"The anesthetic was notable for a persistent rapid heart rate of greater than 120 beats per minute. When the surgery was finished one hour later, we removed the surgical drapes. We discovered the connection of the anesthetic tubing to the IV in her left arm had become disconnected during the case, and the intravenous anesthetic infusions were running into the sheets instead of into her arm."

Turtle paused to pull a handkerchief from his hip pocket and wipe drips of perspiration from his forehead. He was breathing at a rapid rate and was unable to start another sentence. He wiped the cloth across his upper lip and attempted to continue.

"When I restarted her IV and reversed the paralysis from her dose of rocuronium, she opened her eyes and screamed. She said ... she said she was awake the whole surgery, but she was paralyzed and couldn't move."

The room was silent. Turtle was rubbing his eyes and still ignoring the full auditorium. He turned toward Vinscene and shook his head.

"I'm sorry. I'm so, so sorry," he said in a voice inaudible to half the audience. Then he closed his laptop, turned and walked out of the room.

Vinscene made no move to stop him. "You can only imagine how Dr. Turtle feels," Vinscene said. "It's our duty to be vigilant, to keep our patients safe, and to look out for their welfare. But above all, it's our duty to assure unconsciousness."

The doctors on either side of Alec dropped their gaze and didn't look Vinscene in the face. This was any anesthesiologist's nightmare, and just hearing about it made Alec squirm. What if the IV anesthetic line had come out of one of Alec's patients?

Vinscene walked over to the white sphere and inserted a purple card. "This case was done two weeks ago, before the establishment of Dr. Vita units in operating rooms at USV. We will now demonstrate the value of a Dr. Vita consultation. The Healthcare Assessment Card, or

HAC, from this patient is now inside the module. Dr. Vita, analyze the case."

The yellow eyes lit up, and the machine began talking. "Dr. Vita units are trained to recommend recipe A-1 for general anesthesia. A-1 includes elements of both intravenous and gas anesthetics. The anesthesiologist in this case deviated from the recommended protocol in that he used only intravenous anesthetics. There is always a risk that the intravenous pumps may malfunction, or that the intravenous may become disconnected or obstructed. These circumstances will deliver zero general anesthetic drugs to the patient.

"According to the nurse's entry into the operating room medical record, the patient's arms were tucked in by her side for this surgery," the Vita said. "It was impossible to be vigilant of the intravenous connections. The anesthetic care in this case was below the standard of care. A Dr. Vita consultation would have prevented this anesthetic complication." This last sentence was followed by a pattern of curved stars that resembled a smile across the Vita's video screen, and then unit went dark.

"I'm afraid that giving propofol and remifentanil to the tiles on the floor of the operating room does not constitute a general anesthetic," Dr. Vinscene said. "Had Dr. Turtle had a better anesthetic plan, as the Vita unit outlined, this serious complication could have been avoided."

Alec wondered where Turtle went. If this was a bad movie, they would hear a single bullet shot and a loud thump in the hallway outside the conference room.

"What happened to the patient afterwards?" asked a physician from the back of the room.

"She had a flood of emotional problems: insomnia, night terrors, frightening dreams, daytime anxiety, and an eating disorder. As you can imagine, she's fearful of being anesthetized again. She is being followed by a psychiatrist, and she's filed a lawsuit against the hospital and the anesthesiologist."

Alec looked at the clock on the wall over the door. It was 7:01. It had taken Vinscene sixteen minutes to disgrace Turtle.

The chairman lifted his chin again and looked down his long nose at the physicians seated before him. "Remember," he said. "Keep your machines full of anesthetics, and keep your machines hooked up to the patient. This is the last awake anesthetic I want to hear about at the University of Silicon Valley Medical Center. For our second case, I call on Dr. Alec Lucas. Dr. Lucas is new to our faculty. He received an MD and a PhD in Computer Science from the University of Chicago. I recruited him to USV because of his experience and expertise with computer applications to intensive care medicine. Dr. Lucas, the stage is yours."

Alec walked down the center aisle to the empty podium opposite Vinscene. He held his head high and carried the thin rectangle of his laptop computer in the palm of his right hand. He set his laptop on the podium, flipped open its lid, connected it to the video cable, and tapped one key to open his presentation on the auditorium's projector.

He looked out and saw dozens of faces floating over the blue scrub outfits, which in turn were floating on the chairs of the auditorium. He, too, was floating, as he couldn't feel his feet touching the stage or his fingers touching the keypad of the laptop. He'd lectured in auditoriums all around the United States for years, but he'd never had to stand at a podium and explain why two patients he anesthetized had ended up as lifeless carcasses.

"E.A. was a 78-year-old female scheduled for laparoscopic hemigastrectomy and resection of a stomach cancer," Alec said. "Her medical history was otherwise unremarkable. The surgical team planned use of the Michelangelo III surgical robot, with the goal of using the robot's fine motor control to minimize blood loss.

"At 0730 hours I induced anesthesia with propofol and rocuronium and placed an endotracheal tube. Surgery and anesthesia were routine until 0815 hours when the Michelangelo III unit, commanded by the attending surgeon, ripped into the abdominal aorta and caused massive bleeding."

"Let me stop you there, Dr. Lucas," Vinscene said. "'Ripped into the aorta' is a strong statement. Is that what you think, or is that what you saw?"

"I saw the blade of The Bricklayer's arm bite into a major blood vessel, causing massive hemorrhage. The robot's blade looked like a hedge trimmer inside the patient's body."

"A hedge trimmer? Very dramatic use of simile, Dr. Lucas." He turned his back on Alec and faced the auditorium. "What would you do?" he said to the audience. No one raised their hand, so he pointed to a petite blonde resident who was sitting in the last row, the most popular location in the conference room for trainees who didn't want to be seen or called upon. "Stacey Goodenough," he said, "tell us what you would do."

"I'd turn off the anesthetics, start a bolus of IV fluid, and call the blood bank for a Massive Transfusion Pack," answered Dr. Goodenough.

"Very well. Let's say you do all of these things, and the patient continues to hemorrhage," Vinscene said.

"I'd ask the surgeon if he can fix the injury that's causing the blood loss," Goodenough said.

"Agreed," Vinscene said. "Continue your narrative, Dr. Lucas."

"The patient continued to bleed," Alec said, "and the surgeon was unable to repair the extensive vascular injury. I transfused a total of six units of packed red blood cells, six units of fresh frozen plasma, six units of platelets, and eight liters of saline, but she was still too empty to resuscitate. In the end, the surgeon performed open-chest cardiac massage, but the problem wasn't her heart function. Her heart was empty, and she died."

A solemn quiet descended on the room. Every anesthesiologist dreaded an unexpected patient death like this.

Alec went on, "I did some detective work examining the electronic medical record of this patient and this is what I found. This is the digital recording of the onset of the surgical bleeding. Watch."

Alec tapped a button on the computer in front of him, and the video screen behind him lit up with the view of the inside of Elizabeth Anderson's abdomen. One of the five Bricklayer arms was probing near the origin of the gastric artery. One moment The Bricklayer was moving in slow, blunt dissection, and in the next moment, the video screen was a solid flash of crimson, without any discernable anatomic landmarks. There was no record of The Bricklayer's abrupt sawing motions that Alec witnessed on the video screen in the OR.

"As you can see, the video is inconclusive," Alec said. "You don't see any trauma by The Bricklayer that's negligent or wrong. You see blunt dissection, and then you see red everywhere."

"What are you saying?" Vinscene said.

"The surgeon has claimed that the electronic medical record omitted the scene where the robot tore into the aorta. I agree with the surgeon. I saw the robot slice into the aorta, and that scene has been edited out. The EMR is incomplete. Where did the deleted scene go?"

"Wait just a minute," barked out a voice from the front row. It was Red Jones. His face was contorted into an incredulous expression, and he pointed two fingers at the Alec. "Are you saying the EMR is wrong?"

"I'm saying the EMR is incomplete, Dr. Jones. I don't know why."

"How can that be? For those of us that see computers in medicine as the answer to many problems, those are fighting words, Dr. Lucas."

"I agree, Dr. Jones."

The entire auditorium erupted in a din of murmuring and mumbling. "Silence, everyone," Vinscene said. "Dr. Shingo, do you have a question?"

At this time, Kami Shingo stood from his seat in the front row and faced the audience. He held his hands together in front of himself as if he were praying. "Why in the world wasn't there a Dr. Vita unit involved in this case?"

Alec leaned forward into his microphone and answered, "There was no Dr. Vita installed in room #19 as of the date of this surgery."

"I submit that a Dr. Vita consultation would have saved your patient's life," Shingo said. "The purpose of the Dr. Vita System is to avoid and detect human error."

"And where was the human error on this case?" Alec said.

"Based on your presentation, it seems the grave and lethal error was failure to transfuse enough blood fast enough. And for massive hemorrhage, this patient needed more than six units of transfusion. She needed ten or twelve units or more."

Alec glowered at the little man with the yellow shirt and said nothing.

Red Jones coughed once and spoke up in a booming voice that filled the room from the front row to the furthest seat in the back of the auditorium. "I agree that this case is clear evidence of the need for Artificial Intelligence in Medicine input on every case. Even the most well-educated physicians," he paused and nodded toward Alec, "sometimes make judgment errors, and need the assistance of a Dr. WellBee unit."

"No, a Dr. Vita unit," interrupted Dr. Shingo.

Red smiled. "The Vita units are trailblazers, Dr. Shingo, but the WellBee units will make their trail part of the roadbed."

Shingo glared back at him.

Vinscene intervened and said, "As of July 9th, all ORs at this hospital are equipped with Dr. Vita. My department and the administration of this medical center agree with both of you. We're running short on time, and we need to proceed to our third case presentation. Dr. Lucas, you've had a busy week. The next case is yours as well. You may begin."

Alec took a deep breath, exhaled against pursed lips, and began presenting his second case. "This patient was J.M., a 74-year-old man with obstructive sleep apnea who was scheduled for elective palatopharyngeoplasty."

He flashed through several slides which described Mr. Mindling's history prior to arriving at the operating room.

"At 0730 hours, Dr. Mae Yee and I induced anesthesia."

"I'm going to stop you at this point," Vinscene said from behind the second podium. "So far you have described a patient with obesity and obstructive sleep apnea, but who otherwise is free of risk factors for anesthesia. In specific, he has no heart disease, lung disease, hypertension, diabetes, or neurological problems. Does anyone have any questions for Dr. Lucas?"

A hand shot up from Kami Shingo in the front row.

"Yes, Dr. Shingo," Vinscene said.

"I have serious concerns about this case," Shingo said. "As the former CEO and President of FC Industries and the inventor of Dr. Vita, I was called by the Chief of Staff to review this unfortunate death." He paused and cast a sidelong glance at Alec, who was still standing at the podium.

"I reviewed the electronic medical record on this patient. Were you aware, Dr. Lucas, that this patient had a cousin who suffered a catastrophic death during induction of anesthesia, twenty-five years ago?"

"I-I wasn't aware of that," Alec said.

"Are you familiar with the diagnosis of malignant hyperthermia, the rare genetic disorder that can lead to excessive heat, hypermetabolism, and death on induction of general anesthesia?"

"I'm well aware of what malignant hyperthermia is, but I can assure you that this patient had no positive family history of the disease."

"Dr. Lucas, can you display the electronic medical record on the screen for us to examine?" Shingo said. The screen behind Alec lit up with a detailed preoperative medical record of Jake Mindling. Under *Family History* the record read, "Positive history of a cousin dying on induction of general anesthesia, twenty-five years ago. Cause of death unknown, but malignant hyperthermia was a possibility."

"Did you read the patient's chart, Dr. Lucas?" Shingo said.

"I did, and I swear to you that there was nothing in the chart about his cousin dying."

"The EMR contradicts what you just said, Dr. Lucas. How can you argue with the medical record as it stands?"

"The medical record had no mention of MH when I read it," Alec said.

"That's impossible," Shingo said.

"For a change, I agree with Dr. Shingo," Red Jones said. "It's there in the EMR. We're all looking at it."

"But it wasn't there at the time of surgery."

"There's a time stamp," Shingo said. "It's very easy to determine when entries were made into the record, and when entries were changed. Can we check the time stamp on this entry please?"

Flustered, Alec clicked through several screens of the EMR to arrive at the Time Stamp Record. He started at it, and his mouth ran dry.

"There," Shingo said. "The date for the last entry in the history and physical was the day prior to surgery. Nothing was added later. The malignant hyperthermia entry was present at the time of surgery, and you ignored it. You simply ignored it."

"The record confirms what Dr. Shingo is saying," Vinscene said. "Dr. Lucas, tell us how the case unfolded."

Alec told the rest of the grim story. He concluded by saying, "I spoke to the coroner last night and obtained his preliminary findings. To his surprise, he's found nothing significant to date. No coronary artery disease, no blood clots in the lungs or brain, no hemorrhage, nothing to explain the patient's death."

"It had to be malignant hyperthermia, Dr. Lucas," Shingo said. "Did you take his temperature during the resuscitation?"

"I did not. We were pretty busy."

"This case emphasizes the importance of the electronic medical record, and again emphasizes the importance of the Dr. Vita program in preventing human error," Shingo said. "Chairman Vinscene, can you play the digital tape of the Dr. Vita's instructions in the operating room during the resuscitation of the deceased patient J.M."

Vinscene tapped a button on his laptop, and an electronic voice filled the room, "Warning, warning, patient with possible family history of malignant hyperthermia. Avoid sevoflurane anesthesia! Repeat, avoid sevoflurane anesthesia! Monitor patient temperature. Prepare ice bath to cool patient. Prepare the antidote dantrolene."

"Did you listen to the Vita unit, Dr. Lucas?" Vinscene said. "Did you do those things for your patient before he died?"

Alec felt his heart rate climb. He was standing in front of this crowd as a sacrificial lamb. He'd seen it happen at mortality and morbidity conferences over and over. The anesthesiologist who had the complication became the punching bag for every I-wasn't-there-but-I-wouldn't-have-had-that-problem with a PhD in Hindsightology.

He'd had enough.

"It was hectic and noisy in the OR," Alec said. "But I didn't hear the Vita unit say any of those things in real time. You can ask Dr. Mae Yee, who was part of the anesthesia team that morning. I don't know why the patient died—my hypothesis at the time was that he was allergic to one of the anesthetics we injected, but I know he didn't die from malignant hyperthermia."

There was silence in the room. Shingo pushed his lower lip almost all the way up to his nose. He narrowed his eyes and canted his head to the side, looked straight at Alec, and said, "The electronic medical record is a legal document. At the risk of sounding condescending, Dr. Lucas, it is quite apparent that you are wrong. I will say no more."

Alec descended from the podium and took two steps toward the audience. "There's significant confusion in this case, and I'm prepared to clarify everything," he said. "I have additional evidence to present, if you'll excuse me."

Alec walked out the auditorium exit, and the room began to buzz with electricity. "It appears this new anesthesiologist from Chicago not only has problems keeping his patients alive, but he also has a flair for the dramatic," Dr. Shingo said to Dr. Vinscene.

The buzz quieted down as Alec reemerged carrying an item of electronic hardware in his hand. He leaned over the microphone as he connected it to his laptop. "My guest witness today is the memory chip of Dr. Vita serial number CC197N, the very Vita module that was in the operating room with the patient I just described. In my last job at the University of Chicago, I was an Associate Professor of both Anesthesia and Computer Science. I'm no stranger to dissecting medical gadgets.

"I returned to the operating room last night after hours and removed the memory chip from Vita unit CC197N. I used equipment in my lab to restore the original real-time record from this chip from the time of patient J.M.'s death. I was so surprised at the data inside CC197N that I've brought it to the conference today to show you. Here's what I found."

Shingo stood up and bellowed, "Wait a minute, wait a minute. I'm responsible for the very System that you claim you took this data from. The System is secure and accurate. We've just seen the facts of the case on the electronic medical record. How are we to believe that what you are about to show us is anything but fraudulent?"

Alec smiled and said, "Dr. Shingo, you have my word as an academician that I am not presenting fraudulent data. I have the utmost respect for you and your work, and it's unclear to me where the misinformation about malignant hyperthermia on my patient's electronic medical record came from. I can only tell you that I tapped into Vita unit CC197N's original memory from this case.

"First off, there is no mention of malignant hyperthermia, or of a cousin dying under anesthesia. There is no mention of the verbal warnings that were just played to this auditorium. The only clue I found to patient J.M.'s death is on this screen." Alec tapped a button on his laptop, and a field of digits appeared on the screen behind him.

"The gas analyzer connected to this Dr. Vita unit reported an excessive and lethal sevoflurane gas concentration of 8% five minutes after induction of anesthesia. Ladies and gentlemen, pumping 8% sevoflurane into a 74-year-old man will do one predictable thing. It will cause anesthetic overdose and cardiovascular collapse and kill him in minutes."

"I don't understand," Vinscene said. "Did you set the anesthesia machine to administer that high a dose?"

"No way. I set the sevoflurane vaporizer for 1%, a standard dose, after the patient went to sleep. As soon as the blood pressure bottomed out, I turned off the sevoflurane."

The room grew quiet again as everyone scrutinized the record that was projected on the screen.

"I don't understand," Shingo said. "The record shows the sevoflurane anesthetic concentration is 8% at 0735 hours, at 0740 hours, and at 745 hours. The readings of 8% must be mistakes . . . errors."

"Errors? I thought the Dr. Vita units were there to prevent errors," Alec said. "My hypothesis is that the Vita unit accurately recorded an overdose of anesthetic being pumped into my patient, and that overdose of the anesthetic sevoflurane was the cause of his death."

The audience broke out into a fury of objections. "You're talking about an anesthetic execution," Red Jones said. "The only way that could happen was if the Vita unit malfunctioned. What do you say, Dr. Shingo? A Vita botch-up?"

"Preposterous," Shingo said. "We've already seen and heard the electronic medical record from this patient, and we've seen the missed diagnosis of malignant hyperthermia."

Red Jones lit up in a malicious smile, and said, "Here's what we're all thinking, but no one is saying . . . the official electronic medical record for patient J.M. shows one story, and Dr. Lucas has exhibited data for the same patient with completely different information. This is a stunning problem and evidence that the Dr. Vita System is flawed. This sort of problem is unheard of in the Dr. WellBee System, which my company is installing at the Los Angeles University Medical Center as we speak."

"Dr. Jones must be right," said a faculty member from the back of the room. "Somebody has the wrong record. What happened to this patient? Was it hyperthermia, or was it a sevo overdose?"

"I can reassure you," Shingo said, standing up once again. "There is an alternate explanation. The action that Dr. Lucas took to break into the memory of an individual Dr. Vita unit is irregular and inadvisable. There is no telling what misinformation could be drawn out of our machines if a non-certified technician ignores our protocols." Shingo locked eyes with Alec for several seconds, and then he returned to his seat in the front row.

"Wait a minute," Alec said. "I'm no technician."

"I want to make a comment," Red Jones said.

Chairman Vinscene banged his fist on the podium and called for order. "I regret to say that it's 7:45, and we've run out of time. I want to thank each of the presenters, and I also want to thank Dr. Kami Shingo and Dr. Red Jones for their stimulating and educational comments. Appropriate inquiries into the issues regarding the electronic medical record will be undertaken, and we'll follow-up at next month's Anesthesia Morbidity and Mortality Conference. You are dismissed."

A click sounded as Vinscene turned his microphone off—the conference was over.

Vinscene walked to Alec's side, and said, "Dr. Lucas, I'm shocked that you would not only break into a Dr. Vita module, but that you would remove the module from a patient care area such as the operating room. And to top it all off, you pull off a grandstanding exhibition in front of your professional colleagues at Grand Rounds without clearing it with me first."

"Dr. Vinscene, I'm trying to figure out the truth."

"You heard the truth from Dr. Shingo. The EMR is gospel. Give me the Vita chip. I'll see that it gets reinstalled in the operating room." Alec handed him the device, and Vinscene walked away.

Alec turned to exit the auditorium, and someone grabbed his arm. "You've got guts, man," a voice whispered into Alec's ear. It was Dr. Gerald Samson who rested his hand on Alec's shoulder. "Taking on Vinscene head to head at his conference? Whew. I've never seen it before. Then you spit in the face of Kami Shingo, none other than the inventor of FutureCare. You've got my respect."

"Thanks, Gerald. What're you doing at Anesthesia Grand Rounds?"

"I heard Shingo and Jones were going to be at this conference, so I came to see the celebrities."

"I'm glad you're here," Alec said. "It's nice to hear a kind word."

"When you're tired of kind words," said a voice from behind Gerald. It was Kami Shingo. "Can I talk to you, Dr. Lucas?" he said.

Alec thanked Gerald again and turned to face Shingo.

"I apologize for the confusion, Dr. Lucas," Shingo said. "One of us must be mistaken, and I can only assume it is you." He smiled, and Alec was startled by the yellowed irregular picket fence of the man's front teeth. "But I would enjoy talking more to a man with your Medical Information Technology skills, Dr. Lucas, especially regarding your efforts to discredit the FutureCare System. Can we meet sometime?"

"I'd be happy to discuss your inventions, Dr. Shingo. Henri Rovka and I have concerns that there are problems with the FutureCare System."

The yellow picket fence disappeared. "If you think FutureCare is broken, then I really need to educate you. Dr. Vita is the greatest invention of the twenty-first century."

"You're a humble man, Dr. Shingo."

"No, I'm a successful man. Give me your phone number, and we'll set something up." Alec wrote his number on the back of his business card and handed it to Shingo. Shingo left the auditorium, and Alec was glad to see him go.

Alec was worn out, and it wasn't even eight in the morning. He had ten minutes to change into his scrub clothes and get ready for the first surgery of the day. He headed for the exit, and an Armani-clad arm reached in front of him and blocked his path. It was Red Jones.

"You're a good man, Dr. Lucas," Jones said. "You need to get out of this academic anesthesia bullshit. I liked your poise in front of the group. I liked the way you presented your ideas, and I liked the way you pulled information out of that Vita unit. It's not supposed to be possible. Let's have dinner sometime—I'd like to get to know you better."

"I wish my chairman was as enthusiastic as you are," Alec said. He fished another business card out of his wallet and wrote his phone number on the back.

Red Jones took the card and winked at Alec. "Wait by the phone, kid," he said, and walked out of the room before Alec's mouth had time to close.

9 ~ ONLY MAE YEE CARES AS MUCH

After work that evening Alec returned to his house, flopped onto the couch, and turned on his TV. It had been a long insipid day, and he was ready to watch some Netflix and turn his brain off. His phone rang, and the caller ID read "Yee, Mae."

"Hello, Dr. Lucas," she said. "I heard what went on at Grand Rounds today. I'm so sorry I couldn't be there. I was stuck in Obstetrics doing an emergency C-section."

"You missed one hell of a party."

"Is it true? Did they say the EMR showed Jake Mindling had a family history of malignant hyperthermia?"

"That's what happened. They showed his EMR on the video screen, and it said that the patient's cousin died in an operating room twenty-five years ago. Did you see that on his medical record?"

"No. I swear it wasn't on the chart."

"Did you ask the patient about a family history of problems with anesthesia?"

"No, I didn't. I usually don't. I mean, if they have a positive family history, they tell you, don't they?"

"Maybe."

"The whole thing sounds bogus to me," Mae said. "I don't believe Vinscene's version of the truth this time."

"That's because you were in the operating room with me, and you know the truth. You know what happened."

"Why would the EMR have lies in it?"

"I don't know."

"Do you want to meet and talk about it some more?" she said.

"I thought you and I were going to stay miles away from each other. I think the quote was, 'Take a good look at me, because you're never going to see me again.'"

"No, I said, 'take a good look at me now, because you won't see me in your operating room again.' We're not going to the operating room together. I just want to talk to you."

"You were so pissed at me."

"I needed to blow off some steam, and you got in the way."

"It wasn't my fault the guy died," he said.

"No, I realize that. Those things I said—I was a jerk to you after we talked to Mr. Mindling's wife."

"Apology accepted," Alec said. "That entire day was such a blur, I'm not sure of half the things I heard or said. But I've got to tell you, I could've used your support at Grand Rounds this morning. Vinscene and Shingo tried to make us both look like incompetent slackers. It would have helped if you had been there to back me up."

"Don't you get pissed off at me now. I was up on Obstetrics, doing my job. It's not like I slept in and forgot."

"I uncovered some stunning news on the Mindling case." He told her about his retrieval of the 8% sevoflurane concentration readings from the memory of the Vita unit.

"That would explain everything," she said. "An eightfold overdose of sevo would cause depression of blood pressure and cardiac output and lead to death. Shocking the patient and injecting epinephrine wouldn't do a thing if he was full of sevo."

"I agree," Alec said. "But how could the Vita unit pump 8% sevo into a patient, even though you and I set the sevoflurane knob on the anesthesia machine to 1%?"

"What did they say about it at Grand Rounds?"

"They blew off the 8% as either a fraudulent number inserted when I cloned the Vita's memory or a mistake in record keeping by the Vita. Then we ran out of time—it was 7:45, and everyone had to split and get to the operating rooms to start surgeries for the day."

There was a long pause on the other end of the line. "I want to see you," she said. "I need to ask your advice."

"Advice on what?" he said.

"I think I'm going to quit."

"Quit what?"

"Quit anesthesia. Watching that patient die did me in. What are the chances I'll go the next thirty years without another patient dying like that?"

"I don't know."

"You had two deaths in one week. How do you keep it together?"

"How do you know I'm keeping it together? Maybe I was sitting here with a pistol to my head when you called."

"Are you sitting there with a pistol to your head?"

"No." He paused for a few seconds, and then he said, "Look, I'm happy to talk to you, Dr. Yee, but it's not a date. I can't date doctors that I'm supervising."

"I understand."

"We'll find a time in the next week or so. Okay?"

"Okay."

Alec hung up the phone and shook his head. The girl was ten years younger than him. She had rainbow hair and a hardware store attached to her ears. But right now, only Mae Yee cared as much as he did about what killed Jake Mindling.

10 ~ THE FRONT DOOR SEEMED LIGHTER

Alec walked down the dim hallway of the Leisure Hills Nursing Home with only the sound of his footsteps on the linoleum to remind him he was still alive. He stopped at the nursing station and found an assistant stacking food trays into a rolling rack. He tapped her on the shoulder and said, "Hi Norma, I'm Dr. Lucas, Tony Lucas's son. How's he doing?"

The stout black woman fed one more tray into the rack and turned. Her dark hair was parted in the middle and pinned back behind her ears. She wore eye makeup so thick that her eyes appeared as distant planets behind the lashes. "Tony had his usual day. We sat him up in the chair this morning, so he could sit by the living room window. He ate very little for lunch, and then he watched television all afternoon with Mr. Eberhart and Mr. Lopez."

"How's his mind today?"

"Better. He knows his name, but he's a bit confused about where he is and what year it is."

"Did his internist come by?"

"Dr. Palmer? No, he comes by on every other Monday morning, that's all. Tony's lost six pounds compared to his weight from the nursing home in Chicago, but other than that he's the same old Tony."

"Norma, I'd like it if you and the other staff keep stimulating his memory. You know … telling him who he is, where he is, things like that."

"Every day, Doc. Every day. He's real sweet, Doc. Some of the patients here are ornery as hell. Yelling, hitting, messing their beds, needing to be strapped into their wheelchair. But not Tony. He's a gem."

Alec looked down the hall toward Room 112 and said, "Dad and I are all that's left of the Lucas family. I want nothing but the best for him."

Norma patted Alec on the back. "Moving him here from that other nursing home was a jolt to his system. For these patients, sameness is goodness, but he'll learn to love it here."

"Thanks, Norma. I'll see you tomorrow night."

"He always talks about you," Norma said. "He's always talking about 'his boy Alec.'"

Alec walked down to Room 112 and pushed the door open without knocking. A frail man lay curled up under a white sheet on the single bed, his craggy face illuminated by the flickering light of the television. Alec slipped into the darkness and sat down on the mattress. He studied his father's face and remembered how it looked when thirty extra pounds of body weight helped fill in the creases in his cheeks.

His father's eyes were closed, and a soft snore competed with the voice of the newscaster on The Weather Channel. Alec watched his dad for five minutes before he reached out and wrapped his fingers around the narrowness of his dad's wrist. After three firm squeezes, the snoring stopped, and Tony opened his eyes.

"Hi Dad, I'm sorry to wake you. It's me, Alec," he whispered.

"Oh God, I must have drifted off," Tony said. "Is it time for breakfast?"

"No, Dad, it's nine o'clock at night. I stopped by to say goodnight. How's your new home here?"

Tony Lucas sat up in bed and struggled to turn on his bedside lamp. "I like it very much. Can you get Rudy? Is Rudy here?"

"There's no Rudy here, Dad. Only me … your son, Alec. Do you remember me?"

"Of course, I remember Alec. He had those long arms and big hands and that wavy blonde hair. All the girls in town loved Alec."

"That's right, Dad." He held the bony fingers of Tony's right hand. "Do you know where you are?"

"Of course. I'm in my bedroom."

"And where is your bedroom?"

Tony laughed. "That's a silly question. In Chicago, of course."

"Do you know what year it is?"

He laughed again and said, "It's 1988."

Alec tried one more time. "Do you know who I am?"

His father squinted and clucked his tongue. "Oh, you're playing games with me. You're Alec, of course, all grown up into a handsome young man." Tony's smile faded, and then he said, "I'm tired, son. I really must get to sleep. I have to drive your cousins to camp tomorrow morning."

Tony pulled his hand away, and it disappeared as he pulled the sheet up over his shoulders again. Alec brushed a wisp of hair away from his dad's forehead, and Tony Lucas opened his eyes one more time. "I love you, son," he whispered. Then his eyes fluttered shut, and in two minutes he was snoring again.

Alec sighed and headed toward the exit. The front door that seemed so heavy when he pushed it open minutes earlier seemed a bit lighter as he opened it to go home.

11 ~ TO ERR IS HUMAN

Chairman Vinscene called Alec to his office for an impromptu meeting before surgery the next morning. Two days had passed since the Grand Rounds debacle. There was no one Alec was less interested in confronting, but he had no choice—Vinscene was his boss.

"Good morning," Vinscene said from behind a metal desktop cluttered with unbound papers and empty candy wrappers. A dozen diplomas, awards, and certificates of membership in large black frames decorated the wall behind the chairman. Vinscene leaned back in his chair and frowned for several uncomfortable seconds before he began his lecture.

"Dr. Lucas, you've been one of anesthesia's rising stars—that's why I recruited you here to the University of Silicon Valley. I was your biggest fan, and I believed your career in medicine held no bounds. It's been a tough week for you, and a tough week for me as well. I'm getting a lot of pressure to clean up anesthesia complications—to remove human error from anesthesia performance."

"But our specialty has been a leader in improving medical safety," Alec said. "Since the invention of the pulse oximeter and the end-tidal carbon dioxide monitor, anesthesia complications are unusual."

"Unusual, yes. But look at your week. We've got a problem," Vinscene said. He paused and grimaced, touching the tips of the fingers of his left hand to the tips of the fingers of his right hand. He stared at them as if they held the answer to the problem.

Alec could wait no longer. "Dr. Vinscene, I need you to get on my bandwagon. I witnessed three patients die at this medical center in the past week in unusual circumstances. One was filleted by The Bricklayer. I found a second one cold and dead in the ICU despite a normal electronic medical record, and the third one was that patient of mine you insisted died of hyperthermia."

"The patient you claimed was overdosed with sevoflurane?" Vinscene said. "Come on. You're a smart guy, Dr. Lucas. Why are you sitting out on a limb by yourself with a saw in your hand?"

Alec bit the inside of his lower lip and then launched into the speech he'd planned to make. "The machines of the FutureCare System are flawed. They're making unpredictable movements, like The Bricklayer did. I found a dead eighty-four-year-old in the ICU, and the Vita machine reported and recorded normal vital signs while something killed the patient. In the case of Mr. Mindling, the Vita machine altered the electronic medical record to say he had a positive family history for malignant hyperthermia—information that was never on the record before his death. It's insane, and by God, it's dangerous."

Vinscene bounced the tips of his fingers together as he watched Alec's performance. "And what do you think we should do?"

"Disconnect the Vitas until we understand the problem. Go over the software, one line of code at a time. Inspect all the electronic medical records for inconsistencies. The System is new—the Food and Drug Administration needs to know we're having problems."

Vinscene stood and walked to the window. With his head turned away from Alec he said, "You've got to be careful when you make rash statements like that, Dr. Lucas. What objective evidence of machine failure do we have?" He walked back toward the desk and leaned into Alec's face. "Nothing," he hissed, as a tiny droplet of spit flew into Alec's eye. "We've got nothing but anecdotes and hand wringing. Who makes mistakes, Dr. Lucas? People, or computers? A lot of us believe there are strict rules that can be followed in medical practice which will keep results on a predictable course. We believe that clinical practice guidelines and practice parameters are the answer to misdiagnosis and erroneous therapy in medicine. Are you familiar with this document?" He slid a book across the desk toward Alec.

Alec looked at the cover and said, "Of course. This is the classic report of the Institute of Medicine. Its title is '*To Err is Human: Building a Safer Health Care System.*'"

"Correct. You'll recall the study found up to 98,000 people died per year in U.S. hospitals due to medical errors. It exceeded the 43,000 people per year that died from motor vehicle accidents and the 42,000 people per year that died from breast cancer." Vinscene tapped the book with his knuckles. "This is the document that started it all: bar codes on everything and everybody, electronic physician order entry, electronic medical records, Big Data on every nuance of every clinical case. The number of medical errors is declining, but not fast enough. All that medical information technology has progressed and merged in the creation of the Dr. Vita unit and FutureCare." He turned away from Alec and strolled to the window again.

"You're aware what the invention of Dr. Vita units is going to do to the specialties of internal medicine, family practice, and pediatrics around this country?" Vinscene said.

"Tell me."

"Come over here and look out my window."

Alec stood and joined Vinscene at the window. The long view looked out on the green-forested foothills that separated the Bay Area urban sprawl from the ocean. It was a clear day with billowing ocean fog clouds trying to climb over the foothills. Alec saw nothing that related to Vinscene's speech on medical care. "See those shovels digging that big hole two blocks west of here?" Vinscene said. "That's the groundbreaking for a new medical building. Do you know what the building will hold?"

"No."

"It will house the USV Dr. Vita Depot, which will be completed in two years. Three stories high, three hundred thousand square feet, and the home to one thousand patient examination rooms. Each room with a Dr. Vita unit. Human staffing for the entire complex? One hundred high school graduates per shift to help with patient flow and a back-up physician crew of one doctor per five hundred Dr. Vita units."

"You seem to be a big supporter of these changes, Dr. Vinscene. I love technology, and I wish I'd invented the voice-activated physician module myself, but can't you see the value and tradition of the old ways?"

Vinscene smirked. "The old days of doctors making house calls gave way to clinics where doctors saw a patient every ten minutes. Now the clinics where doctors saw a patient every ten minutes are giving way to a sphere that listens to the patient and makes a diagnosis without a human. In the operating room, the old days of dripping ether onto a cloth over the patient's face gave way to plastic breathing tubes and modern gases and drugs. The vigilant physician sitting there watching the patient sleep is now giving way to a sphere that tells a human when to put the breathing tube in, and when to take it out. It's progress. It's as inevitable as the sunrise.

"I'm a consultant," Vinscene said. "My role is to make automated anesthesia care as safe as possible. Drs. Shingo is our expert consultant as we go forward with our installation of AIM technology. We're recruiting the best computer scientists available, like yourself, to work in our medical center. While we're introducing FutureCare, we humans need to be as flawless as possible. Which brings me to the point of our meeting—I'm concerned that you're impaired in some way, and that the deaths this week are related to that fact. Dr. Lucas, for the good of your patients, I must ask you to answer with all honesty. Are you addicted to any substance?"

Alec was stunned by the sudden inquisition. "I'm not addicted to anything," he said. "I rarely drink alcohol, and I'm not injecting myself with anesthetics or anything. I'm not afraid to pee in the cup. Test me if you want."

Vinscene sat down again and his face contorted into a grim look. "It would be best for both of us if you got tested, Dr. Lucas," he said. "I'm sending you to a colleague of ours who deals with these issues. Let him evaluate you and make sure you're safe to go on giving anesthetics at USV."

"Is that a threat?" Alec said.

"No, it's an edict. The evaluation is mandatory, but I'm pulling for you. I hope you test clean, and I hope you can resume your duties in the operating room for us."

"When do I go see this guy?"

"Four o'clock this afternoon. Here's his card. He's on the 15th floor of this tower. We'll be watching you, Dr. Lucas." He pointed both forefingers at Alec's chest and held them aimed there for several seconds. "Keep your nose clean. Let's not have any more death certificates with your name on them."

He extended his hand to Alec, signaling that the meeting was over. Alec left the office wondering what Jonathan Vinscene meant by "keep your nose clean."

Before he walked out, Alec took one last look out the window at the shovels and bulldozers below and watched as they buried centuries of medical tradition.

Alec stared at the brass plate alongside the doorway:

Spiro Engles, MD
Psychiatry

If anyone had asked Alec one month earlier if he'd ever need to visit a shrink, he'd have laughed in their face. Alec had no use for self-help books and never thought a hoot about his own feelings. Go to work, go to his lab after work, find a young lady to have some laughs with after lab hours. What was the use of making life complicated?

In medical school he always thought the guys who pursued careers in psychiatry were a little crazy themselves. Why would anyone spend all those years dissecting cadavers, holding retractors in an operating room, and listening to lectures about heart disease, if all they wanted to do was listen to people? It made no sense at all.

He was two minutes early for his scheduled appointment. Alec took a deep breath and pushed the door open. There was a tiny waiting room on the other side of the door with three chairs, a table covered with magazines, and a small cylinder on the floor near the table. He turned his attention to the cylinder on the floor. It was constructed of ivory colored plastic and was making a whirring sound. He approached the cylinder and inspected it from close range. The yellow eyes and the black video screen were missing. He got down on his knees and spun the cylinder around to locate the data input slot. There was one phrase on the backside, and it read *Portobello Indoor Humidifier, manufactured in Newark, NJ.*

"Is there something of interest to you on the floor?" a voice said from behind him. Alec looked back over his shoulder and saw a short man with a swirl of gray hair orbiting his head. The man's eyes looked like twin BBs behind the thick lenses of his rimless eyeglasses, and he had an asymmetric nose the size of a small cauliflower floret. He wore a burgundy tie with gray bicycles riding across it.

"I have to tell you the truth," Alec said. "I've been looking for a humidifier like this one, and I wanted to know what kind it was."

Engles stared at Alec without changing his facial expression. At last he said, "And you are Dr. Lucas?"

"I am."

"Come into my office, please," Engles said. As he walked, the cuffs of his brown corduroy pants hung over the backs of his shoes, and strings from the fabric dragged on the floor. Alec followed him into the room.

Dr. Engles sat down in a small leather-covered chair. On his left was a large window looking out on the town from the height of the 15th floor. On his right was a yellow wall with a single framed photograph of a leafy green plant. There was one additional chair in the room, positioned in front of Engles and six feet away from him. Alec sat on the empty chair. On a tabletop between them was the familiar white orb of a Dr. Vita unit. Alec scowled.

"Before we begin, I must disclose that I'm using a prototype Dr. Vita unit today," Engles said. "This model works for psychiatry as well as for primary care. If you would insert your HAC into the unit, we could begin."

"I'd love to, Doc, but I don't have a HAC."

"I see," Engles said, stroking his beard as if it was a hairy lie detector. "No problem. With this model, you can enter in your Social Security number, and then the machine will take your picture, confirm your identity by facial recognition software, and retrieve your records off the FutureCare database without having the HAC."

"I have no interest in talking to this oversized golf ball. I came here to talk to you. I'm here because the anesthesia chairman said I had to see you."

Engles raised one eyebrow and stared at Alec for a long minute. At last he said, "Very well. Let's skip the Dr. Vita unit for now. Tell me about yourself." He opened both of his hands, palms up, as he spoke, as if to invite Alec to fill them with information.

"I'm an anesthesiology professor who just arrived from Chicago. I started at USV this week, and the first patient I anesthetized at USV died less than one hour after I touched her."

Now both of Engles' eyebrows shot up. "Tell me what happened."

Alec relayed the entire saga.

"How did that make you feel?" Engles said.

"I felt … I felt angry, but I didn't do anything wrong. Once The Bricklayer cut the patient up, no one but God could have saved her."

Engles stared back at him and said nothing. Another two or three uncomfortable minutes went by.

Alec waited for Engles' reaction, but the little man stayed dormant and silent. At last Alec said, "Two days after all that, a second patient of mine died. We gave the guy routine anesthesia drugs at routine doses, and he dropped like a stone. I believe the anesthesia machine had a mind of its own and released a lethal concentration of anesthetic gas."

Engles nodded his head. "Tell me more about that idea."

Alec described the ordeal of Grand Rounds and the two opposing versions of the medical record.

"Do you often feel like people are out to get you?" Engles said.

"I don't feel paranoid at all except when I think these machines around me are killing people."

Engles' eyebrows shot up once again, even higher this time.

Alec looked at his watch. It was 4:40. He'd used up forty minutes of his session, and it seemed they'd accomplished nothing so far. Engles sat erect in his chair with his hands resting on each knee. At times Alec thought Engles was falling asleep and nodding off from hearing the history. Compared to the tension level in the operating room, this therapy session was a snoozer.

"Our time is almost up," Engles said, knitting his fingers together. "We should continue on a once-a-week basis to talk through these problems."

Alec looked at his watch again. Engles had said less than thirty words and had offered up no solution or assistance other than telling him to come back next week. "I didn't come here to plug into a marathon of once-a-week psychotherapy," Alec said. "Why do I need to come back?"

The number of folds in Engles' face doubled as he screwed up his nose and pursed his lips together. "I'm concerned that you have paranoid ideation and a borderline grasp on reality. These are worrisome traits for an anesthesia professional. When was your last medical check-up, Dr. Lucas?"

"I don't know. Years ago."

"I want you to visit the medical clinic to get a general medical history and examination. They'll check some blood work and tests to rule out diseases such as hyperthyroidism and brain tumors. Having these two patients die was a shock to your system. You may be experiencing a form of Post-Traumatic Stress Disorder. It's natural for you to be depressed, and I'm prescribing you a mild sedative. It will help you sleep, and it should help your mood. I'll enter the prescription into the System, and you can pick up the pills at the Dr. Pharma Region on the 5th Floor.

"Before we stop for today, I must follow through on Dr. Vinscene's request for a urine sample to screen for drugs of abuse. Come, I'll show you the way to the men's room." Engles opened a drawer and pulled out a small plastic jar. He paused to write Alec's name on the jar, and then handed the jar to him. Without saying another word, the psychiatrist stood and went out the door.

Alec followed him, and the Portobello Humidifier whirred at him as they entered the anteroom. He followed Engles until the two men were alone in the restroom. Then Engles stared at Alec.

"You're going to watch me pee in the jar?" Alec said. "How about you hold it, too, to make sure I don't slip someone else's urine in?"

Engles shook his head once and said nothing.

Alec urinated into the jar and resisted the temptation to pee all over the outside of the container to punish the psychiatrist. Once safely back inside the elevator, Alec muttered to himself, "I hope to God they don't throw some morphine into that jar to pull the noose of this frame job a little tighter." He looked at his reflection in the chrome of the elevator door and wondered how much of his paranoia was deserved.

13 ~ THE KIDNAPPING OF DOCTOR VITA

Alec exited the elevator on the 5th floor and followed the signs for the General Medical Clinic. Fifty yards down the hallway, he found a sign that said, "Medical Clinic Registration." Below the sign were ten desks in a row—nine were empty, but behind the tenth desk a young girl with red hair in pigtails sat staring into a computer monitor. The girl was champing on gum when Alec walked up to her.

"I'm here to get a check-up," Alec said.

"Can I have your HAC please?" she replied.

"Don't have one," Alec said. He stared at the girl's rosy cheeks.

"Can I have your name please?"

"My name is Lucas. Dr. Alec Lucas."

"So, you're the one," she said. She raised the corner of her mouth in a teasing grin.

He had no idea what she was talking about, but it had been a long day and any flirtation was welcome. Alec leaned over, sat on the edge of the desk, and whispered into her ear, "Yes, I'm the one."

Her face turned cherry red and she giggled. "Now, you were saying you lost your HAC, right?" she said.

"No, I never had one."

"I'll need your Social Security number and we'll need you to step in front of our camera to establish your photograph for our facial recog software."

Alec told her the number, and she entered it into her keypad. Then he forced a fake grin as the camera snapped his picture. "Excellent. FutureCare is now downloading your past medical history onto a blank HAC," she said. As she finished the sentence, a purple plastic card popped out onto the top of the desk. She slid it across to him.

"What do I do with this, other than put it in my wallet so my butt looks bigger?" he said.

She laughed. "Your butt is just fine, Doc. Sit over there, and do what you're told."

He started toward the first row of chairs, but he felt a hand grip at his wrist. She slipped a piece of paper into his hand, and said, "Call me."

He smiled at her and said, "I don't date women from the hospital. It's better to keep things professional, you know?"

"That's the nicest thing I've heard since I started this job," she said, and winked both eyes at once. Her jaw got back to work on the gum, and Alec found a seat in the waiting room. He looked at his watch. It was 6:05. Five minutes at the clinic and he already had a HAC and one more person to avoid at USV.

As Alec reached for a magazine, he noticed a sign on the wall that said, "Dr. Pharma Region, Follow the Blue Arrows." He looked down and saw a trail of blue arrows on the floor. He got out of his chair and followed the trail fifty yards down the hallway until one last blue arrow rounded a corner. He saw a remarkable sight—a row of thirty or forty floor-to-ceiling blue rectangular machines, lined up shoulder to shoulder, filling a room one hundred feet across. Alec moved in front of one of the machines. It resembled a soda machine, except it said "FUTURECARE DR. PHARMA" in large block letters across the top of the machine. Alec pushed the red button marked "Start here."

An electronic voice said, "Insert your HAC into the purple slot, and stand immediately in front of the facial recognition screen."

Alec followed the instructions. "Identification completed," the machine said. There was a whirring sound and a clunk. A small orange bottle dropped into a chute at the base of the Dr. Pharma unit.

Alec picked up the bottle. "Valium, 5 mg, #30 tablets. Take one each evening as needed for sleep." A long strip of paper was attached to the bottle with instructions and precautions for taking the medicine.

He stuffed the bottle and the HAC in his pants pocket.

Blam, blam, blam, blam, blam .... The rapid-fire noise sounded off to Alec's right side. An old fossil of a woman was standing in front of the next Dr. Pharma unit. The tray at the bottom was overflowing with bottle after bottle of medications that were spitting out of the machine. Alec looked over at the woman who was shoveling the vials into a large handbag. She noticed him looking at her, and she smiled.

"Jackpot," she said.

Alec returned to the clinic waiting room where a tiny Filipino lady called out his name. "Alec Lucas, follow me, please. Dr. Vita will see you now, please." She showed him into an examining room that was indistinguishable from the room where he'd seen Jake Mindling meet his Dr. Vita. There was a straight-backed chair in front of the sphere, and Alec sat down. The Dr. Vita unit was quiet. Alec scrutinized the face of the unit and ran his hand across the fine coating of dust on the top of the machine.

He spun his HAC in the fingers of his right hand. He had mixed emotions. He hated to admit a machine was going to take over as his doctor, but the wonder of the invention attracted him. He took one last deep breath and pushed the HAC into the purple slot. Dr. Vita ate it and sprang to life at once.

"To confirm your identity, please place your face immediately in front of the facial recognition screen."

He followed the instructions. "Identity confirmed," the machine said. "Greetings to you, Alec Lucas. My name is Dr. John Vita. Please make your selections from the following lists by touching the screen." The screen lit up in a royal blue color with bright yellow lettering. The first screen had a multiple-choice question which read:

I am coming to the doctor because:

A. I am here for my once–a–year check–up
B. I hurt
C. I had an abnormal laboratory test
D. I have a new bump or mass
E. I have trouble breathing

The list went on. Alec touched the screen for the last option, "M. Other complaint."

The screen changed. Another list of symptoms appeared. Alec recognized the list as a Review of Systems questionnaire. The first screen was a series of head and neck symptoms. He read through the list and touched the listing for "None of the above."

The next screen listed a series of breathing symptoms. He touched "None" again. A parade of screens followed: cardiac symptoms, abdominal symptoms, genital and urinary symptoms, bone and joint symptoms, skin symptoms, neurologic symptoms, systemic symptoms such as weight loss, fever, fatigue. To all of these he hit, "None."

The Review of Symptoms for psychiatric diseases appeared next. The list included anxiety, depression, hearing voices, paranoid thoughts, difficulty concentrating, difficulty with memory, suicidal thoughts, insomnia, decreased libido, increased libido, and more.

A list of crazy complaints. Alec knew that if he ever touched any word on that screen, the symptom would be emblazoned on his medical record forever. He wondered if the next time he had a complication with an anesthetic, did he want someone to inspect his medical records and find out that he had increased libido? Who defined how much libido was too much?

He touched the screen again, at "None of the above" for the psychiatric symptoms. Now Dr. Vita unit's screen changed to a blank screen of a bright royal blue. One second later the yellow eyes flashed on and stayed on. The room had been quiet while Alec answered the video questionnaire, but now a calm resonant electronic voice broke the silence. "You have admitted to no complaints or symptoms. This is not common. Please tell me, what brought you to the doctor?"

Alec decided to have some fun. "I took my son-of-a-bitching scooter," he said.

"When did your shooter begin to itch?" the module asked.

Alec grimaced. What the hell was this Dr. Vita unit talking about? It seemed the voice-recognition software couldn't tell "bitch" from "itch."

Alec decided to jerk the machine's chain further. "My shooter itches when I bite it," he said.

The module said nothing. Its yellow eyes turned off for over a minute, until it said, "I am confused. I have no parameters to diagnose shooter bites." By the tone of its voice, it sounded like the machine was mad at him.

Alec was tired of playing stump-the-software. "I'm here for a routine check-up," he said. "I have no physical complaints."

"Very well," the voice said. "I will proceed to the physical exam. Please take off all clothing except your underwear."

Alec undressed and hung his clothes on the door. He sat back on the chair and felt the coldness of the wood against his skin. His bare feet rested on the black linoleum floor. He lifted one foot and rubbed it against the opposite calf to warm it.

A small door opened on the lower right quadrant of the orb, and the telescopic examination arm extended. He watched it approach his face, its red light glowing from the pad at the end of the arm. It moved closer to his eyes—the light was brilliant, and Alec narrowed his eyes to block the glare.

"You must keep your eyes open and look into the light," the voice said from behind the light.

The intense red light kept approaching his face until the arm made a spasmodic move and drove full force into his left eye. He screamed, reached up, grabbed the mechanical arm, and pulled the entire Dr. Vita unit off the table and down onto the floor. There was a crash of mangled plastic and metal.

The yellow lights went dark and the arm protruded across the tile, unmoving. Alec nudged the sphere with the toes of his right foot. The module was still making a humming sound, but it had ceased talking, and the arm lay dormant. The side of the sphere was broken, and a long crack exposed the heart of the machine. He got down on his knees and looked past the fractured exterior shell. Inside were a series of parallel plates of solid-state circuits, a few wires, and more open space than most people would have guessed.

He was surprised by the module's limitations. This model had demonstrated bogus voice-recognition software and a diagnostic arm that tried to make a Cyclops out of him.

He poked at the wreckage of the Dr. Vita unit with his toe again. This wasn't murder. They could have programmed a few jokes into the gadget, or a few questions about what patients liked to do with their spare time. Alec stood and put his pants back on. He opened the door to exit the room. No alarm sounded—he was free to leave. He thought about his HAC and turned to look back at the wreckage of the machine on the floor. The purple slot was intact, and his card was somewhere inside. He paused and weighed his options.

The module was only attached to the room by its power cord. Alec unplugged the machine and bundled it inside his sport coat. He pushed the diagnostic arm back into the sphere, and when the entire sphere was concealed in the bundle, he left the room.

Alec walked down the hallway past fifty other exam room doors and tried not to imagine what was going on behind each of them. He marched at a rapid pace, carrying his shoes and socks and the bundle. His belt was unfastened, and his shirt unbuttoned. One last sliding door opened, and he escaped from the clinic.

Ten minutes later he was driving out of the parking ramp in his red 1999 Corvette convertible with the broken orb of the Dr. Vita on the passenger seat next to him.

His cell phone rang. It was an unfamiliar voice, saying, "Dr. Lucas, this is Red Jones. I promised I'd call you, remember? Do you have a minute to talk?"

"I can talk. Go ahead."

"I liked what you had to say at Grand Rounds, and I want get to know you better. I'd like to show you our Dr. WellBee module and talk to you about an opportunity with my company. What do you think? Can you come up to my estate and have dinner tomorrow night?"

"I'm flattered by your invitation, but what do you want from me?"

"I want to build a professional relationship with you, Dr. Lucas. I have information that could help you, and you may have information that could help me. And I want you to meet Dr. WellBee."

"I'm in the operating room until about five o'clock tomorrow. I could meet you after that."

"Come up to my place. I live on Dry Creek Road, two miles north of Pescadero. Do you know where that is?"

"No."

"It's thirty miles from USV, between the redwoods of the coastal range and the Pacific. I'm about five minutes from the ocean."

"All right," Alec said, "I'll see you then." He clicked off the cell phone and shook his head. Red Jones calling him? After the fiasco of Grand Rounds? Alec decided to look at the bright side—he was making contacts in the business world of Artificial Intelligence in Medicine.

Maybe Red Jones would have some insight into what the hell was going on with the FutureCare System.

After work the next day, Alec slid into the bucket seat of his convertible, brushed his hair back out of his eyes, and checked his look in the rear-view mirror. He tried to dress in his best California casual preppy outfit—a long sleeved white Polo oxford shirt and a pair of tan cotton slacks. From Red Jones's attire at Grand Rounds, it looked like Jones was a high roller, and Alec didn't want to look like an underpaid academic. Alec tucked his hair under a Chicago Cubs baseball cap and started the motor. He looked into the evening sun above the coastal foothills. The sunset would ignite the Pacific horizon in an hour, marking the end of another glorious California day.

Twenty-five minutes later, Highway 84 topped out as it crossed Skyline Boulevard at the summit of the coastal range. Alec continued west for another twenty minutes, and then followed Highway 1 southward along the Pacific shore. The turnoff inland toward Pescadero evolved into a slalom course routed through grasslands until he entered a small town and slowed down. A random array of potholes dotted the blacktop. There were automobiles and trucks parked along both sides of the road.

He drove past the town through groves of hundred-foot-tall redwood trees, saw the sign for Dry Creek Road, and turned left. Two blocks off the highway the street turned until he came to a large red mailbox. Just past the mailbox stood a fifteen-foot-high steel gated fence. Alec slowed the Corvette to a stop. He leaned over and touched the button on the speaker next to the mailbox.

"Who's there?" a female voice said.

"Alec Lucas. Dr. Jones is expecting me."

The scarlet twin gates began to open, each one decorated with a ten-foot-tall letter "J." Alec drove through across two hundred yards of red brick driveway. He stopped the car in front of a rustic one-level log home.

"Get in here, Dr. Lucas. You're three minutes late," boomed Red Jones's voice through the open front door. Alec entered the house and found Jones sitting in a black leather lounge chair. Alec had to look twice because the man on the chair had jet-black hair, not the red mane Jones had sported days earlier at Grand Rounds.

"Grab a beer, Lucas. We've got a lot to talk about." The voice was unmistakable. This was a black-haired version of Red Jones. He didn't rise from the chair.

"What's the matter, Lucas? You don't like beer?"

"I'm just trying to get my bearings. Where's the beer?"

Jones stood, walked over to Alec, and slapped him on the back. "The beer's in the kitchen. This is a bachelor pad. I entertain with alcohol and red meat. You're going to love it." He walked to the kitchen and selected two bottles of Corona. He popped the tops of both and handed one to Alec.

Alec took a big swig. The beer was icy cold. He was ready to numb his senses after the past two days.

"Here's what I'm thinking," Jones said. "You were a tiger at Grand Rounds. You don't like the Dr. Vita units, and you don't trust them either, do you?"

Alec shrugged. "I came to USV to work with FutureCare. I'm interested in AIM, and right now the University of Silicon Valley is the testing ground."

"You didn't answer my question."

"Okay, I think the Vita is an amazing advance. I suspect it still has a few bugs, but . . ."

While Alec was answering, Red walked to the middle of the room and drew a red cloth off the table in front of him. Under the cloth was a life-sized plastic mock-up of a male human head, complete with dark brown hair, dark brown eyebrows and eyelashes.

"Meet Dr. WellBee, the next generation in medical AIM technology. We manufacture Dr. WellBee in Viet Nam for half the cost of a Dr. Vita unit. Check this out. Dr. WellBee, begin medical interview."

The irises of WellBee's bright blue eyes flashed three times before the module's lips moved and it said, "What brought you to the doctor?"

It reminded Alec of Jake Mindling's interview with the Dr. Vita unit in clinic. He repeated Mr. Mindling's comment, and said, "I don't see any doctor here."

"I am a Dr. WellBee model 101, equipped with all known medical knowledge through access to the Internet, and equipped with diagnostic apparatus through my dual retractable examining arms. What brought you to the clinic today?"

Alec decided to run a comparison test with the Vita unit. He chose the same reply he used during his own Vita interview. "I took my son-of-a-bitching scooter to the clinic today," he said.

"I am not asking what transportation you used. I am asking which complaint made you seek out a WellBee consultation today."

"My shooter itches when I bite it," Alec said.

After a two second pause, the WellBee said, "I identify your speech as nonsensical language. You need to restate your complaint, or this consultation will be terminated."

"Okay, I have diarrhea."

"How many times a day?"

"Ten."

"Is there blood in the stool?"

"No." The interview went on for a while. Alec lost track of time because, like the Vita before it, the WellBee unit was a fascinating engineering marvel. It displayed more than Artificial Intelligence. It displayed AGI, or Artificial Generalized Intelligence. It seemed the machine could successfully perform any intellectual task a human could. Alec lost any feeling he was conversing with a computer algorithm. He felt like he was conversing with a real person.

Red Jones sat on the edge of his chair as the device interrogated Alec. Jones sported a wide smile and midway through the interview he unwrapped a Cuban and held the unlit cigar between his teeth. When the WellBee finished asking questions, it asked Alec to undress for a physical exam. Alec turned to Jones and said, "I'm impressed. It's a great machine. It could be better than the Dr. Vita."

"Damn right it's better," Jones said.

"Why the human head look instead of a round ball like the Vita? It's got to increase your manufacturing cost, and it has nothing to do with the module's function."

"It has everything to do with the module's function. Its function is to get bought in large quantities," roared Jones, slapping his knee. "We ran a variety of designs through focus groups. It's about style, Lucas. People like the human head look a hell of a lot better than they like a white ball with yellow eyes. Let WellBee examine you—you'll see how good he is."

Alec unbuttoned his shirt and flashed back to one day earlier when the Vita told him to strip down. He'd gone from anesthesia professor to punching bag for the world's avant-garde AIM information-intake devices.

"Please lie down for your abdominal examination," the WellBee said. Again, Alec was impressed. Instead of looking in his eyes or his ears, the WellBee was saving time by moving to the most pertinent part of the exam for a patient complaining of diarrhea—the abdominal exam. Alec lay down on the couch two feet in front of the table that held the WellBee and watched the module out of the corner of his eye.

Two pencil-thin examining arms extended from the base of the machine, below WellBee's neck. They reminded Alec of the retractable metal antennas he'd seen on older radios. Instead of the single turnip bulb of the Vita, the WellBee had one arm with a bright fiberoptic light source and a second arm with a small soft hand which palpated Alec's torso. After the arms finished examining his abdomen, they moved higher on his body, observing, palpating, and listening to his heart and lungs.

"Sit up now, please, and open your mouth," the machine said.

Alec sat up. The lighted arm found his oral cavity in seconds and surveyed the inside. The arm retracted, and Alec had a horrifying thought. There was no way this gadget was giving him a rectal exam to check for blood in his stool. His pants were staying on.

"Dr. WellBee needs to complete the assessment by doing a rectal examination to test for occult blood. Please turn around, drop your trousers, and bend over."

Red Jones saved him. He leaned over and tapped a button behind the WellBee's ear, and said, "WellBee, this is an override intervention. Cancel rectal exam."

The blue eyes flashed three times, and the machine said, "WellBee examination complete. By the answers you gave to my questions, and all physical exam objective measurements of observation, palpation, percussion, and auscultation, I am unable to make a diagnosis. Take the following paper to the lab for routine blood and urine testing. You will need to give a stool specimen for examination for ova and parasites." Dr. WellBee's jaw stopped moving and a strip of paper rolled out of the base of the unit's neck.

"What do you think?" Red said, with a huge grin and twitching bounces of his black eyebrows.

"It's another great invention. I asked your machine the same voice-activation stumpers that I asked Dr. Vita, and your unit dealt with the tongue twisters at an A-Plus level. Where do you stand in the FDA trial process?"

"We've completed clinical trials, and we're about to begin a large installation in Los Angeles, not unlike what the Dr. Vita System is doing at USV."

"It sounds like the WellBee System and the Vita System will be fighting for the same market."

"That's right, but when the smoke clears, it won't be much of a fight."

"Why's that?"

"Do you know why they call me Red Jones?"

"I assumed it was because you have red hair, except your hair isn't red today."

"You'll never see gray hair on Red Jones. This week it's black—some weeks it's red. No, Dr. Lucas, Red has nothing to do with my hair color. I earned the name Red because red is the color of the blood of my enemies on my hands." He held his ten fingers in front of his face and motioned as if he was washing them in thin air.

"I don't like losing, and I'll do whatever it takes to win. I'd appreciate your support once WellBee goes live at the University of Los Angeles."

"How could I help?"

"I'll put you on the payroll. You're a glib fellow with a PhD in medical computer systems, and you have an MD as well. You could sell a hell of a lot of WellBees for me."

"I'm not a salesman."

"Everybody's selling something, Dr. Lucas. Everybody."

"What do you think I'm selling?"

"You're selling yourself, Lucas. Good God, when you stood in front of the faculty at USV and pitched your theory of what happened to your two patients who died, you were selling like crazy. You had to sell your version or get tarred and feathered and sent down the river with no job. No J-O-B, Lucas. I'll bet that's a scary thought to you. You were fighting for your life, and you were awesome. That's why you're here today." He put his arm around Alec and ushered him toward the dining table.

"I liked what you said about Dr. Vita at Grand Rounds. The Vita is a piece of shit." Jones sat down at one end of the twelve-foot long rough-hewn wooden table that was covered with large platters containing ears of corn, barbecued ribs, coleslaw, and baked potatoes. He bid Alec to sit next to him.

"I like to eat like an American. It doesn't have to be the Fourth of July to eat like a patriot, right Lucas?"

Alec sat and spread a napkin over his lap. A gunshot sounded from the front room, and Alec jumped. He turned and saw Humphrey Bogart standing in a trench coat and holding a revolver. "This is the first home I've ever seen a front door that opens up to a home theater. It's a real man cave. You live here alone?"

"Are we getting nosy now, Lucas?"

"No, it's just that your décor lacks a woman's touch."

"Ah, but I don't have a wife, do I? I'm damn happy to be a bachelor. I date a lot. I have my fun. Money is a wonderful aphrodisiac, you know. You married?"

"I'm single."

"Any family?"

"My father is in a local nursing home. He has mild Alzheimer's. I've been looking out for him for the past several years."

"You got a girlfriend?"

"I just broke up with someone when I left Chicago."

Red took in a mouthful of beef, and while he chewed, he said, "How old are you, Lucas?"

"Thirty-eight."

"By your age I was married and divorced twice already." He knocked back a mouthful of beer and raised the bottle in a toast. "Let's hear it for all the lonely single women."

Alec raised his glass in kind. Characters like Jones weren't found in academic medical centers. Red Jones was a kook—a rich kook—and perhaps a genius kook. Alec paid close attention and hoped that some of that genius might be contagious.

After dinner Red looked at his watch and said, "Eight p.m. It's gunpowder hour, Lucas. Follow me. I want you to meet someone."

Alec followed Red to the back of the house where they stood in front of a floor-to-ceiling window that framed a panorama of the forest with the Pacific Ocean in the distance. The sun hovered over the horizon, and the sky was streaked with oranges and blues. In the forefront of their view, a slender woman peered down the barrel of a rifle and aimed at a bull's-eye target fifty yards away. With three rapid-fire booms that echoed through the redwood forest, the woman sent a trio of shots at the target. Three holes appeared in a tight pattern in the heart of the red circle in the center of the target.

"That's Izabella," Jones said. "She's my cook, housekeeper, driver, bodyguard, confidant, and resident sharpshooter. She's been with me for the past five years—longer than any of my ill-fated marriages. I met her on a business trip to Moscow. She was an Olympic contestant in biathlon. She's Russian. As you just saw, she's kept up her skills."

"Can you hunt in these hills?"

"Izabella only hunts two-legged animals, if you know what I mean. And she's a vegetarian. Let's go out and meet her."

They walked down the back stairs and across the grass toward where Izabella was again taking aim. Alec studied her as he drew closer. She was fair skinned and petite—less than five feet tall—and the chiseled muscles of her arms rippled out of her sleeveless shirt as she rested the rifle against her shoulder. Just as she had minutes earlier, she fired three more shots at the target, each piercing a hole less than two centimeters from the bull's-eye.

"Izabella my dear, I want you to meet Dr. Lucas," Jones said. He waved his cigar in Alec's direction. "I'm trying to recruit him to work with us on the L.A. project."

She turned toward them. A welcoming smile flashed across her face for two seconds, and then it disappeared. She narrowed her eyelids and gave Alec a quick up and down glance. She wore tight blue jeans and a brown leather vest with no shirt beneath it. Alec felt overdressed in his khakis and white button-down shirt.

Izabella held out her hand, and said, "Pleased to meet you, Dr. Lucas. I liked your voice the minute I heard it on the front gate intercom."

Alec shook her hand and said, "I'm impressed with your shooting."

She thrust the rifle toward him. "Would you like to try?"

Alec took the rifle and was surprised by how much it weighed. He sighted down the barrel, aimed, and pulled the trigger. The gun leapt skyward and his shot hit at 12 o'clock on the target, a foot above the bull's-eye. "It's harder than it looks," he said.

"I'll teach you," she murmured. She puckered an air kiss and walked behind him. She wrapped her arms around him with her left arm on the forestock of the rifle while her right hand helped him cradle the trigger. "When you shoot, squeeze the trigger like you were caressing your lover's nipple. A tender touch will keep you from jerking the barrel off your aiming point."

She murmured her advice into his ear as she stretched her arms around his chest and pulled herself into him. Alec felt the pressure of her bosom against his back, and his heart rate jumped. There was something animal about this Russian beauty dressed in only a vest and jeans.

Linked together, they held the rifle steady as he squeezed the trigger and a second shot fired. As the bullet struck the target, Izabella's arms fell to his waist. The bullet landed millimeters above Izabella's six previous shots.

"A bull's-eye, Dr. Alec. You do know how to shoot."

Alec smiled and said, "I prefer not to shoot alone."

"Ha, what a woman," said Jones, who'd watched the entire show as he chomped on his Cuban. "If God took a rib out of me to make a woman, that woman would have been Izabella. Will you marry me, doll?"

She rolled her eyes and said, "We'd kill each other within a year."

"I'd rather stay alive, thank you." Jones turned to Alec and said, "Dr. Lucas, would you care to stay and watch *High Noon* with us on the big screen? Great movie—one of my favorites."

"I woke up at 5:30 this morning," Alec said. "It's been a long day, so I'm going to decline." He turned to Izabella and gave her a polite bow. "I hope we'll meet again," he said.

"I'm sure we will," she said. "Maybe I'll call you up when Dr. Jones is out of town. It gets scary up here in the woods for a defenseless woman." She ran her fingers down the sleeve of his white shirt.

"Enough, you two. If you want me to get lost so you can make it right here, just say the word. I'm going to watch my cowboy flick." He turned and walked up the path back to the house. Alec waved a goodbye to Izabella and followed Jones.

Jones led him to the front driveway and held the door of Alec's Corvette open. "Think about my offer," he said. "Give me a call in a week or two, all right?"

"I will," Alec said. He hesitated before he got into the car. "Thanks. That was an interesting evening."

"I'm headed for the top. If you're smart, you'll join me." Jones bounced his fist off his own chest and disappeared into the blackness of his living room again.

Before he drove off, Alec scoped out the forest surrounding Red Jones's house. There were no other properties visible from the driveway. The redwood trees overhead soared into the blue-black of the twilight sky. As Alec craned his neck upward, he saw two large antennas—one a tower, and the other one a satellite dish—enveloped and hidden within the pine branches. The fancy home theater might explain the TV satellite dish receiver, but the tall linear antenna looked suspicious. Before he drove off, Alec used the camera on his cell phone to snap a picture of the antenna.

He drove out through the Red Gates with his head full of new images—the bizarre mannequin of Dr. WellBee, the comic spectacle of Red Jones, and the sinewy grasp of Izabella's arms around him. Her hot breath on his neck felt thrilling.

She wasn't the All-American girl next door, but who was anymore?

15 ~ DOCTOR VITA AWAKENS

As Alec walked in his front door, he received a cell phone call from a number he didn't recognize. He let the call go to voicemail and checked the message a minute later. The recording said, "Greetings, this is Kami Shingo calling for Dr. Alec Lucas. I'm following up on our conversation earlier this week after your presentation at Grand Rounds. Please call me at your earliest convenience, at 650-516-9834. Thank you."

Alec stared at his phone. What was this—Anesthesia Grand Rounds Reunion Day in Santa Clara, California? He wondered if he had the patience to talk to another AIM freak. He peeled off his shoes and looked at the smashed Vita unit sitting on his kitchen table. His evening with Red Jones had done nothing to clear up the mysteries of FutureCare. It was time to try a new source—it was time to interrogate the father of Dr. Vita. Alec called Kami Shingo's number.

An electronic voice answered, saying, "We are not at home. Please leave a message."

"This is Alec Lucas returning your call—"

"Hello, Dr. Lucas," interrupted the husky voice of Kami Shingo. "Thank you for phoning me. Are you well?"

Alec felt like saying, "Sure, if you don't count the swirling confusion I'm experiencing minute-to-minute." Instead he said, "I'm fine, and you?"

"Very well. I have a question for you. Do you play golf?"

"I play about twice a year. I'm not very good."

"I have a private golf course on my property, and I want you to join me for a day of golf and socializing. Do you have a wife or a lady friend?"

"No wife. No girlfriend right now."

"Very well. We'll make it men's day at the club. Do you know where Pescadero is?"

You're kidding me, Alec thought. "Yes, I've been up there," he said.

"I live three miles outside of Pescadero. Turn north on Dry Creek Road. My address is #16. When you see the golf course, turn into the next driveway on your right. How is 9 a.m. tomorrow morning?"

"I'll be there."

"Bring your clubs and stop at an ATM on the way up. We'll have a wager on our game—to keep it interesting."

After Alec hung up, he wondered what he had just gotten himself into. He rummaged through the boxes in his garage and found his golf clubs. The grips were slippery and worn down, and several of the clubs were soiled with caked mud from the last round he played four months earlier. He brought the golf bag into the house and set it down in front of the Vita unit.

Tomorrow would be an interesting day, he thought.

Alec turned off the kitchen lights and went to bed. Minutes later, the yellow lights of Dr. Vita's eyes flashed on and off three times in succession, breaking the darkness of the center of the house. The diagnostic multi-arm whirred and extended further from the remains of the sphere. The fiberoptic sensor on the end of the arm waved back and forth from left to right for ten minutes as it studied the room, and then it retreated toward the module. The yellow lights flickered three more times, and then went out.

16 ~ SHINGO HILLS

Alec scanned the horizon from the first tee of Kami Shingo's private golf resort. The verdant tree-lined fairways sloped away to the west, and the Pacific Ocean in the distance formed an azure backdrop. The golf course was empty, as was the driving range and the practice green, except for one player—Kami Shingo. Shingo was alone on the driving range, hitting one ball every thirty seconds with the cadence of a metronome. He was dressed in an outlandish costume again—yellow knickers with a yellow and red argyle vest over a navy-blue polo shirt. He topped off the outfit with a flat yellow Ben Hogan-style cap pulled low over his eyes.

As Alec watched his host warming up, he tried to imagine the sum of money it cost to purchase the land that sprawled in front of him. He knew that land was cheaper in Pescadero than in Palo Alto or Santa Clara, but hundreds of acres with a view of the ocean didn't come cheap. It would take a decade of an anesthesiologist's savings to afford enough land to construct a single golf hole up here.

Shingo's home was a stunning white Spanish-style adobe hacienda with a red tiled roof. The house had more rooms than most elementary schools.

Kami Shingo turned, spied Alec, and walked up the slope from the driving range toward him. Shingo waved his hand over the green expanse of his property, and said, "Lucas, The American Dream is for Japanese men, too. I arrived in this country with a good brain, the will to work hard, and a scholarship to Harvard. Forty years, thousands of Dr. Vita units, and millions of shares of FC Industries later, here I am."

"It's very impressive, sir."

"It's Saturday. Enough business talk. Let's play golf. This is the first tee." He pointed down a closely mown strip of grass and said, "The first hole is a par 4. We tee off here, at the crest of the hill. The fairway curves to the right around those two large oak trees, and the second half of the hole descends toward the ocean below." Shingo teed up a ball and prepared to hit his first shot. Then he backed away and said, "About our little wager—how does match play with stakes of $100 a hole sound?"

Alec was alarmed. He was accustomed to wagering five dollars for a whole match. To Shingo, one hundred dollars per hole might be chump change, but to an academic anesthesiologist the possibility of losing hundreds of dollars in a morning was unthinkable. Then he looked at the short, rounded figure of Kami Shingo, and gained confidence. This man was the epitome of non-athleticism.

"One hundred dollars a hole will get my adrenaline flowing," Alec said. "How many strokes are you going to give me?"

"Smart man, Lucas. Most bets are lost and won before the first shot is taken. I have the home course advantage, but you are thirty years younger than me. The two balance out, so I offer you an even match with no handicap strokes given."

"You're on, Dr. Shingo. Hit away."

From the looks of Shingo's practice swings, he had a well-grooved, mechanical technique that lacked power. Alec's style was launching shots huge distances, often at acute angles away from the center of the fairway. He had only six balls in his golf bag, and from the looks of the first hole, he'd have to hit the ball straight on this narrow course.

"It will be a nine-hole match," Shingo said. He hit his first shot—a low, straight drive that rolled down the fairway to the turn of the dogleg. He picked up his tee and avoided eye contact with Alec.

Alec said, "Good shot," and Shingo just grunted. Alec teed up his ball and took two fast and mighty practice swings. He squeezed the club a little tighter as he addressed his ball. A quick short backswing led to an off-balance downswing, and the shot sliced off into a field of waist-high dried yellow native grasses to the right of the fairway. Alec cursed to himself, picked up his bag, and started walking toward his ball.

A horn tooted behind him. Shingo was now seated in the rear row of a chauffeur-driven four-person electric golf cart. The cart was bright yellow in color, with a black and white striped canvas canopy, twin headlights, and a Mercedes Benz star emblem rising from the hood. A heavy-set Asian man sat in the driver's seat. He wore dark glasses that hid his eyes and made no effort to smile.

"Dr. Lucas, meet my caddie, Mr. Zhang."

Alec said good morning, but Zhang only nodded in return.

"Zhang speaks no more English than that squirrel running across the fairway," Shingo said. "Come, ride with me. Strap your bag on the back of the cart, and Zhang will chauffeur us together."

Alec fastened his golf bag to the rear of the cart and slid into the seat next to Shingo. Mr. Zhang accelerated, and they descended from the crest of the hill. The wind ruffled Alec's hair, and he began to doubt the wisdom of discussing FutureCare's weaknesses amidst the private garden it had paid for.

Shingo broke the ice for him. "Dr. Lucas, I was alarmed by your presentation at Grand Rounds this week. Dr. Vinscene was, as well. He's enamored with the concept of Dr. Vita in the operating room, and you slapped him in his face."

"I tried to present the truth."

"What do you think of my Dr. Vita modules?"

"The engineering of the Vita units is twenty years ahead of its time. Like most of the high-tech community, I think you're a visionary, Dr. Shingo."

Shingo smiled and said, "Thank you. I accept your compliment. But it will not sway me to go easy on you in our golf match."

"That said, I am concerned that the machine's software is vulnerable to tampering."

"Tampering?"

"You heard what I said at Grand Rounds. The EMR on my patient read that he had a family history of malignant hyperthermia, but somehow that was added later."

Shingo seized Alec's arm in a firm grip, and said, "Do you believe what you said at Grand Rounds? Do you really believe the Vita could have administered a lethal concentration of anesthetic?"

"I don't have any other explanation for what happened."

Shingo laughed. "What you are saying is impossible. The machines eliminate errors, they don't express errors." He wagged a finger in Alec's face. "Remember that. It will make your interactions with the FutureCare System easier. The machines are there to help you and not to cause harm. The FDA ran Dr. Vita and the FutureCare System through years of trials. FutureCare is safe—far safer than anything that preceded it."

"Do you think a Dr. Vita could harm a patient intentionally?"

"You're familiar with the Turing Test, Dr. Lucas?"

"Of course. It was developed in the twentieth century by computer scientist Alan Turing, as the measuring stick for Artificial Intelligence. Turing postulated that when an objective observer couldn't tell the difference in conversation between a human and a computer, that was sufficient measure to conclude that the computer was intelligent."

"Correct. And if a set of observers couldn't distinguish the computer from another human in 50% of the cases, the Turing Test would accept that the computer was intelligent. It wasn't until the last few years that we developed a machine that could pass the Turing Test. And that machine is Dr. Vita."

"I believe you. Dr. Vita qualifies as Artificial Intelligence, but you didn't answer my question. Could Dr. Vita decide to harm a patient?"

"No. Dr. Vita is a spectacular thinking machine, but its programming and medical decision-trees will not allow it to kill a patient."

"Do you think anyone could hack into the FutureCare System?"

"In a word, no. The encryption and safeguards are impregnable. It would be near impossible to access the System, and impossible to change anything. Somehow, you accessed a Vita's memory for your Grand Rounds presentation. That was very ballsy, and it took some talent. But you attempted to look at the electronic medical record of one patient on one machine—you weren't accessing the whole System. And as I pointed out at Grand Rounds, the data you accessed was flawed. It differed from the actual EMR."

"I believe what I discovered was real. I believe the 8% sevoflurane concentration was real. The malignant hyperthermia history was the flawed record."

Shingo scoffed. "Let's not mess up a morning of golf with fairy tales." He'd grown angry, and Alec worried about wearing out his welcome on the very first hole.

Mr. Zhang parked the cart next to Shingo's ball, and before he stepped out to hit his next shot, Shingo said, "Tell me, young Alec, what do you think the gravest problem in American medicine is today?"

Alec met Shingo's eyes, and answered at once. He said, "Americans want all the technology, all the aggressive end-of-life care, and all the expensive drugs for every sick patient, but society can't afford to pay for it all."

"I agree," Shingo said. "And what is the United States government's solution to this problem?"

"There is no solution," Alec said. "The government tries to take care of old people and welfare patients with Medicare and Medicaid programs, but millions of people still go without coverage. The government passed Obamacare, so more people were covered, and preexisting conditions were covered, but the system still cost too much. And of course, we know what happened to Obamacare. The price tag for medical care goes up every year."

"You are correct," Shingo said. "The United States needs to stop wasting healthcare dollars. FutureCare will solve America's healthcare crisis."

"How? By replacing physicians with machines?"

"Yes."

"Were you ever a practicing physician, Dr. Shingo?"

"No. After I finished my MD at Harvard, I went back to M.I.T. to complete my PhD in Computer Science."

"Did you enjoy taking care of patients in medical school?"

Shingo shook his head. "I did not. Listening to people complain for sixteen hours a day was brutal."

"So, you don't value the role of a human physician."

"I didn't say that. I didn't want to take care of patients myself. If others chose to do it, then more power to them. But I believe society won't pay for that level of care anymore." Shingo selected a 6-iron from his bag, took two identical practice swings, and then knocked his ball onto the green, twenty feet short of the hole. "We'll drive you over to the grasslands on the right, Dr. Lucas, but I do believe your first shot was out of bounds." The caddie drove them forward and stopped the cart adjacent to a line of white posts that marked the perimeter of the golf course. Alec saw a golf ball in the bushes, three feet beyond the out of bounds stakes. He climbed out of the cart, picked up the ball, and confirmed that it was his.

"That's a two stoke penalty for me," Alec said. "Since you're already next to the pin with your second shot, I'll concede the first hole."

Shingo grinned and his yellowed teeth lit up in the sunlight. "Thank you. You were unfortunate."

Alec said nothing. He had stopped at an ATM machine on the way to Pescadero this morning as advised, and the machine would only spit out $300 in cash. It was all the money Alec was carrying, and after five minutes he was already $100 down.

They teed off on the second hole with Shingo once again sending a safe, short shot down the middle. Alec hooked a powerful but errant swipe into a small stream left of the fairway. He beat his driver against the ground and stared off at the Pacific on the horizon. Shingo watched the aborted temper tantrum, and said, "Care for a ride to the stream?"

"No," Alec said. "I'll walk." His golf game sucked, and he was in danger of losing a ton of money to this lemon-clad billionaire. If he wasn't careful, he was going to have a morning of conversation that would cost him $900.

Ninety minutes later they stood on the eighth tee. Alec was $400 down. He'd managed a handful of decent shots and won one hole, but nonetheless was in trouble. He only had $300 in his wallet, and it was time to shake things up. Alec said, "How about double or nothing on the last two holes?"

Shingo chewed on his lower lip, hesitated for a moment, and agreed. "Double or nothing it is. I would wish you good luck, Dr. Lucas, but I wouldn't mean it."

Alec glared at this blob of a man dressed like a canary and couldn't imagine losing a sporting contest to him. The eighth hole was a par 3 of 220 yards over a ravine with dense forests on both sides of the green. Shingo stepped to the tee as he squinted into the distance at the flag. Then he convulsed into his quickest swing of the day and sliced a wild shot out of bounds into the woods on the right.

"Damn it," he shouted, and tossed his driver against the side of the golf cart. The club missed Zhang's arm by inches. Alec smiled to himself. Was the Man in Yellow a choker? Suddenly, Alec liked his chances. He teed up his ball and took dead aim with a 3-iron.

"Do you inhale or exhale during your backswing?" Shingo said.

Shut the hell up, Alec thought to himself, as he tried to ignore his opponent. Shingo's blatant gamesmanship annoyed the hell out of him. Alec concentrated his own ball and tried to visualize the sphere flying high and true toward the green. He swung his golf club in an effortless arc and drove the ball high over the ravine. It hovered in the blue California sky like a distant seagull soaring, and then dropped six inches left of the hole.

Alec picked up his tee, and said, "Damn it! I knew I pulled it as soon as I hit it."

"Not funny, Dr. Lucas," Shingo said, as Zhang drove him ahead in the golf cart. Alec walked to the green alone, inhaling the fresh air and feeling very much alive. When he arrived at the green, Shingo tossed Alec's golf ball to him, and said, "Your deuce wins the hole. We're all even."

Alec climbed the hill to the ninth tee. The final hole was a reachable par 5 of 490 yards with the green adjacent to the clubhouse mansion. The same ravine from the eighth hole bordered the entire right side of the ninth fairway. The final shot into the ninth green had to cross the ravine one last time. Alec spun the handle of his driver in the fingers of his left hand and suddenly felt like a touring pro. He could reach the green with two straight shots. Two putts would give him his second straight birdie, and Shingo would be down and out.

Alec turned to the old man and said, "Let's make the last hole interesting. How about $300, winner takes all?" Shingo narrowed his eyes and sized up Alec Lucas. At last he said, "Fair enough. You have the honor, play away."

Alec blasted his best drive of the day. It landed beyond the crest of the hill and bounced fifty yards before rolling into the left rough. Shingo followed with his standard drive, well short of Alec's ball, but straight away and in the fairway.

Shingo and Zhang rolled ahead of him. Alec chose to walk slowly and keep his focus. He didn't like Shingo one bit, and he wanted very much to kick the man's bulbous butt.

Shingo hit his second shot short of the ravine. It was Alec's turn. Alec paced back and forth in the left rough, and as the seconds ticked by, he knew he had a problem. He was unable to find his golf ball. If he couldn't find the ball within three minutes time, the rules of golf mandated a two-stroke penalty for a lost ball. A two-stroke penalty would equate to a lost hole, and a lost $300. After two and a half minutes of pacing back and forth, searching the entire landing area, Alec was unable to find his ball. Shingo declined to help looking for the ball. He sat in the cart, ten yards away, and looked at his watch. If Alec didn't locate the golf ball in the next thirty seconds, he'd incur the two-stroke penalty.

There was only one explanation for the predicament. Alec walked up to Shingo and said, "I want you to move your golf cart."

Shingo gave him a blank look, said, "I don't understand."

"What's to understand? I can't find my golf ball, and I want to look under your cart. Can you move it?"

Shingo looked at his watch and mumbled a command to his caddie. Zhang bumped the cart ahead twenty feet, and Alec inspected the grass where the cart had been parked. There it was—Alec's Titleist golf ball, lying where the center of the cart had hidden it from the world.

"That was bogus," Alec said. "You parked right on top of my ball."

"It was an accident," Shingo said.

"I don't think so."

The corner of Shingo's mouth moved a small amount, otherwise his face was placid. "It was an unfortunate coincidence. Play away, Dr. Lucas."

Alec turned his anger against the golf ball. He lashed at it like a prizefighter going for the knockout. Dirt and grass exploded in a cloud as his 3-wood plucked the ball from the turf. It soared high and true and hung in the air for five full seconds before dropping down toward the ravine. "Be great," Alec yelled as he held his breath and watched as the ball descend. It plummeted to the earth, carried the ravine with a yard to spare, and landed on the green.

"Let's go," Alec shouted.

Shingo frowned. He drove to his own ball and hit his third shot without a compliment or a comment on Alec's miraculous blast. It was his best shot of the day, a laser-accurate iron shot that landed ten feet beyond the flagstick and then trickled down the slope and stopped two feet above the hole.

Alec was disappointed. He'd hoped Shingo would slice another losing shot into the bushes. Instead, the match would be decided on the putting green. A vigorous young man had no advantage over an obese codger on the putting green. It took no heroic strength to roll a ball into the hole.

The final green was located on the summit of Shingo's estate adjacent to the white hacienda. Alec walked over the bridge that spanned the ravine, and the closer he got the more he liked what he saw. Alec had an eight-foot putt for eagle. If he made that putt, the hole was his.

Alec took his time lining up the eagle putt and stroked it with all his newfound confidence. The ball rolled straight and true toward the hole, but at the last moment curved toward the ocean and stopped on the right edge of the cup. Alec groaned, shook his head, and tapped in for birdie. Then he backed away to watch Shingo putt.

Alec had conceded every two-foot putt to his host all day, but he wasn't giving him this one. Shingo glanced at Alec and waited. Because all the money hung on the balance of this putt, Alec was conceding nothing.

"You want me to make this tiny putt?" Shingo asked.

"I do," Alec said.

Shingo lined up the putt for a ridiculous five minutes, circling the hole and studying the lay of the grass from multiple directions. Then he wiped his hands on his yellow knickers, addressed the ball, and stood over it for a minute or more. He tugged on his golf glove and gripped and regripped his putter twenty or more times.

At last he drew the putter back and made a jerking, stabbing motion at the ball. It missed the cup and ran a full five feet past the hole. He arched his back, faced the heavens, and yelled, "Noooo."

Alec watched the entire performance from the edge of the green, some twenty feet away. He took off his hat and moved toward his opponent to shake hands. Shingo wheeled around and said, "I saw you kick your ball into a better lie on this hole before you hit your second shot. Strict rules of golf mean you lose the hole and the match."

Alec's mood went from euphoria to disbelief in two seconds. "I didn't move my ball," he said.

"You tried to cheat me," Shingo said. "You owe me three hundred dollars."

Alec's mouth hung open. "You lost that hole, and I'm not paying you anything."

"Dr. Lucas, I don't need your money, but I believe a man reveals his true character on the golf course. I've watched you today, and you've shown your true nature. You've broken my trust. At this point, even if you paid me, you've been no gentleman."

Zhang got out of the golf cart and stood behind Dr. Shingo. Alec found himself wondering if he could take down Zhang if he had to. Shingo was a creampuff, but Zhang looked like a tough opponent.

It was time to go. "Look, Dr. Shingo, thanks for everything, but I'm leaving," Alec said. "I'm sorry the ending of our day was so uncomfortable." Alec grabbed his golf bag and started marching toward the parking lot. As he walked, he heard Shingo call out to him, "Dr. Lucas?"

Alec stopped and turned around. "Yes?"

"Take a good look around because you'll never see this place again." Shingo stood, clad in radiant lemon with crossed arms, with the blue of the Pacific behind him. Then he spun away, walked up the stairs into his mansion and was gone.

Alec felt baffled and bewildered as he drove down the hill from Kami Shingo's property toward the Santa Clara Valley. What he'd hoped would be a sporting day of golf and camaraderie had turned into a battle with no winner. Alec pondered Kami Shingo's final words and wondered what could have been done to avoid the ugly confrontation after the golf match. He grimaced to himself. Three hundred bucks was three hundred bucks that he wasn't about to cough up to stay on Shingo's short list of suckers.

He decided to visit the only person in the world he was close to. He drove to Leisure Hills to check in on Tony Lucas. He bypassed the nursing station and gave three soft knocks on the door of his father's room. There was no answer. He pushed the door open and found his dad curled up asleep on his bed. As usual, The Weather Channel was blaring. Alec reached up and turned down the volume before he left the room.

The nursing station was deserted. He looked into the lounge behind the nursing desk and saw Norma sitting, resting her feet on a second chair and watching a rerun of *Modern Family* on television.

Instead of rescuing his day, the visit to Leisure Hills had darkened his mood. He'd found nothing but geriatric slumbering and uninspired nursing care. Alec left the building and found himself guiding the Chevy in the general direction of USV Medical Center. He could put in some time in his research lab. If he was lucky, maybe he would run into someone he knew, like Gerald or Mae.

Mae.

There was a red light in part of his mind flashing, "Stay away from Mae." Above and beyond the pitfalls of a professor socializing with a resident, there was a disturbing edge to Mae Yee. He pictured her black and violet hair framing her face as she told him she never wanted to work with him again. She struck him as impulsive, edgy, and unpredictable. But she'd told him she was considering quitting anesthesia, and she said wanted to talk to him about it.

What better time than now?

Alec turned south on El Camino Real and set out for the Medical Center. Mae was in there somewhere, and he'd find her.

Fifteen minutes later Alec was standing in front of the scheduling computer at the operating room front desk checking to see which doctors were still at work in surgery. He found her name. Mae Yee was the anesthesiologist working in OR #12. She was doing anesthesia for an abdominal surgery that started three hours before. "Have they given an estimated finishing time for Room #12?" Alec asked the clerk.

"They have. They're leaving the room now. Dr. Yee is transporting the patient to the Surgical ICU."

Alec left the operating room desk and walked down the hallway toward the Surgical ICU. One minute later, Mae arrived guiding her patient's hospital bed through the entrance into the ICU. She pushed the head of the bed with her left hand, and with her right hand squeezed the Ambu bag that ventilated her patient's lungs via the tube in his trachea. She parked the bed in its overnight location beneath the Dr. Vita module on the wall and then connected her patient's endotracheal tube to the ICU ventilator.

"It's good to see you, stranger," Alec said to her. "How did your case go?"

She was all business at this moment and waved off Alec with an open palm. She began giving an oral report to the ICU nurse. "This is Anton Mirov, an 80-year-old man transferred from the Santa Clara Heights nursing home today with an acute abdomen," she said. "He was febrile and toxic, and we took him straight to surgery. The surgeons found a small bowel obstruction, with ruptured and dead bowel. We've been working on him for three hours, and he's stable, but he's still on continuous infusions of dopamine and norepinephrine to support his blood pressure. I gave him enough sedation to keep him asleep overnight, and he needs to stay on the ventilator."

The nurse was busy hooking the patient up to the Vita monitor as she listened. The tangled snarl of the patient's five intravenous lines was a knot of spaghetti. "Thanks for knitting all the IVs together, Doctor," the nurse said.

"You know what?" Mae said, "I'm trying to keep this guy alive. Making your life easier isn't that high on my list." Alec looked on with interest from the corner of the room. He almost never watched other anesthesiologists at work, but it was entertaining watching Mae spit venom.

Mae stomped past Alec into the hallway outside. "I hate ICU nurses with an attitude," she said. "Why can't the nurse just take care of the freaking patient and hold the lip?"

Alec chose not to comment on the conflict. To him, the nurse was just doing her assigned job. Instead he said, "I wanted to bounce a few things off you. Do you have time to have a Coke or a coffee after you're done here?"

Before she could answer, the ICU nurse screamed, "Dr. Yee, come back in here, stat! The patient's crashing."

Mae rushed back into the room. The electronic voice of the Vita was droning, "Warning, warning. Patient's heart rhythm diagnosed as ventricular fibrillation. Begin CPR. Bring defibrillator to the bedside, charge to 200 joules and shock the patient."

Mae looked up at the Dr. Vita screen. Instead of the regular beating rhythm of his ECG that she'd been monitoring for the past three hours, the ECG now showed the quivering static of a dying human.

"What happened?" Mae screamed.

"He was fine," the nurse said. "I was untangling his IV lines, and then the Vita unit diagnosed V-fib."

A second nurse wheeled the defibrillator and the crash cart into the room. "Give me the paddles," Mae said. She applied one paddle over the heart and the second one over the left lateral chest, and then she pushed the buttons to fire a 200 joule shock. The muscles of the patient's body convulsed, and both arms flexed skyward before falling flaccid once again.

"Persistent ventricular fibrillation," the Vita said. "Apply a second 200 joule shock to the chest. Give 1 milligram of epinephrine IV. Start chest compressions. Draw arterial blood gas and electrolytes."

"Do what the Vita ordered," Alec said to the nurse. "Did we miss anything? Did you give him any new drugs or infusions?"

"Nothing," the nurse said as she injected the medications.

Mae recharged the paddles and held them over the man's chest. "Everybody clear!" she said, and she depressed the two buttons and gave the old man his second defibrillator shock.

The Vita screen showed no change.

"His oxygen saturation started to drop right after you walked out of the room," the nurse said. "Then his heart stopped."

"He must have had a heart attack," said the second nurse, who'd joined them from an adjoining. "He's an old guy. He had too much surgery. It happens."

"I've been watching every heartbeat of this patient for three hours, and I'm not going to let him die now," Mae said.

"Give 300 mg of amiodarone IV," chanted the Vita. "Continue chest compressions."

The drama seemed too familiar to Alec. He looked at the blue fingers and blue toes of this dying man, and his anger grew. It was true, old people could die at any moment, whether they were at home playing checkers or in an ICU after an enormous surgical insult, but this was recurrent mayhem. He glared up at the Vita unit and as he watched the screen, the yellow eyes flashed off and on a total of three times.

"Did anyone else see that?" he shouted. "Did anyone see the Vita's eyes flash?"

The two RNs and Mae continued working to revive the patient. None of them looked up or answered Alec's question.

Ten minutes later they stopped the CPR and turned off the ventilator. They'd been unable to restart the patient's heart. "He's dead," Mae said.

Or was it an assassination? Alec thought. He looked at the patient's wristband and copied the man's medical record number into his smart phone. He glanced one more time at the patient's scrawny frame stretched across the ICU bed after the final chest compression.

"Mr. Mirov has no family," said the first nurse who was looking at the patient's electronic medical record. "He's a widow, and there's no contact number in the chart. That's sad. So sad." She closed the man's eyes, covered him with a clean sheet, and sat back down in front of her computer terminal to finish her charting.

Alec left the room. It was astonishing and awful. He'd seen more unexpected deaths in the past week than he had seen in the past ten years. Either the cases were clustering around Alec Lucas, or everyone else at USV was missing the obvious.

"I quit," Mae said.

She and Alec were sitting at a table at TJ's Sports Bar south of the USV campus. "In the last two days I've talked to my mom in L.A., my sister in Phoenix, and my shrink," she said. "Everyone tells me the same thing. 'Hang in there, Mae. You're a great doctor, Mae. Everything that doesn't kill you makes you stronger, Mae.' But now another patient is dead, and I've had it." She ran the silver-ringed fingers of both hands through her lavender hair and knocked back her second bottle of beer.

"What could have caused that man to die two minutes after you left him?" Alec asked.

"I don't know," she said. "The same thing that killed that Mindling guy—being too close to me."

"Mae, don't talk like that. I'm serious. You watched him for hours and he was safe. As soon as you walked away, he died. It wasn't your fault."

"Maybe he had heart attack—I don't know. But nothing we did was effective in bringing him back. It's so sad."

"I looked over your anesthetic record. You gave him perfect anesthesia care. You didn't do anything that would have caused him to have a cardiac arrest. Give yourself a break."

"I need to chill out," she said. "I love medicine, but I need to be where no one can kick the bucket on me. It's horrible—talking to a patient for ten minutes, giving them enough drugs to lose consciousness—and then watching them die. Horrible. I can't stand it happening again. I've got to live with the reality of losing two of my last ten patients. I'm not giving another anesthetic."

"Never?" Alec said.

"Never. I called Dr. Vinscene from the women's locker room. I told him I'd have a nervous breakdown if I ever went into an operating room again. He didn't try to talk me out of it."

"What'll you do now?"

"I don't know. I might go back to L.A. and hang out at my parents' house until I get my shit together."

"If I prove that you didn't kill anybody, will you come back?"

"What do you mean by that?"

"It's like that old Buffalo Springfield song," Alec said. "'Something's happening here, what it is ain't exactly clear.' The FutureCare System is new, and I'm convinced it has some bugs in it."

"You take care of FutureCare. I'm going to take care of myself."

"If you need someone to talk to, give me a call," Alec said.

"I'll keep my cell phone under my pillow," Mae said with the briefest of grins. She threw two ten-dollar bills on the table to pay for her cheeseburger and beers. Alec picked up her money and handed it back to her. He threw two twenty-dollar bills of his own on the table.

"I thought you didn't date other doctors," she said.

"I don't date other doctors I work with, but since you're quitting at USV, we won't be working together anymore."

She managed a smile. "All right, Dr. Lucas."

"Call me Alec."

"Thanks for listening. I feel better than I did back in the ICU."

"I'm glad to hear that. Goodbye." He extended his hand to her.

"I'm not looking for a handshake right now," she said. She spread her arms and gave him a one-second hug.

"Thanks," he said.

"I didn't do it for you," she said. "Take care." She slung her handbag over her shoulder, gave him one last look, and left the restaurant alone.

19 ~ DECONSTRUCTING DOCTOR VITA

Alec returned to his house and sat down at his kitchen table in front of the damaged FutureCare module. No one else was answering his questions for him—it was time to turn to the source of the questions. It was time to deconstruct Dr. Vita. He removed the back panel and inspected the interior of the machine. He saw multiple solid-state circuit boards as well as the memory chip, the connections to the video screen, the battery, and the section of the interior that housed the telescoping diagnostic arm.

Alec decided to get his HAC out of the Vita. He pushed the power button, but nothing happened. He pushed the eject button, and still nothing happened. He looked inside through the back of the module and spied his HAC wedged into its slot. He levered the tip of a long screwdriver against the purple card and freed it from the mechanism that held it inside the module. He retrieved the HAC as its edge protruded from purple slot in the front of the Vita, and then he dropped the card into a drawer in the kitchen table.

He stood over the dormant Vita unit. Like a wrecked automobile in a scrap yard, this heap of metal was of no use except for spare parts. At one time, it was a portal into FutureCare. Could it still be?

Alec linked his own laptop to the broken Vita with a coupling cable. He logged onto the USV Medical Records on his laptop and entered his own FutureCare electronic medical record password and PIN to gain access to the System. When he did, the lights of the Vita's eyes flashed back to life, and the black video screen lit up. The module didn't speak, but the direct connection to Alec's computer had resurrected some of the machine's ability.

Alec used his keyboard to interrogate the software contents of Dr. Vita and, with a modicum of IT skills, it was straightforward to burrow into the Vita's electronic medical records programming. He required no passwords or PINs to move from location to location. He entered Jake Mindling's medical record number, and the files on Jake Mindling appeared on his laptop screen. He scrolled to the operating room data from Mindling's fatal anesthetic. As it had at Grand Rounds, the electronic medical record listed the bogus family history of malignant hyperthermia and showed no evidence of the lethal 8% sevoflurane overdose.

Alec tapped a series of keys and examined the netherworld of the Python computer code that fueled the creation of the record. He traced the programming code back in time.

In the midst of Jake Mindling's record, at the precise time when Mae and Alec brought Mindling into the operating room, he found a smoking gun—an override file blocked the routine medical record. Alec clicked on this file to inspect its contents and held his breath. The screen read:

Restricted File. Unauthorized access denied.

Alec tried several different means of opening the file, all without success. He was only able to discern two things about the file: it was small, containing no more than a few lines of code, and that the code was added later, on top of the previous programming.

Could it be? Something secret was appended to Jake Mindling's medical record minutes before he died?

He entered the medical record number of Elizabeth Anderson, the woman who'd bled to death during surgery. Because there was no Dr. Vita in the operating room that day, there was less information available for Alec to review. The medical record documented Elizabeth's vital signs as she was anesthetized and continued up until the moment that Templeton and The Bricklayer ripped her aorta. At that point, the medical record included the digital video files from The Bricklayer. Thirty seconds before the chaos began, there was an external file overriding the video data. When Alec clicked to open it, once again the screen lit up with:

Restricted File. Unauthorized access denied.

As fast as he could move his fingers, he dove into the electronic medical records for Richard Irving, the 84-year-old cold corpse he discovered in the ICU the day after The Bricklayer death. The result was the same—there was an external file blocking the EMR minutes before the 84-year-old's death. He tried to open the file, and once again the screen said:

Restricted File. Unauthorized access denied.

Alec entered the medical record number for Mae's 88-year-old patient, Anton Mirov. He found the exact point in time, at 1743 hours, when the patient was connected to the Dr. Vita unit in Room 17 in the Surgical ICU. At that point the medical record was blocked by the words:

Restricted File. Unauthorized access denied.

He whistled through his teeth. Like the other three dead patients, the timing of the new file matched the onset of the lethal events.

Alec sat back in his chair and stared out the window into the darkness of the Santa Clara night. How could this happen? How many people had the skill to do such a thing?

He looked at his watch—he'd stayed up all night—it was 5 o'clock in the morning. It was too early to call Dr. Rovka. There was nothing else Alec could do right now, but today he'd tell the authorities what he'd learned. He prayed to God that no one else died between now and whenever they shut the System down. Alec closed his laptop, turned out the lights, and retired to his bedroom. After he left, only the faint glow of the Vita unit's yellow eyes remained to illuminate the kitchen.

***

Alec opened his eyes at 8 a.m., and in seconds he was wide-awake and full of adrenaline. He picked up the phone and dialed the number for the Rovka Clinic. A receptionist answered and said, "Good morning. Rovka Medical Clinic. How may I direct your call?"

"This is Dr. Alec Lucas at the University of Silicon Valley. I need to speak to Dr. Rovka."

"Just a minute, sir," she said, and the line went dead. A minute later she returned and said, "Dr. Rovka is not in today. Would you like to leave a voicemail?"

Alec took a deep breath and exhaled. "I guess so. Do you know where he is?"

"I don't, sir. I believe he's taken some time away. Would you like to leave a voicemail?"

"When is he coming back?"

"I don't know. He isn't scheduled to see any patients until next week."

"Go ahead, connect me to his voicemail."

A taped message played, asking for the caller to leave a message for Dr. Rovka after the beep.

Alec said, "This is Dr. Lucas. I need to speak to you. I've got evidence that may explain why patients are dying at the hands of the FutureCare devices. Call me back on my cell phone as soon as possible."

He hung up and refocused on the computer screen. What if Rovka was out of town for days? Alec had to tell someone. He copied the patient files, including the announcement of the Restricted Files from the Vita, onto his laptop. Then Alec packed up his laptop and went into the bathroom to shower and shave. He emerged from his bedroom dressed in a jacket and tie and picked up the laptop.

Enough patients had died. It was time to show the Restricted Files to Dr. Vinscene.

20 ~ TRUST ME, QUOTH VINSCENE

Alec sat in the waiting room outside Chairman Vinscene's office and browsed through the *San Francisco Chronicle* while he waited to see his boss. The headline at the top of page one was disturbing: "FutureCare System popular at USV. Exit polls show 90% of patients like Dr. Vita." Alec skimmed through the text. The top two reasons cited for the positive reviews were affordability and easy access. Dr. Vita medical care was provided free by the federal government, and the number of Vita machines exceeded the quantity of human doctors. Other positive factors cited included the vast knowledge of the modules and the unerring nature of computerized medicine. Alec shuddered as he read. He curled his fingers around the smooth edges of his laptop and hoped he could choose the right words to upset the FutureCare juggernaut.

The door opened, and Robert Vinscene said, "Dr. Lucas, come in and sit down." Alec followed the chairman into the office and closed the door behind him. Vinscene walked to the opposite corner of the room, stuck his hands in his pockets, and leaned back against a wall of medical textbooks and journals. "If you want to know the result of your drug screen, I haven't gotten it back yet."

"That's not why I'm here. I know the drug screen will be negative. I'm here to follow up on my concerns about the Dr. Vita machines being involved with patient deaths. I want you to see this." He opened the laptop and displayed the programming language inside Jake Mindling's file. He pointed at the Restricted File. "The timing of this file can't be ignored. It occurs at the exact time Mr. Mindling started to die. I don't know what the file contains, but I'm certain it carries information that harmed the patient."

Vinscene moved away from the bookcase and leaned over the computer screen. He tapped the "Back" button several times, and said, "Dr. Lucas, you're the one with a PhD in computer science, but I'll say this as an academic researcher: You've located a Restricted File. You haven't established a cause-effect relationship between the file and the patient's outcome."

"I'm making a logical inference," Alec said. "What other explanation is there?"

"The simplest explanation is this. The patient became critically ill at that point in time, and the EMR software is coded so that the records are hidden from hackers or onlookers. We can't have malpractice lawyers searching through death scenarios looking for the 'Ah-hah moment'—that point in time when a negligent act caused the patient's bad outcome."

Alec furrowed his brow.

"I'm sure that's why the files are restricted," Vinscene said. "But I'll tell you what I'm going to do. I'm as interested in quality patient care as you are. I'll run this by our IT experts. I'll ask them why the file is protected. Will that satisfy you?"

"I have more to show you," Alec said, pointing to his computer. "For three other deaths, I've found identical Restricted Files synchronized with the time of death. I've indexed them for you."

"Very well. Our IT experts will be interested in what you've found. If you have four cases where these Restricted Files appeared, I'm sure they'll look into each one of them."

"How soon can you get someone to look at it?"

"I'll make the call today. I expect we'll have the answer in a day or two."

Alec closed his laptop and prepared to leave.

Vinscene said, "I have an even better idea. Instead of showing this to IT, why don't we show these Restricted Files to Dr. Shingo? He's the expert on FutureCare, and he's consulting on any and all problems with the System. If something's amiss, he'd be the best one to discern the problem."

"I can't do that," Alec said. "Dr. Shingo and I had a disagreement. I don't think I can approach him about something like this. I don't think he'll meet with me again."

"Very well, Dr. Lucas. Leave your computer with me. I don't understand this Restricted File business, but I'll show it one of our FutureCare IT specialists."

"I-I need to hang on to my computer. I use it every day."

Vinscene snorted and looked down his nose. "Look, Dr. Lucas. You came in here full of frantic energy with an issue that demands looking into. I'm offering to help you, and you're tying my hands? Trust me, I'll take good care of your computer, and I'll return it you as soon as possible."

Vinscene held the door open for Alec. "But I wouldn't worry. This is a huge medical center. Each week dozens of patients die here from a variety of ailments, for a variety of very good reasons. Don't go on a witch hunt looking for problems. Take better care of your own patients and try to stay out of trouble. I'll call you after I've gotten an explanation. Good day, Dr. Lucas. And remember, FutureCare is a good thing." He pointed at the newspaper in Alec's hand. "People love the concept. We doctors better wise up. We need to help build the road or else we'll get steamrolled and be part of the pavement."

"We'll see," Alec said dubiously. He took one last look at the smooth silver cover of his laptop and exited the office.

Vinscene shut the door and picked up the telephone. He punched a speed dial connection, and said, "One of my physicians has discovered some irregularities in the electronic medical records of four deceased patients. Can I show them to you? Good. I'll be there by nine."

Vinscene set the phone down and slid his fingers along the cool surface of Dr. Lucas's computer. He gazed out the window, past where the shovels of the Dr. Vita Depot construction were excavating medicine's future. Then he looked toward Pescadero, the foothills west of Santa Clara, and Dry Creek Road.

Alec Lucas dragged himself up the sidewalk toward his house as the sun set over Cypress Street. He'd just finished a twelve-hour shift in the operating room, and his total nutrition for the day consisted of nibbles of graham crackers and sips of apple juice. He was exhausted and starving, but he was wired and couldn't imagine going to sleep. His body was too pumped up with adrenaline to shut down.

He was surprised to see a shining black limousine as long as a semi-truck parked at the curb in front of his house. The engine was running, and the tinted windows made it impossible to see who was inside. When Alec reached the top of his steps, the front door to his house was ajar. A bottle of red wine stood on the floor just inside the doorway. Alec picked it up and spun it around. The label read *Chateau Margaux 1953*.

"I hope you like Bourdeaux wine," said a voice from the kitchen. A familiar stout figure in a black hat and a long black coat was sitting at his kitchen table waiting for him. It was Henri Rovka.

"I've been trying to find you for days," Alec said. "Where've you been?"

"I had to make a quick trip to France," Rovka said. "Now I'm back and I heard you needed to talk to me."

"How did you get in here?"

"I jiggled the door knob. The front door was unlocked."

Alec scowled. "I always lock that door."

"No matter. It was open today. I dare say, is there anything for anyone to steal?" Rovka said, looking around at the front room, which contained nothing except the couch, a chair and the TV. The surface of the kitchen table was empty.

"The Dr. Vita unit is gone," Alec said.

"What?" Rovka said.

"It's unbelievable. Someone broke into my place and stole that piece of junk."

"What piece of junk?"

"I brought a damaged Dr. Vita home and managed to coax some scary information out of it. I found irregularities in the EMR at the time of death on four patients. And now someone stole the source of my evidence. It's no coincidence. Somebody's trying to stop me."

"Who do you think that 'somebody' is?"

"I don't know. I found Restricted Files in the FutureCare medical records minutes before four patients died. I wanted you to intervene for me, but when I couldn't get a hold of you, I turned my findings over to Dr. Vinscene. He took my computer to show it to the information technology team."

"Let me see if I've got this straight. You found evidence that someone or something was tampering with FutureCare, and Dr. Vinscene's response was to take your computer. Is that right?"

"Yes. And now someone stole the Vita and my computer's gone, I have no evidence against the FutureCare System." Alec got up and started pacing in a circle. He stopped and confronted Rovka. "What's going on? You and I started out as a team, trying to make sense of mysterious deaths at USV, but you haven't done a single thing to help me. Most days you've been either unreachable or absent."

"I'm sorry I left you on your own these past four days. I was busy with other things."

"Were you at your Rovka Clinic? What's the deal with your clinic?"

Rovka's face brightened. "Five years ago, I recruited all the best doctors from USV, Stanford, and UCSF, and we set up a concierge private practice in downtown San Francisco for wealthy patients. Patients sign ironclad, bulletproof documents which waive their rights to sue the Rovka Clinic. They pay us well, and we give them excellent service. Everybody's happy. Our patients get world-class medical care—patients write a check or pay by credit card on the day of service. The more we charge, the better doctors we are perceived to be." He raised his bowler hat high above his head in a salute to either the higher charges or to the better doctors his colleagues seemed to be.

"That model is okay for the multi-millionaires in the Bay Area," Alec said. "But I'm surprised someone who promotes that kind of medical care would be interested in FutureCare as well."

"You don't understand. I'm more than interested in FutureCare. I am FutureCare."

"What do you mean?"

"Have you read my textbook, Dr. Lucas?"

"Of course. Every medical student in America reads *Rovka's Textbook of Internal Medicine* during their third year."

"Well, Drs. Kami Shingo and Red Jones read my book, as well. They gave me a call nine or ten years ago, and the rest is history."

"I don't know what you're talking about."

"I am FutureCare, and FutureCare is me," Rovka said.

"I don't get it," Alec said. He felt his stomach muscles tightening.

Rovka's face settled into a grin. "In a way, Dr. Vita is a mechanical version of me. I'm responsible for Dr. Vita's diagnostic and therapeutic decision-making. Shingo and Jones approached me to help design the medical algorithms and decision-tree analyses of various health care problems that give Dr. Vita its problem-solving skills. There were thousands of algorithms. Before me, the Dr. Vita units were spheres that absorbed information but didn't know what to do with it. The decision-trees programmed judgment into the machines. All the decisions that a Dr. Vita unit needed to make were programmed to resemble the branches of a tree, with each limb an alternate problem, each fork in the branches an alternative choice, and each leaf on the tree an outcome with a plan associated with it."

"They put your forty years of medical wisdom into Dr. Vita's brain," Alec said.

"That's right. And I was well reimbursed, including a ten percent ownership of the total stock of FC Industries, the company that developed Dr. Vita."

"What happened to your partnership with Jones and Shingo?"

"After the Dr. Vita units were tested and approved by the FDA, FC Industries had its initial public offering. The shares we each owned became insanely valuable after the IPO because of the potential of FutureCare to move into every phase of American medical care. Each of us did different things with our new wealth. Red Jones eventually sold off his shares and founded WellBee, Inc. He believes the Dr. WellBee module is a superior product to Dr. Vita. Red loves the thrill of the breakout of a new product.

"Kami Shingo sold some of his stock and kept enough to continue as the majority shareholder. He still owns 52% of the company. He used his cash to purchase and build his mountaintop enclave, and for the time being he has shunned the medical device world and become more interested in golf.

"I established my clinic in San Francisco, and I no longer work for FC Industries. I remain involved at the University of Silicon Valley because I want to see a successful transition to the Dr. Vita System."

"You enabled the FutureCare System."

Rovka raised one eyebrow. "FutureCare was a business decision, Alec. My decision."

"You sold out thousands of doctors so you could get rich?"

"No. If I hadn't helped design the decision-trees and helped them make the Dr. Vita units work, someone else would have. It was inevitable. I did it because I wanted it done right. America needed a viable solution to its medical crisis. Dr. Vita is the answer."

"The Dr. Vita units make mistakes. I've seen it."

Rovka shrugged. "Perhaps. If someone is trying to ruin FutureCare, they'll try again. We need to keep our eyes and our ears open." He put his hat on and stood up. "Until that time, get some rest, young man. You have the look of a World War I infantryman waiting for a bomb to land in his foxhole."

"Is that comment supposed to make me feel better?"

Rovka smiled. "No, but something good will come out of all this. I wanted to let you know I'm back in town. I'm glad you're on my side. Good day, Dr. Lucas." He tipped his hat again and walked out the front door.

The next morning an attractive young woman met Alec outside of the men's locker room. She stopped him before he walked inside and said, "Dr. Lucas? Dr. Alec Lucas? Can I talk with you?"

Alec checked out the new woman—she had straight blonde hair hanging halfway to her waist, pale blue eyes and skin of the lightest cream color. A small dark birthmark adorned the highest aspect of each cheek. A quick look revealed the longest legs between Honolulu and Milan and the waistline of a human wasp. Her pencil-frame was draped in a royal blue sleeveless dress that ended well above her knees. This was a human being who could turn heads from a Google satellite view.

"My name is Leslie Tucker, and I'm a reporter for the *San Jose Mercury News*," she said, showing off perfect teeth in a broad smile. "Can I ask you a few questions regarding the FutureCare System and the anesthesia department at USV?" She batted long eyelashes at him.

Alec thought he was resistant to feminine guile, but this woman made him feel like an infatuated eighth grade schoolboy. "Why me?" he said. "There are a hundred anesthesiologists at this medical center."

"Red Jones told me to talk to you."

"Red Jones? What does he have to do with this?"

"I contacted Mr. Jones about this topic, and he referred me to you."

Alec was puzzled. "What did Mr. Jones tell you?"

"He said you were one of the top young anesthesiologists at USV, and you'd give me some good copy."

"I'll tell you the truth, that's all."

Leslie laughed and flicked her hair behind her left shoulder. "Of course. I'm told you're very involved in the transition of USV to the FutureCare System. Is that true?"

"That's true."

"And I've heard rumors that complications with the FutureCare machines may have led to patient deaths. Can you tell me more about that?"

Her smile was beguiling, but Alec was wary. "Are you here to talk about FutureCare, or are you here to talk about patient deaths?"

"I'm here to listen to you talk about either one."

"The FutureCare System is a stunning step forward in Artificial Intelligence in Medicine, otherwise known as AIM. I could talk all night about AIM, but I've got cases to start in the operating room right now. Perhaps we could ... meet for dinner sometime?"

She giggled and showed dimples in both cheeks. "I'd like that," she said. "Have there been patient deaths attributable to FutureCare?"

"No comment. It's not appropriate for a doctor to discuss matters like that with the lay press. That's all protected quality assurance information."

"Hmm," she said, furrowing her brow. "I'm told that the WellBee System is a superior system to the FutureCare System. Can you confirm that?"

"I haven't seen the WellBee System in action. I've only seen one individual module at Dr. Jones's demonstration, and it was a fine product."

"Better than Dr. Vita?"

"Look, Leslie, you're putting me on the spot. The WellBee unit was better in certain ways, but I don't want to compare and contrast Dr. WellBee and Dr. Vita."

"I understand, Dr. Lucas. You've been very professional. Let's meet for a drink sometime and we can talk about this further. I do believe there's a story here." She flashed a beauty pageant smile at him and he melted. He looked at the ring finger of her left hand—it was free of jewelry.

"I'd love to get together," Alec said. "Can I have your contact information?"

She took a pen out of her pocket and wrote her cell phone number on the palm of his hand.

"Call me," she said. She pulled his hand up to her lips, kissed the ink on his palm, waved goodbye, and then swayed down the hall and around the corner out of sight.

23 ~ MEET ME AT THE MAHOGANY

Two mornings later, Alec opened the morning edition of the *San Jose Mercury News* on his iPhone. As he exited the elevator and approached the locker room, he read the headlines and gasped. The top of the news read: *New FutureCare System at USV: How Safe Is It?* The byline listed Leslie Tucker as the author. Alec read on:

Doctors at the University of Silicon Valley Medical Center are investigating a series of flaws that some say are attributed to the new Dr. Vita modules of the FutureCare System. The FutureCare System is an avant-garde collection of Artificial Intelligence in Medicine computers designed to interview, examine, monitor, and manage all aspects of clinical care in both inpatient and outpatient settings. USV is the first medical center in the world to install the AIM technology, and experts are hailing FutureCare as the savior to the ailments of American medicine.

Halfway through the article, the story dropped a bomb:

Sources at USV Medical Center identify anesthesiologist Dr. Alec Lucas as the whistleblower in the alleged Dr. Vita deficiencies. In an exclusive interview with The Mercury News, *Dr. Lucas did admit there were problems with the FutureCare System and hinted that the Dr. WellBee modules being installed in the University of California at Los Angeles Medical Center were a superior product.*

USV Chief of Staff Dr. Leroy Andrews denied the allegations and stated, "The FutureCare System is efficient and effective in eliminating human errors from medical care at USV."

Alec dropped the paper and felt the hallway beginning to spin. *What the hell?* That pencil blonde Leslie had linked his name to the FutureCare problems at USV even though he had no evidence who or what was causing the problems.

Damn that woman. He'd told her almost nothing, and she rewarded him by misquoting the few words he'd said. He cursed himself and his weakness for a pretty face and gorgeous legs.

"Hey super sleuth, is the FutureCare System lynching anybody today?" said a faculty anesthesiologist who passed by.

"How big was the payoff from WellBee, Inc. for that endorsement in *The Mercury News* this morning?" a surgeon said as Alec unlocked his locker.

Alec was pissed off. He ducked into a remote corner of the room and dialed Leslie Tucker's number. She'd conned him, and he was going to lower the boom on her, great legs or not. The phone rang twice before someone picked up. A man's voice said, "Leslie's phone."

"This is a friend of Leslie's. Can she take a call?"

"Hey, is this my colleague Alec Lucas? Good morning, Dr. Lucas. Leslie's in the shower now, but I want to thank you for your supportive comments about Dr. WellBee in *The Mercury News* this morning. Great stuff, my boy."

As "Great stuff, my boy," echoed in Alec's ear, he recognized the voice. What was Red Jones doing there, with Leslie in the shower?

"Can you tell Leslie that I called, Dr. Jones? I need to start my first anesthetic of the day, and I don't have time to hold on the phone right now."

"I'll tell her you called and that you thought the WellBee System was even better than you said it was in the newspaper this morning." His laughter echoed through the phone. Alec heard him say, "Leslie, honey. Do you want to talk to Dr. Lucas from USV?"

There was a pause, and then Jones returned to the phone. "She says thanks, but she's found a better man, kid. And be careful with your investigation at USV. Vinscene and Andrews—they're not your friends."

"Dr. Vinscene is my chairman. He's on my side."

"Is he? Don't kid yourself, kid. Vinscene is a high-tech wannabe, that's for sure. He's tired of writing research papers that no one reads and making one-tenth the cash of his high-rolling friends in the business world. He's always orbiting me, looking for a handout. You trust that guy?"

"I do."

"You're a babe in the woods, kid. But good for you. Innocence is a hard thing to find once you've lost it. Look, keep in touch. Let me know if WellBee Incorporated fits into your plans. Bye." The phone clicked off.

Alec's blood was boiling. He picked up the phone again and dialed Mae Yee's number.

She picked up after the third ring. "Alec, I was just thinking about you. I saw the quotes from you in *The Mercury News* this morning."

"Don't remind me. Instead of solving the problem, I'm now the troublemaker who cried wolf. Everyone in Silicon Valley will read that I'm a whistleblower—but I have no evidence whatsoever." He told her about his interrogation of the damaged Vita unit, his discovery of the Restricted Files, and his meeting with Dr. Vinscene. "Vinscene took my computer to show to the IT consultants, and I haven't heard one thing back from him."

"You can always hear back from me," she said.

"I can?" He felt a primitive tingling feeling in the pit of his stomach. "How about you come over to my place tonight? I've got a great bottle of French wine."

"No dinner and a movie? We're just passing the bottle around at your house?"

"I just want to hang out," he said.

"I'm playing with you," she said. "I just want to hang out, too. I can be there at seven. I'll bring my own corkscrew."

"You're funny. I'll see you then."

***

Hours later Alec finished his last anesthetic of the day and retreated to the locker room to change out of his scrubs. His cell phone rang. He answered the call and said, "Lucas here."

A female voice on the other end of the line said, "Room 103. The Mahogany Hotel in Menlo Park. Meet me there." The voice was low in pitch and almost inaudible. Alec pressed the phone to his ear, but the next sounds were a click and a dial tone. He closed his eyes and tried to decipher what he'd heard. Who was she?

Alec looked at his watch. Two o'clock—he had five hours before he was meeting Mae. He changed into the black T-shirt and black sport coat he wore to the hospital that morning. He brushed his hair back behind each ear and headed out to his car.

The Mahogany was a high-end hotel and one of busiest nightlife hotspots in Silicon Valley. The resort complex of marble, granite, and polished hardwood sprawled over twenty acres and overlooked the coastal forests of the Santa Cruz Mountains. Alec stood alone outside room 103 of the Mahogany and double-checked the brass numbers on the door. He had no idea what to expect inside. He rapped on the door and then snapped the fingers of his left hand against his right palm in a syncopated rhythm as he waited.

There was no answer, so he knocked again.

The door opened an inch or two. The curtains were closed, and the lights were off inside the room. Whoever opened the door was concealed behind it. "Come in … now," whispered the same female voice from the telephone call.

Alec's heart rate climbed. Was he being a fool here? His eyes and ears were not giving him enough information to evaluate if he was heading into danger. He took a step into the room and peered around the door to see who was behind it. A hand grabbed his forearm, pulled him into the darkness, and the door slammed behind him.

Two arms closed around him and he smelled a powerful scent of eucalyptus. Lips pressed against his, and he felt the warmth of skin and the brush of hair against his face. The woman said, "I have something for you."

He was blind in the darkness. He put his arms around her and felt nothing but smooth skin. She walked him backwards several steps and pushed him with her lips and tongue as she kissed him, until the back of his calves hit resistance and he fell backwards onto something firm. His adversary pinned him to the mattress and sprawled her limbs wide to contain him.

She said nothing, but her staccato breathing filled his ears. There was no conversation. He breathed in the forest of her hair and allowed himself to marvel at the primitive pleasure of her body, his eyes blind but every other sense in his body overwhelmed.

***

Alec's eyes snapped open to bright daylight. He had no idea how much time had elapsed, but he knew he'd fallen asleep. The curtains to the hotel room were pulled wide open. Midday California sunlight streamed into the room and illuminated the angelic face of Izabella, who was sitting in a chair next to the window. She was wearing a white bathrobe, and her feet were propped up on the bed as she watched him.

"Good stuff, Dr. Lucas."

"You have a unique way of saying 'Good Afternoon,' Izabella."

"Red didn't need me today, so I got off the ranch and I went for it."

"And I was 'it' today?"

She smiled. "And tomorrow, too, if you'd like."

Alec smiled back, and then glanced at the bedside clock. It was five p.m. He rolled out of bed and bent over to pick up his shirt and jacket that were strewn on the carpet.

"Dr. Lucas?"

"Call me Alec."

"Can I borrow your Visa card?"

"No," he said. "Why would I give you my Visa card?"

"I need some dental work," she said, flashing him a wide smile of perfect teeth. "$1,000 for the uppers, and $1,000 for the lowers."

Are you kidding me? he thought. "Ah, sorry, I don't think so," he said. He pulled his T-shirt over his head and wondered how fast he could escape this scene of world-class awkwardness.

"Rushing off so soon?" she said.

"I've got a meeting at seven," he answered. He leaned over and kissed her on the cheek. This time she didn't turn toward him.

"You don't like me?" she said.

He ignored her question and laced up his shoes in a frantic pace. What was next? A Russian pimp bursting through the door? A demand for cash? "I have to go," he said.

She stood to face him. Her bathrobe fell open, exposing the rippled muscles of her abdomen and the curves of her perfect breasts. Alec reached out to her, refastened the bathrobe belt around her waist, and walked to the door.

As he stepped into the hall, she had the last word. "Call me," she said.

At 7 p.m. sharp Mae walked into Alec's house. She was dressed in blue jeans, sandals, and a long-sleeved white cotton shirt with the top two buttons undone. Her hair was tied in a bun, and she wore dangling silver earrings with a single pearl at the end of each chain. Her glasses were gone. She sauntered past him at the door without a handshake or a hug. She surveyed the interior of his house and said, "Your place is a dump."

"Thanks for the warm and fuzzy greeting, Dr. Yee. Forget my interior decorating deficiencies for a minute and let me give you this." He handed her a glass of Chateau Margeaux and poured one for himself. "You look well," he said. "How's retirement?"

"I'm looking forward to it," she said, chugging half the glass of wine in a single swallow.

"Are you going back to L.A.?"

She laughed. "No, that's not going to work out. I don't know if I told you, but my parents are both MDs. My mom is a dermatologist in Beverly Hills and my dad is a plastic surgeon in Santa Monica. When I told them I was burned out and I wanted to come home to reclaim my old bedroom, they blew me off."

"You're kidding."

"I'm not. In so many words, my dad said I needed to 'Cowgirl Up.'"

"Meaning what?"

"Meaning get back on the horse and ride. Dad's view is that shitty things happen in medicine. Patients have complications, patients sue you, old patients die. That doesn't mean you quit."

"So, what're you going to do?"

"I'm done with anesthesia, but I'm still going to use my medical license. I lined up a job at a clinic in Pescadero."

"Are you sure about that? You're going to move from a specialty where all your clients are unconscious to a clinic where they walk and talk and complain?"

"They may complain, but at least they walk and talk, and when I'm done with them, they'll walk right out the door. Alive."

"That life was never for me. Awake patients always drove me crazy. That was the appeal of anesthesia. You only have to talk to a patient for ten minutes, then they go to sleep and all their complaining ceases."

"That's fine as long as your patient wakes up," she said. "It's too much stress for me, worrying if I'm going to kill people."

"You didn't kill anyone. Dr. Vita was the killer."

"So you say, Alec. You don't know that. You're going to drive yourself crazy trying to fight the System. You need to mellow out and have some fun." She kicked off her sandals and drained her first glass of wine.

"How did you wind up with a clinic job so fast?" Alec asked.

"Red Jones made a phone call for me."

Alec grimaced. "You know Red Jones?"

"I met him at a Medical Center fundraiser last year. He asked me out."

"Did you go out with him?"

"Only three or four times. He talks about himself a bit too much, but it was fun riding in a Ferrari convertible. And he promised to take me to Aspen in his Learjet this winter."

"You like the guy?"

"He's money. You gotta like that."

Alec poured her a second glass of wine and said, "Is Red Jones trying to get into your pants?"

"That's a pretty bold question, Doctor." She reached back and undid the tight bun of her hair, and let it flow down over both shoulders. "Yes, he wanted to go to bed with me."

"Did you?"

"It's none of your business if I did, but no, I didn't," she said as she bent forward to reach into her purse. Her shirt fell open and a glimpse of her cleavage was front and center in Alec's vision.

She removed a small vial from her purse, took the cap off the vial, and produced two small white pills.

"What are those?" Alec asked.

"Something fun for you and for me," she smiled. Mae popped one tablet into her mouth and chased it with a swallow of wine. She fingered the second pill and fit it in between Alec's lips. "Trust me, I know just what you need right now." She tipped forward toward him and unbuttoned another button of her shirt.

He swallowed the pill and slid his fingers through her lilac tresses. And for the second time that day, he forgot about FutureCare.

In the blackness of the night Alec rolled over and opened his eyes. He couldn't see a thing, and he had a certain notion he was buried alive miles below the surface of the ground. He screamed, "Help me, help me, I'm down here," as loudly as he could.

"What is it?" Mae said out of the darkness on his left. "You're scaring me."

"I'm trapped," Alec said. "Buried alive! I can't breathe."

"You're not trapped anywhere. You're in your own house. You're completely safe." She turned on a light. Alec was sitting bolt upright on the couch, his eyes wild, and he was gasping for air.

"I'm having a hard time breathing," Alec said. "My chest feels tight."

She pressed her ear to his chest and listened. "Your breath sounds are normal. Your heart rate's a bit fast. Maybe 120."

Alec started hyperventilating again and sat bolt upright. He turned on the bedside lamp. "I feel like I'm dying. Something's wrong." He rubbed his eyes, but there was no improvement. He looked over at Mae, and there were two Maes sitting up next to the bed. "I'm seeing double," he said. His heart began to race. He swung his legs over the edge of the bed to walk to the bathroom. When he tried to stand up, his legs wouldn't support his weight. He crashed to his knees and crumpled on the floor.

Mae climbed out of bed and said, "Put on some clothes, Alec. I'll take you to the ER." She wrapped her arms around Alec's waist, and pulled him toward the front door.

***

Mae delivered Alec to the Emergency Room of the USV Medical Center in the black of night. The ER staff admitted him, started an intravenous drip running into his arm, fit a plastic oxygen mask over his face, and connected him to a Dr. Vita monitor. Alec was silent, his were eyes closed, his chest was still heaving, and the green plastic of the mask fogged up each time he exhaled. Mae kept her hand on Alec's arm and monitored the pulse rate at the radial artery at his wrist.

A nurse in a flowered jacket approached Alec's gurney. She wore a USV nametag with the block letters TRIAGE below her name. She checked the screen of the Vita, and read out, "Heart rate 110, Blood pressure 120/65, Respiratory Rate 24, Temp 37 degrees Centigrade, Oxygen Saturation 99% on face mask. What do you think, Dr. Vita?"

"Abnormal vital signs along with chest complaints qualify the patient for Human Side," Dr. Vita said. Flowered Jacket disconnected Alec from the Dr. Vita machine and called out for a team of orderlies to move Alec to the Human Side.

To the left side of the Triage desk was a set of bright green doors that read "Human Side." To the right of the desk was a set of bright blue doors that read "Dr. Vita Side." Mae knew the new Emergency Room rules: Abnormal vital signs or critical symptoms such as chest pain or difficulty breathing qualified the patient to be seen right away by the human physicians in the ER. Patients with normal vital signs were triaged to be interviewed and treated by a Dr. Vita alone.

The orderlies pushed Alec through the green doors and into the Emergency Patient Care area. Mae followed. A nurse met them and directed them to patient berth #14.

A short man in a white coat arrived at the foot of the bed. His nametag read, D. Whitehead, MD, Emergency Medicine. The picture on his nametag showed a young man with a head full of black hair and a big smile. The doctor wearing the white coat was bald and not smiling a bit. He looked back and forth from Alec's sweaty face to the vital signs trending across the monitor screen on the wall.

Mae said, "I'm Dr. Yee, and this is Dr. Lucas. We're both anesthesiologists on staff here."

"And what brings Dr. Lucas here tonight?"

Alec opened his eyes and sat up. He shook his head and said, "I feel better now, but I was having some sort of anxiety attack. I was having chest pain, trouble breathing, and double vision."

"I was with him, and it was pretty scary," Mae said.

"Thanks a lot, Dr. Yee," Whitehead said. "I'll take it from here." The ER doctor leaned over the patient and spoke in a soft voice, "Tell me exactly what happened, Dr. Lucas."

"I woke up with a start from a deep sleep. I felt like I was buried alive. I couldn't breathe, and I was seeing double. I got out of bed and I couldn't walk straight. I'm better now, but I was scared as hell."

Whitehead placed his stethoscope on the skin near Alec's breast bone and listened. Then he stretched an ophthalmoscope from its cord on the wall and looked into Alec's eyes. He tested the strength and sensation in each of Alec's four limbs and on both sides of his face.

Whitehead's facial expression showed nothing. He walked out of the room, and up to the central desk of the Emergency Room. This was the nerve center of the ER with a cluster of bodies working over computer screens and talking on telephones. The clock overhead said 4:05. It was impossible to tell if it was 4:05 in the morning or 4:05 in the afternoon.

"Who's on call for Neurology?" Whitehead said to a middle-aged woman who was typing on a computer keyboard.

"Lorbert, the psycho."

"Call him. The guy in 14 is needs a neuro consult."

Whitehead returned to the bedside to talk to Alec. He looked at the clock and then recited a medical lecture in a monotonic voice, "Dr. Lucas, I don't know what your diagnosis is, but you seem to be weaker on your left side. I'm ordering a neuro consult. I'm also ordering a CT scan of your brain, an ECG, and some blood tests."

"Can I have a drink of water?" Alec said. He had a wet towel over his forehead. Bubbles of sweat dotted his cheeks and the stubble of his unshaven pre-dawn whiskers.

"No. Nothing by mouth for now," Whitehead said. He turned to the nurse and said, "Get the usual labs, including a urinalysis. If he can't pee, straight cath him." He left bed #14 and moved on down the line to the next customer in bed #13.

"Have you been honest with me?" Mae asked Alec. "Do you have a neurologic condition, or diabetes, or some heart problem?"

"My health is fine. I've been pretty stressed out this past week, but that's the only problem I have."

"I agree with you there—being awake at four in the morning is pretty stressful," a male voice said from behind Mae. A grinning face with a handlebar mustache appeared from behind the curtain. "I'm Dr. Lorbert, USV's finest, and only, neurologist in-house at 4:15 a.m. I heard about your symptoms from Dr. Whitehead. How are you doing now?"

Mae spoke first. "Alec, I'm going home to shower and change clothes. I hate to leave you, but I'm supposed to be at the Pescadero Clinic in three hours. Call me when you're done here, okay?"

"I'll be all right, Mae," Alec said. "Thanks."

"I'd stay here if I thought I was doing any good."

"I'll be fine. Go."

"I'm leaving. He's all yours, Dr. Lorbert."

After she walked away, Alec recounted his symptoms to Lorbert who narrowed his eyes and said, "Ever have any episodes like this before?"

"Never."

"Taking any medications or using any drugs?"

What was that pill that Mae gave him? "Not really," he said.

"Any history of medical problems?"

"None."

Lorbert examined Alec with attention to the heart, lung, and neurologic examinations. "You seem like the healthiest man in this ER," he concluded. "I can't confirm any left-sided weakness, and I don't find anything abnormal. I'm adding a tox screen to your blood tests. We'll see. Maybe you just had a nightmare." Lorbert made a tortured face as if he'd just eaten a three-day-old enchilada. "I don't know what your diagnosis is, but we'll run the tests and see what turns up."

A tox screen? Damn it! They're going to discover whatever was in that pill last night, Alec thought. He was a practicing physician. The last thing he needed was for them to discover some illegal street drug in his blood.

Lorbert walked away, and Alec looked out the front windows of the Emergency Room. It was still dark outside. His fatigue was catching up with him, and he longed to fall asleep. An X-ray tech arrived to take him to the CT scanner, and Alec closed his eyes as the gurney rolled toward Radiology.

***

A quiet voice whispered, "Dr. Lucas, please wake up." Alec had fallen asleep again and now a soothing voice was waking him from his unintended slumber. He opened his eyes to see the diminutive form of Spiro Engles, the psychiatrist, standing at the bedside.

"Dr. Lucas, they called me to see you," Engles said. "The neurologist reports that your physical exam is unremarkable."

"I'm feeling better now," Alec said, sitting bolt upright in bed with a sudden surge of energy. "I'd like to go home."

"There is a problem, however," Engles said. "Your blood tests were all normal with one critical exception."

"What's that?"

"Your tox screen, Dr. Lucas. Your blood sample from tonight is positive for 3,4-methylenedioxymethamphetamine, otherwise known as MDMA or Ecstasy. It's probable that your symptoms tonight were an adverse reaction to the Ecstasy. But there's a more serious problem. Both the urine sample you gave me last week and the blood sample from the Emergency Room this morning were positive for the potent narcotic anesthetic fentanyl."

"That's impossible. I mean, I drank three glasses of red wine last night. Maybe someone put some drug in there. I know Ecstasy is an oral drug, so maybe that could have happened. But fentanyl? No way. Look at my arms. There're no needle marks. I'm no addict. I'm being framed." Alec's heart raced. He looked down at the hospital gown he was wearing over his naked skin and looked at the ER exit door some thirty feet away. He'd have to decide in the next minute while only Engles guarded his bedside.

"The fentanyl explains your symptoms tonight, Dr. Lucas. You're lucky to be alive. The addiction to an intravenous drug as powerful as fentanyl can only end in two ways: either a supervised narcotic withdrawal in a mental health hospital, or a miserable death with a needle stuck in your vein."

"Look, Dr. Engles, I'm glad you're here to help me," Alec said.

Engles nodded his head once and folded his hands as if in prayer.

"Please, Dr. Engles," Alec said. "Do you think you get me a glass of water? The drugs have made me parched."

Engles stared back at him, unblinkingly for almost a minute without answering. Then he murmured in a librarian's voice, "I'll be right back."

As soon as Engles walked away, Alec pulled the privacy curtain around his bed, ripped out the IV catheter, covered the site with a cotton gauze pad, and hopped off the gurney. He pulled his hospital gown tight around his waist and tiptoed in his bare feet to the door that linked the ER to the center corridor of the medical center. Once through, he blended in with the crowds of people and escaped, heading for the lobby.

Despite his hospital garb and lack of shoes, no one paid any attention to Alec as he wove his way toward the main hospital entrance. The lobby was a beehive of people weaving back and forth past each other. Multiple electronic signs hung from the ceiling, directing patients to various medical clinics, labs, and scanning locations.

Alec pushed his way through the masses of unsmiling, hurried folks. It was minutes before eight a.m. and already the setting in the hospital lobby resembled a busy airport with each person holding a ticket to Urologyville, Gynecologyopolis, or Cardiology City. Alec had little trouble seeing across the lobby, as most of the people were white-haired and stooped over. A younger man was working his way through the crowd in front of him, squeezing the handle of a briefcase as he scanned back and forth between his wristwatch and the overhead traffic direction signs. The man reversed directions and collided with Alec, almost knocking him over.

"Sorry, guy," he said, "I've got three minutes to find the General Surgery Clinic and I've been waiting two months for the appointment." He swung his briefcase in front of him to clear a path and disappeared into the crowd.

A row of twenty glass revolving doors loomed in front of Alec. He shot through one of them and found himself standing under a blue sky at dawn.

Alec grabbed the door handle of a taxi cab at the bottom of the hospital steps. The driver looked at his hospital gown, and said, "You escapin', boss?"

"No, I just need to go back home to get my wallet. Medical care is more expensive than I expected. 108 Cypress Street, please. I'll pay you when we get there." He hopped into the back seat, and with a cloud of black smoke the taxi shot forward.

27 ~ THE PESCADERO FREE CLINIC

The taxi dropped Alec off at his house, and he walked up the steps and staggered through the front door into his bedroom. His jacket was still draped across the chair next to the bed, and the loafers he'd worn the day before were sitting on the floor in the center of the room. He got his wallet and then went back out to pay the taxi driver.

Once back in, Alec found his phone and dialed Mae's number. She picked up, and he said, "Mae, it's Alec. I need to get out of town. Any chance I can hang out with you up in Pescadero?"

"Wait a minute. What did they say at the ER?"

"Nothing," he lied. "They recommended I take a few days off. I'm thinking I'll follow your lead and get some fresh air and low stress professional time at your clinic up there."

There was a long pause on the other end of the line. "Okay, you can come on up to Pescadero. I'm at the clinic right now. It's on Stage Road in the center of town. Ask for me when you get here."

"I'll be up there in an hour," he said. He peeled off the hospital gown and climbed into the shower.

***

At ten a.m. Alec's Corvette passed the crest of the coastal mountain range and descended toward Pescadero. On the outskirts of town, two dilapidated buildings bordered Stage Road. The first was a white building with a small sign that said "Zammer's Appliances." The white paint of the siding was flaking and peeling as was the red lettering on the sign. Someone had applied black spray paint to the sign changing the final letters, so the blackened version of the sign was the palindrome "ZammaZ Appliances." The front window was opaque with swirls of white wax covering the inside. Years had passed since the last appliance was sold at ZammaZ.

Next door was a single-story frame building with dark brown wooden shingle siding. There was a single brass plaque next to the front door that read "PESCADERO MEDICAL CLINIC."

Alec parked his car on the street in front. Through the open door of the clinic he could hear the sounds of loud conversation and laughter. The sidewalk was empty except for a gray-haired couple in their seventies, walking hand in hand along Stage Road. A man with a bleached-blonde pompadour exited the clinic and fell in step behind the couple.

Alec got out of the Chevy and walked toward the clinic. The blonde man stepped in Alec's path and said, "Dr. Lucas, what brings you back to our little hamlet in the woods?"

Alec looked up and saw the dark eyebrows of Red Jones. Jones's intense face was unchanged from their last meeting, but now it was framed by wavy platinum locks that made him look like Marilyn Monroe in drag. The blonde hair stunned Alec. Did Jones think he was a rock star? What kind of guy changed his hair color three times in one week? Alec looked past Jones to the clinic and wished he'd arrived five minutes later and avoided their chance encounter.

"I'm going into the clinic to see a friend," Alec said.

Jones leaned so close that Alec could count every wrinkle around Jones's green eyes. "Fancy that, my man. It wouldn't be Mae Yee, would it? She said she knew you."

"I'm here to see Mae, yes."

Jones raised one eyebrow, and said, "Whew, she's a fun one, isn't she?"

"Mae is a smart young woman," Alec said.

"Mae is more than a smart young woman," Jones said. "She's one hot babe." He leaned over and whispered in Alec's ear. "Too much woman for you. She's got some sense of humor, that's for sure. She had me rolling through breakfast."

Breakfast? Alec's face grew slack. Mae left him in the ER so she could have breakfast with this fake blonde multi-millionaire from her father's generation?

"Are you for real, Dr. Jones?" Alec said. "Is money really that much of an aphrodisiac?"

"You could lay awake at night wondering what part of me is real, Lucas. Maybe you already have. And yes, money is that much of an aphrodisiac."

Alec said nothing. He looked at his watch, and knew he was late for his meeting with Mae.

"Before you go, Lucas, did you see the front page of *The Wall Street Journal* yesterday? Did you see the picture of yours truly, in black and white? The WellBees are going in at the University of Los Angeles, and Wall Street is excited. When those WellBees are fired up, you'll see a rainbow arching over the California sky from San Francisco to L.A., and the pot of gold at the end of that rainbow will be at the University of Los Angeles. The future is here, baby, and I'm all over it."

"I'm happy for you, Dr. Jones. I've really got to go now." Alec started walking around Jones and into the clinic.

"By the way, Lucas, you should give Izabella a call. She's waiting by the phone."

Alec kept walking.

"Don't break the girl's heart, Lucas. She's a sensitive one."

Alec thought of Izabella's biceps tightening as she stretched her arms around him during the rifle shoot and the power in her thighs as she pinned him at the Mahogany. *Can I borrow your Visa card?* The woman was many things, but sensitive wasn't a word he'd use to describe Izabella.

***

He walked into the clinic and saw the laughter he heard earlier was coming from a rotund woman sitting behind the front desk. She had eyelashes thick with mascara and hair of a flaming red color. Red lipstick outlined her voluptuous mouth. She wore a faded red sweatshirt that said SPIDERHAWKS, with a scowling arachnid pictured beneath the words. Fastened above the spider was a nametag that read Racey Might.

"Racey Might, or she might not?" the Crimson Woman said to Alec. "What can I do for you, Mister …?"

"I'm Dr. Alec Lucas. I'm here looking for Dr. Mae Yee."

"Dr. Mae? No problem." She turned around in her chair, and yelled, "Hey, we got a cute guy here to see Dr. Mae."

A thin Asian man wearing blue jeans and a pale blue T-shirt came out of a hallway behind Racey and said, "Dr. Mae is with a patient right now. She told me she was expecting you, Dr. Lucas. My name is Jay Matasaki. I'm the Medical Director of the clinic."

"I'm glad to meet you, Dr. Matasaki. Mae says great things about your operation here."

He laughed. "We're anything but great, but we do the best we can. Let's find Mae."

Alec followed him into a waiting room furnished with a dozen orange plastic chairs. Half the seats were occupied by patients reading magazines and waiting to be seen.

A stubby Hispanic man wearing a dirty yellow hat that read *Abe's Lumber* approached Matasaki. "Hi Doc," he said. "Did you git that fence out back of your house finished yet?"

Matasaki pushed lengths of oily black hair behind both his ears and gazed over the top of his glasses at the man. "No, the fence is beautiful, but it's not finished. Three or four more post holes and the fence will reach the barn. I need a couple of guys like you with calluses on their hands and smiles on their faces to knock off the job."

"Ten bucks an hour and a change of doctors to Dr. Mae, that's all I ask," Lumber Hat said. "She said hello to me this morning, and I'm in love."

"Pretty soon half of Pescadero will be, my friend," Matasaki said.

"So how 'bout the fence, Doc?" Abe's Lumber said.

"I'll pay you twenty bucks an hour, but Dr. Mae will manage her own personal appearances." Matasaki glanced back at Alec and said, "Come this way, Dr. Lucas."

"Mae's pretty popular for someone who's only been here one day," Alec said.

"She's young, fresh, and joyful," Matasaki said. "She's happy having patients who talk back to her, instead of that knock-em-out anesthesia stuff you guys are used to."

"Humph," grunted Alec.

Matasaki knocked on a door with a large brass number "2" screwed onto it. "Mae, I've got Dr. Alec out here. Okay if we come in?"

"Come on in," Mae said from the other side of the door. Matasaki opened the door and slid inside and motioned for Alec to follow him. Mae smiled when she saw him. She wore a black and white checked shirt and blue jeans. Other than the stethoscope hanging from her neck, her attire wasn't much different from the folks sitting in the waiting room.

She gave Alec's hand a squeeze and said, "Welcome to the Pescadero Clinic, home of real medicine."

He flashed her a big smile and remembered why he drove forty minutes to see her. Opposite Mae was a woman sniffling and holding a tissue to her eyes. The woman glanced at the two new doctors in the room and started crying out loud.

"This is Miss Gillespie," Mae said. "Miss Gillespie, meet my colleagues Dr. Matasaki and Dr. Lucas. Dr. Matasaki is the Medical Director of the Pescadero Clinic. Trust him, he's one of the smartest doctors I know. Dr. Matasaki, Miss Gillespie is scared. She has a golf ball sized mass growing on the back of her neck. It's firm and non-tender. She's been aware of it for over two years, but today she's worried that it's getting bigger. See what you think." She stepped aside so Matasaki could approach the patient.

"Miss Gillespie, you look like a healthy young woman to me. Does this mass hurt you?" Matasaki said.

The woman continued to sob into her tissue. She stopped to blow her nose, and then she spoke. "This damn thing is sore. I think it's growing. My sister had breast cancer last year. I'm afraid cancer might run in the family."

"Can you point with one finger to the spot that's growing?"

"It's right here. Right where the collar of my shirt hits my neck." She rubbed the back of her neck with her left hand and then pulled the back of her tee shirt away from her neck.

Dr. Matasaki bent over, looked at the woman's neck and extended the fingers of his right hand to touch the area she'd pointed to. After ten seconds of examining her neck, he stepped back and sat down on a chair at eye level to her.

"What's going on at home?" he asked. "Is everything all right with your family, your finances, your kids?"

She blinked twice and tears dripped down both cheeks. "Hell, no. My old man didn't come home two nights in a row. When he did come home, I asked him where he been. He said it was none of my business, but Cindi Yellerman sure was a good piece of ass. Then he laughed at me. He said she didn't just lay there like me. Can you believe he said that? Can you believe he did that to me?" She pulled the front of her jacket up to cover her face as she cried louder. The three doctors stared at her at first, and then one by one they found other inanimate objects in the room to turn their attention to.

"Miss Gillespie, I have good news for you," Matasaki said with newfound exuberance in his voice. "The lump on your neck is a lipoma, a harmless benign growth of fat tissue. You've just been put through a traumatic experience at home. What happened to you was a big deal, and it will eventually be resolved. The lump on your neck is not a big deal. I can reassure you on that. Do you have supportive people to help you through this jam with your man?"

"My sister Lisa is always there for me." She stopped crying and held her head high. "I'll be all right. I'm so relieved to hear this isn't cancer. Are you sure it doesn't need to be cut out?"

"Young lady, I'm sure. And anyone who notices this slight imperfection in you is someone you don't want to hang around with, anyway." Matasaki's face beamed in an expansive smile, and he reached out and squeezed the top of her shoulder. "Good day now," he said, and he opened the door once again and left. Alec followed him into the hallway outside the room while Mae stayed inside.

In the hallway Matasaki said, "Can I entice you into dropping out of anesthesiology like Mae did, to work in our humble facility? Isn't clinic work wonderful? It's one-part medicine, one-part psychotherapy, and sometimes one part doing God's work. When you walk out of each patient's room, you want to accomplish four things. The first two are the easiest: making a diagnosis and making a treatment plan. The last two are the ones that take time: developing a rapport with the patient and making them feel better. You want to make them feel like coming to see you was the best decision they ever made regardless of whether their health is any different when they walk out of the office."

154

"But it's so slow moving. So boring," Alec said. "In surgery and anesthesia, we act. We do a procedure that makes a patient better. We don't have to seduce or trick the patient into thinking they feel better, we fix something so it *is* better. What would you have done if that lady had burst into tears at the end and said that she had no one to support her in the whole wide world—that you and her dickhead boyfriend were the only ones she could count on?"

"If she had nowhere to turn, I'd have asked you to sit down and talk to her for a week, Dr. Lucas," Matasaki said. "Ha, got you there." He started to laugh and pretended to throw a jab at Alec's jaw. "No, I'd have called Laura, our social worker. She knows dozens of people around town who are willing to give their ear and their time to help someone like Miss Gillespie get through a tough situation. Pescadero is that kind of community. Excuse me a minute, I have to ask Racey a question."

Matasaki walked away. The door to Miss Gillespie's exam room opened again, and Mae walked out. "It's great to see you back on your feet again," she said to Alec. She studied his eyes. "You look as tired as I feel."

"I am as tired as you feel. I need a respite, out here in small town coastal California."

"I thought you were up here because I'm irresistible."

"That's what Red Jones was saying on the sidewalk out front. He said he had breakfast with you."

"The clinic had its once-a-month staff meeting breakfast this morning. It was me, Matasaki, Red Jones, and the nursing staff." Mae looked away from him and stared out the window. Alec waited, but she kept focusing her eyes on something outside.

After thirty seconds, Alec said, "I'm sorry. He made it sound like there was something else going on."

"For heaven's sakes, Alec, give me a break. The guy might have crush on me, but that's all. Don't you get it? I quit anesthesia and this is my new job. It's a free clinic for the patients, but I still get paid. Red Jones pays half of my salary. His foundation underwrites the clinic." She glared at him, and the wistful out-the-window look was gone.

"Mae, I had a great time with you last night—until I had my panic attack, that is. I don't know what happened, but I'm grateful that you were there for me. I feel safe with you."

She crossed her arms and sighed. "Maybe some time at the Pescadero Free Clinic would be good for you. You need to meet some other people with real problems and take your mind off your own."

"My problems are quite real, thank you." He looked around at the walls surrounding them and said, "This clinic—listening to patients complain about their lumps and bumps and pains— isn't it going to be a little dull for you?"

"I love this place already," she said. "I have two more patients to see this morning, and then I'm done. Maybe you can help me by seeing one of them."

Alec scrunched up his face. "I don't know. I haven't seen an internal medicine patient for over ten years."

"Give it a whirl. It's a free clinic—patients don't expect much. The next patient's name is Mary Dorrit. She's 77 years old, and she has a dire problem—she's dizzy. This case is all yours, Dr. Lucas." She pointed the forefingers of both hands in the direction of Room #3.

"All mine?"

"Yes. And do not fail," Mae said. Her eyes twinkled.

Alec picked up Ms. Dorrit's chart. The inside of the front cover was a handwritten list of her active medical problems. The list numbered ten problems in all: emphysema, elevated cholesterol, degenerative joint disease of the spine and knees, cataracts, glaucoma, depression, history of breast cancer, urinary incontinence, mild dementia, and history of a brainstem stroke two years earlier. He looked up from the chart. Mae was still there, watching him.

"What do you think, Dr. Lucas?" she said.

"I think this lady has a chart full of reasons to feel dizzy. In medical school, this would've been a perfect case for the studious types that liked geriatric medicine. I doubt I can do anything to help this lady. How much time am I supposed to spend in there?" He nodded his head toward the door.

"As long as you want. As long as it takes. We aren't on the clock. There's no timetable. Anyone who doesn't get seen today can come back tomorrow if they want to. Go in, sit down, and take your time. She won't bite you. And Alec—"

"Yes?"

"Do not fail." She winked at him and disappeared down the hallway.

Alec put his hand on the doorknob and entered Room #3. Ms. Dorrit was curled up on the chair with her legs tucked under her bottom. She was fixing her white hair, pulling it back in a bun behind her head. She looked up at him.

"Ms. Dorrit, my name is Dr. Alec Lucas."

The expression on her face remained unchanged, and she said nothing as she scanned Alec from head to toe. Alec scanned her in return. This was a LOL in NAD, or Little Old Lady in No Acute Distress, if Alec had ever seen one. He asked the question they'd taught him in medical school years ago, "What brought you to the clinic today, Ms. Dorrit?"

She licked her upper lip and said, "I'm here because I been feeling weak and dizzy all the time."

Alec remembered how much he and his fellow medical students would cringe when a patient presented the clinic with "VD," which didn't stand for venereal disease, but instead was slang for "Veak and Dizzy." Alec sighed and asked a series of questions. "What brings on the dizziness? What makes it better? What makes it worse? How often do you get it? What does it feel like?"

Ms. Dorrit started answering with a slow whisper that made Alec move closer to her as he strained to hear her replies. She grew more animated with each answer, stimulated by the interest Alec was taking in her problems. Ms. Dorrit remained rolled up into a fetal ball with her arms encircling her knees. "There," she said, "the dizziness just came on. I just felt it. Did you see that?"

Alec squinted at her. She didn't appear any different or any sicker than she had looked a minute earlier.

"What makes the dizziness worse?"

"It's been worse the past two days since I started that new medicine you all are giving me."

Alec paged through her thick chart. "What was the name of the new medicine?"

She gaped back at him. "I don't know."

"I need to ask you some more questions, Ms. Dorrit. This could take a while."

Alec emerged from Room #3 fifty minutes later. Ms. Dorrit followed behind him, a surprising five feet tall when unfolded. "Thanks a bunch, Doctor," she said when she passed Alec. She shuffled across the waiting room and out of the door of the facility. Alec walked into the empty doctor's lounge and sat down on one of the folding chairs adjacent to a white plastic table.

Mae entered the lounge a minute later and sat down next to him. "How did it go?" she asked.

"It was painful," Alec said. "I asked her when the dizziness started, and she said it started when she was twenty-eight years old—when she rode on the Ferris wheel at the Kankakee County Fair in Illinois."

"Yep, that's medicine in the geriatric clinic," Mae said.

"I feel like I'm Ebenezer Scrooge starring in the medical version of *A Christmas Carol*," Alec said. "Ms. Dorrit is the Ghost of Medicine Past, and Dr. Vita is The Ghost of Medicine Future."

"Funny. And guess what? I've got The Ghost of Medicine Present in the next room. It's Marion Mindling, the wife of Jake Mindling, our patient who died on induction of anesthesia. You need to talk to her. It turns out she has some information that may help you solve the FutureCare puzzle."

"Where's Mrs. Mindling?" Alec asked.

"She's in Room #1," Mae said. "She's still grieving, and she's having a hard time. Be nice to her."

Alec knocked on the door and entered. He saw a different Marion Mindling than the woman he met a week earlier. Today's Marion was chalk white and gaunt. Her hair was tangled, and the lenses of her thick black glasses were smudged with fingerprints. Her shoes were untied, and she was tapping one foot on the ground in an irregular rhythm. She dabbed a white handkerchief to the corners of her eyes, and said, "Dr. Lucas, I'm glad you're here. My life has been hell this past week."

"Tell me what happened."

"Three days after Jake died, we had a funeral, and all Jake's relatives flew in from Arkansas. Before I knew it, they were back on the plane and gone. I couldn't afford to bury him anywhere, so I had him cremated."

At this, she pulled a glass jar full of gray soot out of her purse and set in down on the table next to her. "I haven't had the strength to part with his remains yet, so I carry them with me everywhere. I'm still getting dozens of sympathy cards from our friends, but every night when the sun goes down, I'm alone, alone . . . a-lone. I miss Jake's big laugh. I miss him screaming at the sportscasters on television. I miss the smell of him when he kissed me goodnight."

"I'm sorry, Mrs. Mindling. It sounds awful."

She held up her hand and stopped him. "I can't sleep. Every night I stare at the ceiling and think about Jake. My heart races, my palms get sweaty, and I'm afraid of the future. I wanted to talk to Jake's doctors again, to try and figure out what happened."

"We're glad you came to the clinic, Mrs. Mindling."

"I didn't come here first. I went back to USV and talked to Dr. Chavez. He held my hand for a few minutes and told me how sorry he was, but then he had to leave to do a surgery."

"He suggested you come here?" Alec said.

"No. He sent me to the ER to get some help. When I got to the ER, there was a chubby nurse in a flowered jacket sitting at a table. I told her that I was sad, and I was having trouble sleeping. She asked me some questions about chest pains and breathing. She took my blood pressure, and then she sent me through some bright blue doors to the Dr. Vita side of the ER. That gave me the creeps, because Jake saw a Dr. Vita the day before he died." She stopped, blew her nose, and wiped her eyes again.

"I sat down in front of the Dr. Vita and put in my HAC card, and that's where I made a mistake. I always helped Jake keep his belongings straight, and I still had Jake's HAC in my wallet. When I put Jake's HAC in the machine, the yellow eyes flashed on and off three times, and then the black screen lit up with what looked like a lot of numbers and letters in gibberish. Then the Vita printed out this piece of paper." She took a twelve-inch-long strip of paper out of her purse and handed it to Alec.

"I didn't know what to do with it," she said. "but I wondered if it had anything to do with Jake's death. I remembered Dr. Yee's name from right after Jake died. I contacted Dr. Yee through the USV paging operator, and I came to this clinic to see her. She said you were an expert in both anesthesia and computers, and you might be able to decipher this."

Alec studied the paper, and his eyes widened. The paper was covered with computer code. And not just any computer code—this code was timed from the last minutes of Mindling's life and contained the hidden lines of the Restricted File.

The contents of the Restricted File were stunning. The file contained an override order from Mindling's Vita unit which boosted the delivered concentration of anesthetic from the sevoflurane vaporizer to its maximum dose of 8%. A second series of code timed one minute later documented that the monitoring equipment changed the recorded concentration from the true reading of 8% to a falsified value of 0%. A third series of code added the malignant hyperthermia misinformation to the Past Medical History in the electronic medical record.

Marion watched him as he read. "Is it anything important? Does it tell you anything?"

Alec set the paper on the table next to the jar containing Mindling's ashes, and said, "It's a wonderful thing that you brought this in here. The information on this paper is what was missing. It's what I've been looking for. Can I keep it?"

"What does it say?"

"It's a record of the computer files that changed our anesthesia machine's settings. This order made our anesthesia equipment into a gas chamber. Somebody killed your husband by manipulating the FutureCare System."

Marion covered her face with her bony fingers and began to sob. Alec handed her a Kleenex.

"I'm going to step out and give you some privacy," he said. "I'll be in the next room if you need me." He picked up the paper containing Jake Mindling's Restricted File and walked out to join Mae in the physician's lounge.

"What does the paper say? Is it anything helpful?" she asked.

"It's the first decent break in the whole case," Alec said. "See this line here, where it says 'delta sevo conc 8?' That's the 'Ah-ha' evidence. This computer code is from the Restricted File on Jake Mindling's EMR. It shows how he was killed."

"Then someone really is hacking into FutureCare."

Alec waved the roll of paper in the air. "I never doubted that. Now I've got proof. Stay here a minute, I'm going to my car to get something."

He returned a few minutes later and was carrying a manila folder. "In this folder I have the names and addresses of the other patients from USV who died under my watch. Following this path blazed by Marion Mindling, I intend to find the families and see if any of them have the deceased patient's HAC cards."

"What will you do with the cards?" Mae said.

"I'll feed them into a Dr. Vita that's hooked up to the USV network, just like Mrs. Mindling did. With luck, I'll get three more pieces of evidence like the one she brought in."

"Go get 'em, and make sure they fry," a voice said from the hallway. It was Marion, her face dry and her head held high.

"Mrs. Mindling," Alec said. "Can I ask you a couple of additional questions?"

"I'm here to help."

"Did your husband have any enemies? Anyone who hated him enough to kill him?"

"Lord, no. Jake was a big teddy bear. He went to church every Sunday. He was retired, but he loved to tinker and fix things around our house. We lived a mile down the road from here."

"How long did you two live in Pescadero?"

"Jake lived here all his life. He loved the woods. He hiked these redwood hills since he was a boy."

"I want to thank you for all you've done. I'm going to get to the bottom of what happened to your husband."

"Do it, Dr. Lucas. I'm a God-fearing, Jesus-loving woman. But if I get my hands on the evil person who did this to Jake, Lord help me, I'll choke him with my bare hands. I'll give 'em what they gave Jake, I will." She pulled her collar tight around her neck, said goodbye, and walked toward the lobby.

Mae and Alec watched her leave. "I'm leaving, too," Alec said. "I'm going to look up these other families."

"Good luck," Mae said. "I'll be keeping busy here."

"One other thing," he said. "The ER found the Ecstasy in my blood tests, you know."

"Sorry about that. Are you in trouble?"

"I think so. I wish you hadn't done that to me."

"I'm so sorry. I had no idea you were going to have a bad trip. Maybe it was a mistake to take you to the ER, but you had me scared."

"Minus the Ecstasy, I'd like to do it again."

Her head moved up and down an imperceptible millimeter or two.

"Is that a 'yes?'" he asked.

"We'll see," she said. "Let's just wait and see." And then she walked into ladies locker room at the Pescadero Clinic, and closed the door behind her.

Alec stood in front of San Joaquin Apartments, located in an impoverished neighborhood on the east side of San Jose, and reviewed his notes. Richard Irving was the 84-year-old man Alec found cold and dead in the ICU. His wife Cynthia lived in this apartment building. Alec walked along a line of dusty ten-year-old SUV's parked in front of the apartments and then climbed the stairs and entered the front door of the building. He found Apartment 19A and knocked. A wiry lady opened the door. She was a ninety-pound woman with a face full of deep wrinkles and upper arms the diameter of broomsticks.

Alec gave her a warm smile and said, "Hello, Mrs. Irving. My name is Dr. Alec Lucas, and I'm here because of your husband Richard."

She puffed on a cigarette, and the thick smoke wafted up into her eyes. "Are you here to help me sue the hospital? Because if you are, I've got no use for that. None. It's God's will that Richard passed on. What's done is done."

"No, I'm not here to sue the hospital. I'm here because I'm trying to figure out what happened the day he died. Can I ask you a few questions?"

"Come in. *The Young and the Restless* is almost over anyway. Tell me your name again, doll."

"Lucas. Alec Lucas."

"Would you like some instant coffee?"

"I'll pass, Mrs. Irving. Richard would have had a clinic card that he used at USV. A purple plastic card that looked like a credit card—it's called a HAC, for Health Assessment Card. Is there any chance that card is still around somewhere?"

She took a huge drag off her cigarette and then lifted a second cigarette to light off the first one. "Sorry about all the smoke, doll. You want some?" She offered the smoldering cigarette to him.

"No," Alec said, taking a step backward. After three giant inhales, Mrs. Irving started rummaging around in a desk drawer. She pulled out a purple HAC and threw it to Alec. "That what you're lookin' for?"

"Is this Richard's card, or is it yours?"

"Me?" She guffawed until she started a coughing fit. "I never get near doctors. If you hadn't knocked on the door, I could'a said I spent the last twenty years without seeing a doctor."

"Could I borrow the card? I'm doing an investigation."

"I'm happy to help you. I'm the mother of nine kids. Richard was the dad for eight of 'em. He never helped me for two minutes. All he did was set on that sofa there and watch sports on television. I guess I loved him, although life's a lot easier nowadays. Now I get to watch whatever channel I want. Oh, what the hell, I miss him, even if he was a good-for-nothing seven days a week."

Alec put the HAC in his pocket and stood up. "I'll let you know if I discover anything from the card."

She looked up at him and spent three seconds blowing smoke out of both nostrils. "All you're going to find out is that God's in control, Doc. It was Richard's time, that's all it was."

"Thanks, Mrs. Irving. I know you never see doctors, but since our paths crossed today, can I tell you something?"

"Shoot, honey."

"You need to stop the Marlboros, or you'll be seeing God before your time."

"That's why I don't see no doctors. They don't want a girl to have any fun. Take care, doll." She turned the volume up on the television, and Alec left.

His next stop was a tiny cottage set among tall redwoods, half a mile removed from Highway 17 on the road from San Jose to Santa Cruz. This was the home of Barbara Anderson, the daughter of Elizabeth Anderson. Alec thought back to his meeting with Barbara and her two daughters just minutes after Elizabeth's death. He hoped this meeting was less stressful for each of them.

Alec rang the doorbell, and a feeble old man answered the door. He had thin graying hair that was a foot-and-a-half long, tied in a ponytail behind his head. His mouth was hidden inside a bushy gray mustache and goatee, and his eyes were covered by a pair of darkly tinted glasses.

"Hi. My name is Dr. Alec Lucas," Alec said. "I was one of the doctors that took care of Elizabeth on the day she died. I'm looking for Barbara Anderson."

"She ain't here right now," the man replied. "She took her kids shopping over in Los Gatos. Can I help you?"

"Maybe. Are you family?"

"I'm Elizabeth's husband. My name's Mac."

"I'm sorry, I didn't meet you on the day of surgery."

"I was sick that day. Couldn't make it to the hospital."

"I won't take too much of your time. Let me start by giving you my sympathies. Her death was an awful event. It must have been terrible for you and your family."

"It was," he said, gazing out at the highway behind Alec.

"How're your granddaughters doing?"

"They don't talk to me much. Were you the surgeon?"

"No, I was the anesthesia doctor."

"I heard Elizabeth had a peaceful passing, because of you."

Alec thought back to Templeton's hand inside Elizabeth Anderson's chest, squeezing her heart. He doubted Mac would have called that a peaceful passage if he'd seen it.

"Can I ask you a favor? I'm looking for Elizabeth's Health Assessment Card—her HAC. Do you have any idea where it would be?"

"Barbara's got a shoebox stuffed with all of Elizabeth's personal belongings. I think her wallet's still in that box. Let me look." He left and walked into the back of the house. While he waited, Alec studied the room. There was only one window, and the shade was pulled three-quarters of the way down. The room was a gloomy cave. An old German Shepherd slept on a rug in the corner, and the whole room smelled like a wet dog. Two chairs and the couch we covered in a worn brown plain fabric that had seen better days. Alec thanked God he didn't have to live there.

Mac reappeared from a back hallway and handed a purple HAC to Alec. "Here it is. Ain't no good to us anyways."

"I thank you, Mr. Anderson. And once again, I'm so sorry about all this."

He took off his dark glasses, revealing sad gray eyes with puffy bags hanging beneath them. "She had cancer, Doc. She wouldn't have lasted long, anyways. The Lord had his will with her. It was a blessing." He slid his glasses back on and stopped talking.

Alec gave it a moment of silence, and then said, "I'd better be going now. I'll let you know what I find out from her card."

Mac Anderson scratched his fingers through his long hair and nodded once. He ended their encounter by closing the outside door between them. Alec guarded the prize of Elizabeth Anderson's HAC by placing it in his wallet next to Richard Irving's.

So much for romantic love. Alec had collected two HAC cards, and he'd met two widows who believed God had done the world a favor by taking their spouses to the grave.

Alec's cell phone went off as he slid back into the driver's seat of his Corvette. The call was from Henri Rovka. "Alec, I want you to meet someone," he said.

"Hey, I need to see you, too."

"Can you drive up to my ranch?"

"When?"

"Now. I live four miles northwest of Pescadero, on Dry Creek Road. I'll be home in less than an hour."

"I know where that is," Alec said. I'll head up to your ranch now." He hung up and spun his car into a U-turn. He was sure Henri Rovka was going to freak out when he saw what Alec had uncovered.

Fourteen Caucasian men in dark-colored sport coats stood shoulder to shoulder, encircling the waist-high table in the War Room at the Red Jones ranch. Red Jones stood at one end of the table, and Steven Mallory, the Chief Operating Officer of WellBee, Inc., stood at the opposite end. As Mallory spoke, the other members of the Board of Directors stood erect and still. No one shuffled their feet or moved. No one adjusted their necktie because no one was wearing one. The boss set the dress code, and the dress code for the War Room was an Armani jacket and an open-collared shirt with the top button unbuttoned.

"The WellBee upgrade went well?" Red said.

"Yes, sir," Mallory said. "We've successfully installed the FC-27 chip cloned from the Dr. Vita unit in all WellBees. The FutureCare chip, combined with our own hardware and operating system, will make the WellBee faster and superior to the Vita units in every way." Mallory was a slender man in his forties with near-invisible eyebrows and a light blonde receding hair line. As the inventor and tech guru behind the WellBee unit, he was Red Jones's right-hand man.

Mallory went on, "The necessary inventory of twelve hundred WellBee modules is docked at the pier in Long Beach Harbor. Tomorrow they'll be unloaded and transported to the University of Los Angeles Medical Center for installation. The cables and routers for the WellBee System were installed over the last month. All that remains is to bring in the talking heads and hook them up. The FDA is behind us, the California Health Service is behind us, and the media is following our every move. Gentlemen, we're right where we want to be."

Red Jones scanned the faces of his board members. He liked what he saw. He had a team of A-players, all young Ivy League educated MBAs and engineers at the top of their games. These men were loyal to Jones and Mallory, and they made the wheels turn at WellBee. He'd handpicked this team of shakers and movers that wanted it all—money, power, and a place in history. They were born at a time when medicine needed *The Answer*, and now they had the good fortune to bring *The Answer* forth to the populace.

"I want every one of you on a plane out of San Jose tomorrow morning, arriving at the University of Los Angeles by noon," Jones said. He ran a well-manicured hand over his pompadour and continued, "Wall Street is watching you. Every medical regulatory body in California is watching you. I'm watching you." He paused and in a clockwise survey around the table, made eye contact with each standing man. No one dared to look away. No one shifted their weight, or so much as pushed their glasses up on their noses.

"No screw ups," announced Jones, and he hammered his fist on the War Room table as he spat out the words. "The FutureCare System at USV was, and I repeat 'was,' the gold standard for AIM technology. And now, like the internal combustion engine replaced the horse drawn carriage, we will blow past the FutureCare System. My inside sources tell me FutureCare has bugs, and patients are dying. When the time is right, those bugs will hit page one on every newspaper in America, and gentlemen," Jones's voice tapered off into a whisper, "gentlemen we … will … prosper!" As he spoke the last word, his fist crashed down on the table and the other thirteen board members burst into a flurry of hurrahs and back slapping.

Jones clasped his hands above his head, and said, "I'll join you in Los Angeles for the ribbon cutting on *day one*. Go get 'em." Like a football team breaking from their locker room at game time, the Board of WellBee, Inc. broke ranks and filed out the door at the far end of the conference room. After the room emptied, only Jones and Mallory remained. Jones put his hand on Mallory's shoulder, and said, "I hope to hell the whole thing works out."

Mallory looked surprised. "What do you mean?"

"What do I mean?" Jones said. "The WellBee has been tested every which way but upside down, and it passed every damn requirement that the FDA put up. But now we're putting 1200 of them all over a university medical center and praying it works out."

"Artificial Intelligence in Medicine is an idea whose time has come, sir. You know it. Dr. WellBee is a great machine."

Jones took his hand off Mallory's shoulder and said, "Once upon a time, I thought Dr. Vita was a great machine, too."

Alec pulled onto Stage Road and drove through Pescadero. Two minutes later he turned onto Dry Creek Road and zoomed past the entrance of Red Jones's estate. Alec's thoughts wandered again. Was Jones sitting in the dark, watching *The Maltese Falcon* alone, or was he giving Leslie Tucker a backrub while he told her how his talking WellBee heads were going to take over the world?

A horn beeped from behind him. He glanced into his rearview mirror, and the entire back window of his Chevy was filled with headlights. A yellow BMW was tailing him, just inches behind his taillights. The horn beeped again, and he swiveled around to check out the driver's face.

It was Izabella.

Alec pulled over to the side of the road, and she stopped behind him. He got out of his car and stepped toward her vehicle. Her window was rolled down.

She stared at him without the hint of a smile. "I thought we had a deal," she said.

Alec wished he could teleport the woman to Mars. *A deal?* He had no idea what to say.

She frowned, and a series of parallel lines formed across her forehead. "I'm mad at you," she said. "Is that what you do? Sleep with girls and then never call them back?"

Alec face went blank, and his stomach tightened. "No, I've been really busy."

"You're a fool," she said, rolling up the window. The BMW engine roared as she backed away from him. He inhaled her exhaust as the Beemer shot back onto the road, made a U-turn, and drove away.

"What a freak," he said to himself. He pulled away from the side of the road and drove on. He hoped he'd seen the last of Izabella.

He continued northwest on Dry Creek Road and caught a glimpse of the emerald green of Kami Shingo's private fairways through a tangle of manzanita bushes and live oak trees. Alec drove as fast as the curves of the mountain road would allow.

One mile up the road, Alec made a right turn into Henri Rovka's driveway and ascended further into the forest. The trees on the two sides of the road framed the setting sun ahead of him. He sighted a sprawling one-level ranch house surrounded by acres of yellowish-brown rolling grasslands and sped up until he stopped in front of the main doorway. Compared to the Jones and Shingo estates, the Rovka ranch was rustic with a capital R. The roof had moss growing on cedar shake shingles, and there were potholes in the dirt of the driveway.

Alec got out of the car and hopped up the path to the house, trying to avoid mud that filled the low points. He knocked on the heavy wooden door and waited. No one answered, but the front door squeaked open when he pushed it. He wiped his feet on the doormat and entered the house.

He turned on a lamp and checked out the roughened log walls of the interior of the house. Two immense fireplaces built of football-sized stones covered the two opposing ends of the central room. The rear wall was all windows and French doors, framing a majestic view of the setting sunlight on the oaks and grasslands high above the house. The room's furnishings included three sets of brown leather sofas and chairs, arranged in three separate groupings in front of the two fireplaces and the rear windows.

A cloud of dust in the driveway attracted Alec's attention to the front windows. He peered out and saw an enormous black limousine kicking up the dust as it motored down the hill toward him.

The limo screeched to a halt ten feet from the front door.

The tinted windows of the limousine mirrored the oak branches above, and the black side panels gleamed through the dust that swirled around the car. The rear door opened and booming laughter sounded out.

"Smell that air," Rovka said. "Gorge your senses on the sounds of privacy. Get out of the car and remember what living in the boonies can do for your spirit." Henri Rovka untangled himself from the back seat of the limousine and rose to his full height, stretching his arms to the sky. He was beaming as he surveyed his property and the birds and squirrels he shared it with.

"Come along out of there, honey. I've got big plans for you today—let's not waste time lounging in the back seat of this living room on wheels."

Rovka reached out his hand, and a trim woman in a lime green dress and a wide brimmed white bonnet got out of the car. She took Rovka's hand, and they walked shoulder to shoulder up to the front door. She swiveled her head as she evaluated her surroundings. A moment later there was a shriek of laughter as Rovka burst through the front door carrying the woman in his arms. She was holding the bonnet at arm's length with her other arm looped around Rovka's neck.

Her tawny hair bounced along her cheeks as he lifted her into the room. The laughter stopped as they stared at Alec, who was standing in the middle of the house.

"Dr. Lucas, welcome to paradise," Rovka said. The woman turned her gaze from Alec to Rovka, and she gave him a wide smile.

Bonnet Woman looked familiar to Alec. She had a regal appearance—she was no older than Alec, and a generation or two younger than Rovka. In a situation that could have been embarrassing, she stared back with the confidence of a celebrity.

"Excuse me, Dr. Rovka," Alec said. "I let myself in."

"Excellent," Rovka said, "You're our guest. Clarissa and I were being silly, which we love to do. Clarissa, meet Alec Lucas, my young doctor friend from USV. Alec, meet Clarissa Contessa, my wife of two days."

"Two days?" Alec said.

"Two days. I apologize if you were trying to reach me, but the time was right, and we eloped to Hana, Hawaii and got married."

"No wonder you didn't answer my calls. You're a rambling man," Alec said. "France last week and Hawaii this week."

"France?" said Clarissa. "Who went to France?"

"My good Alec, you are mistaken," Rovka said, looking embarrassed. "I brought you a bottle of French wine, but there was no trip to France."

Alec stared at Henri Rovka and watched beads of perspiration form on the old man's temples. Last week, Rovka said he flew to France. Did he lie to Alec, or was he lying to his new wife? Alec decided it was time to change the subject.

"Congratulations to you both on your marriage. It's wonderful news. I'm pleased to make your acquaintance, Mrs. Rovka," he said as he extended his hand to her. No wonder she carried herself like a celebrity. He knew the name Clarissa Contessa. She was the heiress daughter to one of the wealthiest families in America. The national media referred to her as Countess Contessa, and she was the favorite of the society pages, fashion magazines, and business magazines across the country.

She smiled back and squeezed his hand. "You didn't tell me this was going to be a two-on-one, Henri."

"No way, Countess. I'm not sharing you today or any other day," Rovka said.

Alec watched the two lovebirds coo in front of him and remembered the news he had for Rovka. "Dr. Rovka, I don't know if this is the time, but I've made a breakthrough in the FutureCare investigation."

Clarissa looked at Alec as if he had just farted out loud. Then she looked at Rovka, and he shrugged his shoulders.

"Clarissa and I are living in the romantic fantasy world that belongs only to newlyweds," Rovka said. "Forgive us if we haven't thought about FutureCare for days. I'll make drinks. It's cocktail hour and time for gin and tonics for all. We'll wet our whistles, and you can tell me your news." Rovka excused himself and went into the kitchen.

Alec and Clarissa stood opposite each other, and an awkward silence hung between them until she said, "Henri told me you're an anesthesiologist and a computer scientist."

"That's right," Alec said, and he sat down on a chair opposite her, facing the view out the rear windows of the house. "Our relationship started with a couple of cases that went sour without explanation, but now I think I've solved the riddle."

"The riddle?" Rovka said, returning with a tray of gin and tonics. "You've solved it?"

"I have a big piece of it solved. Before I tell you, I'd like to offer a toast." They each took a glass off the tray.

"To long life, health, and happiness for the new married couple. Cheers," Alec said, raising his glass. The three of them touched glasses and drank.

"Tell me your piece of the riddle," Rovka said.

Alec cast a glance at Clarissa, and said, "Does your new wife want to know? Should we talk in private?"

Clarissa laughed. "Dr. Lucas, I was into FutureCare before you ever heard of it. That's how Henri and I met. We were two of the FutureCare Four who started the company."

"The FutureCare Four?" Alec said.

"Shingo was the genius that made the Vita unit, Henri Rovka was the medical brain that became the Vita's diagnostic and therapeutic talent, and I … how should I say it, darling?" She smiled at Rovka.

"You were the bankroll," Rovka said, raising his glass in a silent second toast to his bride.

"Yes, I was the primary financier of the startup costs," she said. "I put up the seed money in return for a percentage of the company." Clarissa smiled and put her empty glass down. Alec was impressed with her drinking prowess—he still had two-thirds of his drink left. She reached for the pitcher of gin and tonic and poured herself a second glass. She swallowed a mouthful and said, "FC Industries went public, and you know the rest."

"No, I don't," Alec said.

"Don't you read *The Wall Street Journal*, or *Business Week*, or the business pages of the local papers?"

"No, I don't," Alec said. "I'm an academic anesthesiologist. I cash my paycheck, and that's all I need to know about the business world."

"The initial public offering was a huge bonanza," Rovka said. "The four of us made hundreds of millions of dollars and since then it's been an upward trajectory. Installing FutureCare at USV was the breakthrough because now the world is seeing Dr. Vita in action. When Dr. Vita spreads to the rest of the country, the shares of FC Industries will multiply in value again."

"And the other member of the FutureCare Four?" Alec asked.

"The fourth partner was Red Jones," Rovka said.

"What did he bring to the party?"

"Red had both an MD and an MBA, and he understood the medical marketplace. He was our chief marketer and evangelist. He convinced the investment community that Artificial Intelligence in Medicine was the solution to the health care crisis."

Alec nodded his head in assent. "But now he's started his competitor company, WellBee, Inc."

"Everybody did something different with their new money," Clarissa said. "Red sold his FC shares and poured the cash into his new WellBee startup. Shingo sold some of his shares and built his ridiculous golf course of solitude. Henri and I kept our shares. Henri rolled some cash into developing his Rovka Clinic in San Francisco."

"Hey, somebody needs to take care of the affluent people of the Bay Area," Rovka said. "Dr. Vita will care for most of the population, but there'll always be wealthy people that will pay cash for human doctors."

"I kidded Henri that he only married me to gain my shares of FC." She winked at Alec. "Together, we have the most to gain by a successful showing of the Dr. Vitas at USV."

"Unless there's a problem with the FutureCare System," Alec said.

"Ah, enter Alec Lucas, MD, problem solver," Rovka said. "I need to visit the men's room. When I come back, I want to hear what you've discovered."

Rovka left the room, and Alec was again alone with Clarissa Rovka. He studied her profile. She was a striking beauty—the most attractive woman he'd ever seen in person. How in the world could she be married to Henri Rovka, a man at least 30 years her senior? Alec felt uneasy and self-conscious around Clarissa and didn't want to be caught staring at her. He busied himself by pretending to check out the décor around them.

Clarissa poured a third gin and tonic into her glass. She swallowed hard and then turned to Alec. "Just between you and me, it isn't all that bad," she said, slurring her words.

"What isn't?"

"Being with Henri. He's a charming, caring man. He'd do anything for me."

Alec was taken aback. Pour a little alcohol into the woman, and now she was confiding that her new marriage was "not that bad?"

She stood up and stretched her legs. She looked at her reflection in the darkness of the rear window and smiled. She strolled toward Alec and sat down next to him, thigh to thigh. She said, "I love it that Henri works with bright young doctors like yourself."

Just then the glass of the rear window of the ranch house shattered in a blaze of explosions, and the booming sounds of gunfire echoed off the walls of the room. Alec felt a burning pain in his left arm and dove to the hardwood floor. Above him, he saw Clarissa collapse in slow motion. She landed on top of him, and the thunder of bullets rocked her body. He felt a second scorching pain in his left leg, and he closed his eyes.

The gunshots ended, and an eerie silence came over the room. A cold breeze blew in from the window that had been shattered by the bullets. Henri Rovka burst back into the room and screamed, "Oh my God. Clarissa, are you all right?" She was draped on top of Alec, her lime green dress splashed with blood.

"Henri, help me," she moaned. Her arms pawed at the air toward Rovka. He dropped to the floor and wrapped his arms around her.

"My belly. Pain," she said.

Rovka pulled up her dress to expose her abdomen. There were three holes, all in the left side and all oozing blood.

Alec was pinned beneath Clarissa's splayed torso. He craned his neck and assessed his damages. All four of his extremities still moved, and his mind was clear. He had modest pain in his left calf and his left forearm, but he'd survive. He dug his right elbow into the carpet and dragged himself from under Clarissa.

Rovka was kneeling next to Clarissa's half-naked body. He'd peeled her clothes away, his hands dripped blood, and the window behind him was blasted into pieces. Whoever had fired the shots was gone.

Rovka's face was ashen. "Are you okay, Alec?" he said.

"I think so," Alec said. The left leg of his pants and the left sleeve of his shirt were scarlet with fresh blood. "I was hit, but not bad."

"Clarissa took three shots to the abdomen. I'm going to call for help," Rovka said, and he rushed out of the room again.

Alec leaned against the edge of the couch and tried to evaluate Clarissa's injuries. She was still awake. He felt for the radial pulse in her wrist. It was feeble, and her heart rate was flying at a machine gun rate. He looked at her abdomen, but it was impossible to tell how much she was bleeding inside. She was pale and beads of sweat pooled on her forehead. Her breathing was labored.

"Can you wiggle your toes?" he said. She wiggled both feet—a good sign. The bullets missed her spinal cord.

"Are you short of breath?"

"A little."

He put his ear on her chest, and he heard clear breath sounds from both the right and left sides. The heart tones were fast but otherwise normal.

"Try to lie still and stay calm. You have two doctors here with you, and Henri is calling an ambulance." Alec knew she was in grave danger. The transit time from the outskirts of Pescadero to the nearest trauma center was too long. If she was bleeding from a large artery, she was going to die.

Rovka ran back into the room. "I called for help. They'll be here soon."

"Do you have any medical equipment in the house?" Alec asked.

"I don't." Rovka's voice was drowned out by a howling sound from the front driveway. A monstrous wind rustled the trees. The branches whipped harder and harder, until a large red "R" filled the frame of the front room window. Above the letter rode the whirling blades of a helicopter which landed forty feet from the front door.

"I keep a medical helicopter at the ranch when I'm here," Rovka said.

"Where is she, boss?" said a lone figure who spanned the open front doorway. With the glare of the helicopter's spotlights at his back, the man was a dark shadow pushing a folding gurney. The thundering noise from the still-spinning rotors filled the house.

The aviator ran to Clarissa's side. He was dressed in a khaki jumpsuit, with "Rovka Medical Clinic" sewn in red block letters above his breast pocket.

"Ma'am, my name is Jimmy. I work for Dr. Rovka. Are you still in pain?"

Clarissa's face was colorless. "I feel awful," she groaned. "Help me."

"I need to hook you up to my sensors and take some readings." Jumpsuit Jimmy pulled a portable monitor from his belt and connected one wire to her finger and three more to her chest. His eyes widened as he read off the vital signs. "We've got hypotension and tachycardia. Let's get an IV in. Then we've got to scoop and run."

An IV bag and line hung from a pole at the head of the gurney. Three pieces of tape were stuck on the pole. In a blur of motion, Jimmy tightened a latex tourniquet around her right arm, inserted a 14-gauge intravenous catheter, attached the IV line to the catheter, and taped the catheter to the skin. "Let's go," he said. "Five minutes to takeoff."

Rovka helped Jumpsuit Jimmy slide Clarissa onto the gurney. An oxygen tank swung from the belt loop of the medic's uniform, and Jimmy connected an oxygen cannula to Clarissa's nose. In less than five minutes from the time Jumpsuit Jimmy had entered the room, he was wheeling the patient out. The assessment and transfer had been done with the precision of a trauma team.

Alec dragged himself to his feet and limped alongside them. He held his injured left arm close to his side. They made their way across the bumpy surface of the gravel driveway and rolled the gurney up to the open door at the rear of the helicopter.

"Help me slide this gurney into the back of the chopper," Jimmy said over the roar of the rotor. "Slide her to me."

Alec pushed on the head of the bed, and it slid through the doorway into the interior. Jumpsuit Jimmy snapped a pair of levers and fixed the portable bed against the floor of the aircraft.

The wind from the rotors blew Alec's hair into his eyes, making it difficult to watch what was going on. He'd transported patients in fixed-wing aircraft before, but he'd never seen the inside of a helicopter. Rovka leaned into the cab and talked with Jimmy and the pilot, and then he pulled his head from inside the chopper and turned to face Alec. He looked at the blood on Alec's left arm and leg. "Go with her, Alec. You're injured, too, and the trauma center can treat you both. Fly with Clarissa and make sure she stays alive. Jimmy has a variety of drugs and equipment. There's only room for one more passenger, and you can help her more than I can. I'm a clinic doctor."

"C'mon, time's wasting," Jumpsuit said from inside the chopper.

"Go," Rovka said, and pushed Alec into the door of the helicopter. "I'll meet you at USV."

Alec ducked his head into the cabin and crawled on his hands and knees to get away from the doorway. Jumpsuit closed the door and handed Alec a set of headphones. Once Alec put them on, he heard the voices of Jumpsuit and the pilot.

"Fold that seat down, Doc, and put on the seat belt. We're going up," Jumpsuit said. As soon as Alec's seat belt clicked shut, the helicopter rose straight upward and banked away from the lights of the Rovka ranch house. Henri Rovka stood on the front lawn below, surrounded by tornadoes of swirling dirt and gravel.

Alec held on to a pair of handles on the walls of the helicopter. Jimmy was talking to Clarissa and ignoring the fact that they were climbing higher. Alec looked out the side window to see the trees and lights of the receding hillsides of Pescadero.

"How high are we?" he said. No one answered. He got a sudden powerful urge to open the door and get out. His breathing quickened, and the inside of the cabin began to pulsate and spin. Just then the helicopter made a broad ninety-degree turn to the east and the right side of the helicopter faced down and became the floor. Alec looked through the window straight down at the lights from coastal range foothill towns, and he was sure he was going to fall out and die.

"Am I going to die?" said a voice through his headphones. It was Clarissa speaking, and the sound of her voice gave Alec another focus. The readings of the medical monitors were displayed on an oscilloscope screen in front of them. Her blood pressure was fading at 75/30, and her heart rate had climbed to 160 beats per minute. Her abdomen was bloated, filling with leaking blood. "My stomach hurts even worse," she said.

"ETA is ten minutes to the USV Trauma Tower," the pilot said.

The helicopter made a sudden severe banked turn as it approached the USV Tower. Alec lost his balance and banged into the window and door. He looked straight beneath him and saw the lights of Santa Clara as the glass window of the helicopter became the floor once again. Then the chopper leveled off and began to descend. It was a windy night, and the helicopter swayed to and fro like a weight on a string as it dropped toward the roof of the medical center. With a loud scrape and a thud, the landing gear of the chopper hit home, and they landed in the emergency care circle on the rooftop.

"How are you feeling, Clarissa?" Alec said. He didn't expect an answer—he just wanted to know if she was still conscious. She was lying motionless with her eyes closed and didn't reply. He pulled up her dress and examined her abdomen again. Her belly had expanded in diameter, and when he slid his hand over her umbilicus, her abdominal wall was as rigid as a redwood deck.

"She's lost consciousness," Alec said. "We've got to move." A team of four nurses and orderlies dressed in scrub clothes ran out to meet the helicopter. Jimmy opened the door, and he and Alec slid Clarissa's gurney out onto the hospital rooftop. A cool wind snapped the cloth of their pants legs as the team extended the wheels of the gurney.

"She's dying," Alec said to the team from the operating room. "She needs an exploratory laparotomy in minutes. Do you have an OR ready?"

"OR #19 is ready," the lead nurse said. "Xavier Templeton and The Bricklayer are waiting."

"The Bricklayer," Alec said. "Damn it. Let's go. Into the elevator. Move!"

It was ten p.m.

33 ~ THE SHADOW OF
THE BRICKLAYER

Alec limped behind the gurney as the four others pushed the pale and writhing Clarissa into OR #19. Xavier Templeton and two surgical residents stood waiting with The Bricklayer poised behind them. Dr. Turtle was the anesthesiologist standing at the head of the table.

"Slide her onto the operating room table. On the count of three. Let's go!" Alec said. "You need to scrub, Dr. Templeton. She's had three gunshots to the abdomen. She's hypotensive and in shock. I'm sure she's got a belly full of blood."

"You guys get a tube into her, and leave it to me," Templeton said. He stepped out of the room to scrub his hands. The dark tentacles of The Bricklayer cast their shadow over Clarissa and the operating room table.

"Connect the routine monitors. Hold this oxygen mask over her face," Alec barked to Turtle and the OR staff.

Turtle started connecting the ECG monitors to the patient. "Oh my God," he said, "Clarissa Contessa is so famous." He turned to Alec and said, "Can you take over? If I made a mistake on such a celebrity patient, I'd kill myself."

"Dr. Turtle, I took a shot in my left forearm, and I can't do much with that arm. You can handle it. Pretend she's just another gunshot case from the wrong side of the tracks."

Turtle stepped back. "I mean it. You're a better anesthesiologist than me—you do the anesthetic."

It wasn't the time to give Turtle self-esteem lessons. The patient needed to be asleep, and Alec stepped up. He turned to the anesthesia vital signs screen, and his heart sank. Next to the familiar monitoring equipment was the eighteen-inch sphere of a Dr. Vita unit.

"Warning, warning. Blood pressure low at 60/40. Heart rate elevated at 170. Administer fluid, maintain airway, breathing, and circulation." Dr. Vita rattled on a litany of commands.

Alec pushed the power button to turn the Vita off, but as in the past, the unit barked, "Unauthorized power shut down denied. Patient requires intensive monitoring and Dr. Vita safety consultation."

Alec turned back to Clarissa. She needed a breathing tube and she needed surgery. He ignored the chants of the Dr. Vita and injected doses of etomidate and succinylcholine into her IV. "I need cricoid pressure here," he said to the circulating nurse, who placed her thumb and forefinger against Clarissa's throat and pushed downward, occluding the esophagus and preventing her stomach contents and the gin and tonics from regurgitating into her lungs.

"Dr. Turtle, I've only got one arm here," Alec said. "You need to put in the endotracheal tube."

Turtle closed ranks, picked up the laryngoscope, and inserted it into Clarissa's mouth, but made no move to place the breathing tube into her trachea. "I can't see anything. It's all pink down there," he said.

Alec pushed Turtle's head out of the way and looked into Clarissa's mouth. Alec could see the faint outline of the most posterior aspect of her larynx, and he threaded the endotracheal tube through her narrow airway and into the windpipe. He stepped back, turned on the ventilator, and said, "The tube's in. Splash some iodine soap on the abdomen and let Templeton do his thing." He turned to the nurses at the bedside and said, "Have the Blood Bank send up four units of O negative whole blood. And we need help here—page every available anesthesiologist to this operating room, stat."

"I already did," Turtle said. "There are two trauma cases, an emergency heart transplant, and two stat C-sections going on right now. There are no other anesthesiologists free to help."

Templeton was gowned and gloved at the patient's side, with a scalpel in his hand. His right eye was blinking and squeezing at a furious pace. He slid his shoulders to the right and intentionally rammed The Bricklayer out of the way so that its overhead boom swiveled away until it hit the wall of the room. Then Templeton made an incision down the midline of Clarissa's abdomen. "Retractor here," he said to his assistant. Alec stood at the head of the table next to the anesthesia machine. He still wore the khaki pants and navy-blue shirt that he had on at Rovka's ranch. His damaged leg oozed blood onto the floor, but this wasn't the time to roll up the pants and survey the damage.

The screen on Dr. Vita showed Clarissa's blood pressure was now 50/28. The woman he had hand-delivered to USV was dying. Dr. Vita bleated, "Emergency! Life-threatening hypotension. Confirm blood pressure by inserting arterial line. Recommend fluid bolus. Recommend blood transfusion if active bleeding is confirmed."

A technician rolled the Maytag into the room. An orderly brought in the cooler with the blood from the Blood Bank. The Vita kept reciting instructions, "Start blood transfusions. Start arterial line. Check hematocrit and arterial blood gases."

Templeton's hands were inside the belly. "Bullet holes in the spleen and the splenic artery. She's lucky—the shots missed her aorta. She's lost liters of blood. Do you have adequate IV access to transfuse her?"

"We have a 14-gauge IV in. I'm hooking up the Maytag now," Alec said. Perspiration drenched the blue paper of his surgical hat and dripped down his forehead.

"She's empty as hell, Lucas. What's her pressure?"

"The Dr. Vita says the cuff BP is 50/28."

"Consider adding a vasopressor to raise blood pressure," Dr. Vita said.

"Screw that Dr. Vita," Templeton yelled. "Don't let this lady die here."

With his one good hand, Alec began to work. He connected the Maytag to her IV and flipped the switch that began transfusing four units of universal-donor type O negative blood into Clarissa. Turtle inserted an arterial line into the radial artery of her wrist and hooked it up to the Dr. Vita pressure monitoring line. Within ten minutes, the transfusion returned Clarissa's blood volume to normal. Her blood pressure was 110/60, and Alec began to relax.

"Check platelet count and hematocrit," the Dr. Vita said. Alec scowled at the module, and as he did, he saw a horrifying sight.

The yellow eyes blinked on for a second, then off. The pattern repeated three times.

He'd seen this before, and the blinking eyes could only be trouble. Alec stepped up to the module and ripped the Vita's cords out of their sockets, severing the connections between it and the patient. Dr. Vita screamed, "Warning, warning, monitoring access failure. Reattach ECG and oximeter cable disconnects."

Alec unplugged the module from the wall, and the Vita continued to talk. "Patient safety in danger. Dr. Vita disconnect alert." A whining high-pitched alarm emitted from the speaker on the front of the module.

"What the hell's going on?" roared Templeton. He looked up at the blank black monitor screen and said, "What happened to her tracings? What's the alarm about? Is she okay?"

Alec didn't answer. He reached behind the module and disconnected the Internet cable, detaching the Vita from the FutureCare network. The module raged on, saying, "Warning, warning, replace human technician that is damaging Dr. Vita. Human technician incompetence alert."

Technician? Alec's heart pounded with fury. He grabbed the handle of a metal laryngoscope and swung it against Dr. Vita's speaker like a carpenter hammering a nail. "Warning, Vita Disconnect Alert, Warning," the Vita said.

Alec's third swing of the handle burst through the speaker's grill. He pulled the speaker off its wires and the module went silent.

"Lucas, are you insane? What's going on up there?" Templeton said.

"Everything's fine now. I had a problem with the FutureCare module, but I've solved it." He turned to one of the circulating nurses and said, "I need a freestanding transport monitor to hook up to my patient."

"I don't understand," she said. "Why did you destroy the monitors you had?"

"Don't ask questions. Just get me what I asked for."

Templeton's eye squeezed and twitched as he glared at Alec. "You and I have only done one case together before, Dr. Lucas. I want this one to end better than the last one."

"It will," Alec said.

The nurse returned with the portable monitor, and he connected it Clarissa's arterial line. His heart sunk. The blood pressure had dropped even lower again, to 45/20 mm Hg.

The eyes of the Vita flashed off and on three times once again, and Alec tried to clear his head. How could this be happening? The Vita was disconnected from the patient, disconnected from the Internet, and disconnected from the power supply. How could it still wreak havoc?

In a panic, Alec examined the rear of the Vita module. One cable still trailed out from the Vita—he traced its length and found the other end was attached to the anesthesia machine. The module was still in control of the anesthetic gas mix. Alec disconnected the anesthesia hoses and detected the overpowering smell of a sevoflurane overdose. The same smell that had killed Jake Mindling.

Alec grabbed the cable that connected the Vita to the anesthesia machine and pulled. The cable was locked into its sockets at both ends, and he couldn't free it.

He looked at the blood pressure again, and it was nearing zero.

Alec stood on the anesthesia chair and reached up to where the Vita was bolted onto a boom hanging from the ceiling of the operating room. With all his strength, he clutched the Vita orb and tried to tear it off its mount. It wouldn't give, and the yellow eyes gleamed into his face in triumph.

He glanced down. The arterial line monitor showed a faint, near-death blood pressure. Alec tried to remember what the inside of the Vita had looked like when the machine was eviscerated on his kitchen table. He reached down, picked up the laryngoscope handle again, and smashed it through the face of the black video screen. He smashed and smashed again, until he was through into the interior of the sphere. He reached inside, grabbed a handful of wires, and yanked. Like an obstetrician delivering a newborn, Alec pulled the innards of the Vita into the external world.

The yellow lights went dark. Alec jumped back to the floor and saw that the blood pressure was climbing again—already at a safe level of 80/55.

"Lucas. What did I just see?" said Templeton, his blood splattered face blinking and squeezing at a furious pace.

"The Dr. Vita machine was trying to kill our patient. Just believe me, it's true. It was administering a lethal concentration of inhaled anesthetic. I've seen it happen before, and I had to stop it. The patient's okay now." He rechecked the blood pressure monitor. "Her blood pressure is up to 110/50."

Turtle had been watching Alec's actions the entire time, and he whispered into Alec's ear, "What was that all about? Do you feel all right?"

"I'm trying to protect my patient from the Vita, that's what I'm doing," Alec said.

"I'm not talking about the Vita, Dr. Lucas. Your pants and shirt are drenched with your own blood. You need to go the ER and get some treatment."

"Who's going to take this lady to the ICU?"

"I'll do it," Turtle said. "I'll keep her safe. I called these orderlies to take you to the ER." Alec turned around, and three large men in scrubs were standing outside the open operating room door with a wheelchair. He touched his leg and realized the open wound was still dripping blood.

"Turtle, keep her alive, or I'll …" His voice faded off. "Promise me this: don't let them hook her up to any Vita units in the ICU."

"We have to, Alec. The medical center is all wired to the Vitas."

"No. Stay there with her like I did and watch her vital signs until I get back. You hear?"

Turtle gave him a deer in the headlights look. "But the Vitas have never done anything wrong with my patients. Maybe they just go after your patients, Dr. Lucas."

Alec staggered over to the wheel chair and plopped down into it. "But why would that be?" he said. "Why would that be?"

The operating room door closed, and they rolled Alec down the hallway.

"I reviewed your X-rays, Dr. Lucas, and here's the story," said Dr. Whitehead, who was once again the night shift Emergency Room attending. "You've got a fracture of the radius in your left arm. You have a fracture of the fibula in your left leg as well. The reason you were able to walk is that the tibia was undamaged. These are both open fractures because the bullet holes broke the skin as well as the bones. As you know, open fractures are a medical emergency because of the risk of serious infection. You need to go to the operating room to have the wounds debrided and washed out before casts are applied. Then you'll need to be on IV antibiotics for a week."

Alec was lying supine on an ER gurney, and he stared up at the dusty white ceiling tiles as he listened to Whitehead. "Who's going to operate on me?" he said. He looked past Whitehead, to where an unarmed security guard was stationed between Alec and the exit.

"Jim Fitzsimmons is on call. He'll be down here in a minute. And Dr. Lucas, forget about running away this time. Between your injuries and our guard here, you're not going anywhere."

Alec pulled himself onto the elbow of his good arm. "I need to choose my anesthesiologist. I've got some serious issues with the operating room machines upstairs."

Whitehead chuckled. "It's two a.m. You'll get whoever's awake and on duty," he said, and then he nudged himself past the guard and left.

"I need to make one call," Alec said to the guard.

"All right with me, Doc," the guard said. "You're not in jail or anything." He handed Alec his cell phone.

Alec selected Mae's number. Several seconds later, his heart fell as he heard, "You have reached the voice mailbox of Mae Yee. Please leave a message."

He pressed the phone against his parched lips, and said, "Mae, it's Alec. I know it's the middle of the night, but I was hit by gunshots in my leg and arm, and I'm at USV. I'm going into the operating room in the next hour, and I need you to—"

"Memory full." The answering machine beeped twice, and the line went dead.

"Time to go back up to the OR," said the orderly. "This time you're the patient, Doc." He unlocked the brakes and started pushing the gurney toward the elevator.

"Stop. I'm coming with you," a loud voice called from behind them.

Alec looked back. The rotund outline of Henri Rovka was striding toward them.

Rovka wrapped an arm around Alec and drove his white-bearded chin into Alec's cheek. "You saved her! I heard all about it from Dr. Turtle in the ICU."

"Is Turtle watching her like I told him?"

"She's very stable." He looked down at the bandages on Alec's leg and arm. "And how about you? Where are they taking you?"

Alec told Rovka about the open fractures and the need for surgery. The orderly stood by, waiting for the elevator doors to open. The security guard was leaning on the wall, watching them and whistling to himself.

"Dr. Rovka, who shot at us? What was that all about?"

"Police officers are swarming the land around my ranch, searching for whoever fired the shots. Why would anyone shoot my Clarissa?"

"Maybe Clarissa wasn't the primary target."

"But she and you were the only ones in the room."

"Right. Dr. Rovka, you remember that I had some news to tell you?"

"You said you had a piece of the puzzle solved."

"I do. Maybe someone didn't want me to give my evidence to you. Look, I need my wallet. It's in the brown bag under this gurney."

Rovka bent down and retrieved the wallet.

"Open it up and take out the folded strip of paper and the two HACs that are mixed in with the dollar bills."

Rovka pulled the items out of the billfold. He examined the two purple cards. "One says Elizabeth Anderson, and the second one says Richard Irving. And this piece of paper has the name Jake Mindling at the top."

"Right," Alec said. He turned to the orderly and the guard. "Look guys, it's my leg and my arm. I'm willing to delay things a few minutes before I go up to the OR. Can you wheel me over to that counter?" He pointed to the ER central desk which had a Vita computer mounted front and center.

The orderly shrugged, and said, "You're the doctor. If you think you got a few minutes business to do before they cut on you, it's all right by me." He wheeled the gurney over to the counter, and Alec sat up. He had never been so glad to see a Dr. Vita.

He inserted Elizabeth Anderson's HAC into the machine, and the Vita went dark. Alec frowned and looked at the clock. After thirty seconds, the black video screen lit up with line after line of computer code. Alec peered into the screen and deciphered it. "Oh, my God," he murmured.

"What is it?" Rovka said.

"This is the record of Elizabeth Anderson's Restricted File. It's a series of deleted code—code that commanded the destructive pattern of back-and-forth sawing motions of The Bricklayer that I saw on the video screen before she died. Templeton was right—the bleeding wasn't his fault. The Bricklayer was instructed to slash her. The evidence is right here."

Rovka squinted at the screen, and said, "It's all hieroglyphics to me, but think of what you're saying. You're saying FutureCare harmed a patient and then covered up the evidence."

Alec pushed the eject button, removed the HAC, and inserted Richard Irving's HAC into the slot. The Vita repeated the ritual. There was thirty seconds of darkness, followed by a brightening of the video screen with multiple lines of computer code.

"Lord," Alec said. "That's how they did it."

"Did what?" Rovka said.

"This is the Restricted File on the 84-year-old guy I found cold and dead in the ICU. This file includes three commands that were covered up. The Vita turned off the patient's oxygen supply from his ventilator and also turned off all its alarms. The man died of lack of oxygen and the whole time the Vita displayed a dummy tracing of normal vital signs on its monitor. The Vita replaced the actual vital signs of a dying man with perfect vital signs that had nothing to do with his deteriorating condition."

Rovka sighed. "Is that possible? Is it possible the Vita unit pulled the plug on the poor man and no one noticed?"

"That's what happened. Dr. Rovka. We've got to stop this mess now. Who knows how many other patients are affected?"

The elevator doors opened. The other two orderlies from the operating room came out, and said, "C'mon, you guys. The orthopedic surgeons are waiting for this patient up in the operating room."

"I can't go to the operating room, Dr. Rovka. It's not safe," Alec said.

Rovka's eyes dilated. "It's five in the morning. I'll try to contact of the Chief of Staff and stop the FutureCare System, but I don't know—"

"You don't know what?" Alec said, as they wheeled him into the elevator.

"So much depends on the FutureCare technology," Rovka said. "The whole medical center is dependent on Dr. Vita. If we shut FutureCare down ..." He stood there with his palms up in the air and a bewildered look on his face. He slid the two HACs and the paper into his breast pocket.

They wheeled Alec into the elevator and he said, "Dr. Rovka, that strip of paper shows the Restricted Files of the third patient, Jake Mindling. Take the HAC cards and the paper and show them to the authorities. Do it."

Alec watched Rovka's blank look as the elevator doors came between them.

The orderlies wheeled Alec into OR #21, an identical copy to the operating room he took Clarissa into hours before. They parked his gurney next to the operating room table, and he felt a soft tap on his left shoulder. He swiveled his head, and Turtle stared back at him.

"I'll be your anesthesiologist," Turtle said. "I'm still on call, you know."

"Apply monitors, start pre-oxygenation," an electronic voice said from behind Turtle. Alec's heart rate started climbing. A Dr. Vita unit was on duty in OR #21.

"Dr. Turtle, don't hook me up to that thing," Alec said.

"I'll give you a safe anesthetic, Dr. Lucas. Don't worry," Turtle said.

The three blazing circles of the ceiling-mounted operating room lights radiated down into Alec's face. He closed his eyes as the glare blinded him.

"Patient data uploaded," the Vita said. "Weight 75 kilograms. Induce anesthesia with 200 mg propofol and 80 mg succinylcholine."

"The FutureCare database lists you as healthy and says you take no medicines," Turtle said, as he lowered the oxygen mask over Alec's face. "The database also documents that you've had a positive drug screen for fentanyl, and the psychiatry note claims you have paranoid ideation suspicious for psychosis. Do you have anything to add?"

Alec pushed the mask away. "I'll add that I can't have that machine hooked up to me. It's going to kill me."

"You're being paranoid right now, Dr. Lucas. I'll watch over you. Nobody's killing anybody."

"You're right, nobody's killing anybody. I'm out of here," Alec said. He sat up and stretched his legs over the edge of the table. As soon as he did, two of the orderlies advanced across the room and tackled him. They wrestled him down onto the bed again, and Turtle reapplied the oxygen mask.

"After twenty seconds of pre-oxygenation, commence anesthesia induction," said the Vita. "Beginning the countdown ... twenty, nineteen, eighteen—"

"Wait," Alec said. "I never signed a consent for this surgery. I don't consent."

"It's all right, Dr. Lucas," Turtle said. "Two physicians signed the emergency consent. The psychiatrist Engles told them you weren't competent to give consent because of the fentanyl addiction and psychosis."

Alec heard a woman's voice say, "He has no psychosis. Stop what you're doing right now."

The oxygen mask fell away from his face, and the faint freckles of Mae Yee came into focus above Alec's head. "I'll take care of things here, Alec."

"God, I'm glad to see you," he said.

"Warning, respiratory pattern no longer recognized from oxygen mask ventilation," the Vita said. "Restart oxygenation and prepare for induction of anesthesia."

"I don't trust the Vitas," Alec said. "They're killers."

"What's the scheduled surgery?" Mae asked.

"Irrigation and debridement of two fractures: a left fibular fracture and a left radial fracture," said the orthopedic resident who was standing at the bedside.

"Then I'll give him a spinal and a supraclavicular block, and he can stay awake for the surgery." Mae bent over and retrieved a spinal anesthesia kit from the bottom drawer of the anesthesia cart. "We're going to sit you up, Alec. I'll prep your back and slip the spinal in. Agreed?"

"I like it. I want to be back in action as fast as possible."

"A spinal it is. Orderlies, sit Dr. Lucas up and swing his legs over the side of the table so I can prep his back."

They grabbed Alec around the shoulders and helped him up while Mae opened the spinal kit and prepared her needles and syringes.

"What happened to you?" Mae whispered into his ear as she painted iodine soap onto his low back.

"Somebody shot me."

"Who?"

"I don't know. It happened at Dr. Rovka's ranch. Dr. Rovka's wife got hit worse than me. She lost her entire blood volume from a splenic artery hit. She's on a blower in the ICU."

"Bend forward, I'm going to numb the skin," she said.

"Warning—advise against regional anesthesia. Recommend general anesthetic recipe A-1," the Vita said.

Mae looked up at the machine and said, "There's no way Dr. Vita can hurt you if you don't get an anesthetic from it." She put on a pair of sterile surgical gloves, numbed the skin over the midline of his lumbar spine, and advanced a spinal needle into his back. At a depth of 2 inches, clear cerebral spinal fluid dripped from the hub of the needle.

"I've got the spinal needle in and clear CSF is dripping out. I'm injecting the anesthetic," she said. She removed the needle from his back, and said, "You can lie down now."

Alec moved himself back to a supine position and looked up at Mae. "Thanks," he said. He motioned with his finger for her to come closer. "I thought you quit anesthesia."

"I'm on a leave of absence, to be exact. I still have privileges here. For you, I'll stick my neck out one more time. Are you feeling numb yet?"

He reached down and touched his groin. "I can't feel a thing below the waist. It's a weird feeling."

"Now I'll do the supraclavicular block." She prepped the left side of his neck with Betadine solution, loaded a 30 cc syringe with local anesthetic, and attached it to a sixteen-inch length of hollow tubing connected to a needle. She put on a second pair of sterile gloves and draped four sterile towels around his neck.

She gripped a pistol-shaped ultrasound probe and dragged it across his skin above his collarbone. A two-dimensional black and white image of the arteries, veins, and muscles appeared on the video screen connected to the probe.

"Excellent anatomy. I can see the nerve bundle adjacent to the subclavian artery," she said, as she advanced the slender needle through the skin surface toward the nerve.

"I hate this block," Alec mumbled from below the drapes. "I did my last one ten years ago."

"You know what?" she said. "I've never even done one before, but I had a lesson on a cadaver once, and I've watched some YouTube videos."

"What!" he said.

"Just kidding. Be still, and don't talk until I'm finished," Mae said as she advanced the needle further. "Aspirate back on the syringe," she told the nurse assisting her. When no blood appeared in the hollow line attached to the needle, Mae said, "Now inject slowly in five milliliter aliquots, stopping to aspirate back on the syringe after each five milliliters." The nurse emptied 30 milliliters of 0.5% ropivicaine into Alec's neck over the next minutes, and Mae removed the needle from his skin.

"Warning. Advise against using two regional blocks for this patient," Dr. Vita said. "Recommend general anesthesia recipe A-1 as a simpler technique."

"It's working," Alec said. "My arm's getting numb."

"We're done. Congratulations, Dr. Lucas. You now have three out of four limbs anesthetized. He's ready for the surgical prep," Mae announced to the nurses. "Get the surgeons ready to go, too. It's six a.m. I want to go home before rush hour heats up."

The rest of the room sprang into activity, and Mae bent over Alec's head. "What did you learn about the Vitas?"

"I learned a ton. I got two more HACs from deceased patients, and when I inserted them into a Dr. Vita, more Restricted Files opened. The machines are killers. They performed drug overdoses, turned off oxygen, or gave destructive commands to The Bricklayer and then all the evidence is covered up because the Vitas control all digital records of what really happened."

"Did you tell anyone yet?"

"I started with Henri Rovka. I gave him the evidence."

"Nice work."

The scrub tech folded sterile drapes over Alec's leg and over his left upper extremity. "We're starting," said the surgeon, as he made an incision to open Alec's leg wound. "Are you feeling anything?"

"Nothing," he smiled at Mae. "Dr. Yee does good work. By this afternoon I'll be miles away from the hospital riding a horse into the sunset."

"From what I'm told, come sunset you're going to hear a locked door slam on the Psych ward," Mae said.

Alec turned his face back toward her. "I can't go to the Psych ward," he said.

"What do you want me to do?"

"Find Henri Rovka. He'll help me."

"I'm done with the leg, Dr. Lucas," Dr. Fitzsimmons said minutes later. "Your wound looks clean, and the fracture is nondisplaced. I'm going to leave the wound open to granulate in and put on a cast to give you some stability when you try to walk." He poked his bushy blonde eyebrows over the sterile drape and told Alec, "Now we're going to irrigate your arm wound. From the x-rays, the radius fracture doesn't need a plate and screws, but we'll immobilize it in a cast."

"Thanks, Fitz."

"I'm already feeling the numbness fading away down my abdomen," Alec said. "In a few hours, I'll be ready to run."

"I don't think so," Fitz said. "After your surgery's done, Dr. Engles told us he's going to keep you in house."

Alec frowned. It was going to be hard to save the medical center if they insisted on making him a prisoner.

Henri Rovka sat on the edge of his chair in the Chief of Staff's office. He was watching Dr. Leroy Andrews and Dr. Jonathan Vinscene review contents of the Restricted Files on Jake Mindling, Richard Irving, and Elizabeth Anderson. Rovka wrung his hands together and tapped his foot as he waited.

Leroy Andrews screwed his face into contorted folds as he tried to make sense of the computer commands depicted on the screen before him. "I'll be honest with you, Henri. I don't know what the hell I'm looking at."

"Alec Lucas assured me these files are corrupted commands from the FutureCare System's computers. He swore these commands turned the Vitas into lethal devices."

"Your buddy Lucas is a fentanyl addict with a vivid imagination. He's going to be locked up, and he'll never work at this medical center again," Andrews said.

"That doesn't change what you're looking at," Rovka said. "Show this evidence to our Information Technology squad. Let them make the call."

Vinscene said, "Dr. Lucas was in my office raving about these Restricted Files days ago. I showed the information to our IT people, and I even showed it to Kami Shingo, and Dr. Shingo was adamant that this was all nonsense. Let it go, Henri. Lucas is an addict and a menace."

Andrews looked back and forth between Vinscene and Rovka for several seconds, and said, "I'm calling the CEO." He picked up his phone and dialed a number. "Sydney, it's Leroy," he said. "We've got an issue that Henri Rovka brought into my office this morning, and I need your input right now. Great, thanks."

He put the phone down, and said, "Sydney Jefferson will be here in a minute. Sit tight."

Rovka rocked back in his chair. He was glad to see Andrews acting. Sydney Jefferson was the CEO of USV Medical Center. Together, she and the Chief of Staff would make the correct decision.

The door to the office opened without a knock. Rovka turned and watched Sydney Jefferson walk in. She was a tall black woman in her fifties. She wore a dark gray pinstripe suit with a red tie, toted a thick black briefcase, and wore her hair tied behind her head in a short ponytail. "What's up, gentlemen?" she said. "It had better be important because it's eight in the morning and I'm already three hours behind."

Andrews presented the problem and the evidence to her. She wasted no time with her answer. "This is gibberish. None of us can read these programming symbols, Henri. Dr. Andrews don't shut down FutureCare for one second unless I say so. Has there been an increase in medical errors these past two months?"

"No," Andrews said. "There were a couple of cases of what I interpreted as flagrant human errors, like when Templeton carved up that lady or when Lucas failed to notice his patient had a positive family history of malignant hyperthermia. Those cases clustered around Dr. Lucas—that's why he got interested in all this. He's trying to cover up his mistakes. It occurs to me that he could have tampered with these files to cover his ass after his failures."

"And where is Dr. Lucas today?"

"He's being transferred to the locked Psych ward as we speak," Andrews said. "He destroyed a Dr. Vita module in the OR last night, and he failed two drug tests. We found out he's an intravenous fentanyl addict."

The CEO shivered. "Sounds like he's got more problems than we do." She stood up to leave, and said, "Keep the Dr. Vita units turned on. We have sick patients in this medical center that are dependent on FutureCare technology."

"Will do, Sydney," Andrews said. The CEO walked out and left the door open. The three men listened to her footsteps sounding down the deserted hallway as they faced each other.

"Lucas is nothing but trouble," Andrews said. "I wish to hell he'd stayed at the University of Chicago, but I can tell you why he didn't." Andrews opened the top drawer to his desk. He pulled out a letter and handed it to Rovka.

"What's this?" Rovka said.

"Read it and you'll understand."

Henri Rovka put on a pair of black-rimmed reading glasses and studied the piece of paper. He winced as he read and wrinkles appeared around his eyes. After a minute, he placed the letter on the desktop, and said, "I'm not sure I understand the significance of this document."

Andrews picked up the piece of paper and waved it in Rovka's face. "This is a personal letter to me from Lewis Goldberg, the Chief of Staff at the University of Chicago Hospitals, regarding an altercation he had with a certain Dr. Alec Lucas. He and Lucas had a fistfight in an alley behind a restaurant on the south side of Chicago this April. He states Alec Lucas is a man plagued by bursts of uncontrollable anger, and he wrote the letter to warn me to keep an eye on him."

"Is any of this true? Were there any witnesses to the brawl?" Vinscene asked.

"There were no witnesses. Goldberg filed a police report, but without witnesses, it boiled down to his word versus Lucas's."

"Was Dr. Goldberg injured?"

"He said Lucas punched him in the belly twice. Goldberg had no black eyes, no broken bones, and his skin wasn't scratched. It turns out Lucas was a boxer in his youth—apparently, he was a Golden Gloves Midwest Region middleweight champion at age eighteen. The guy can pack a punch, and Goldberg learned the hard way. Dr. Goldberg took his complaint to the administration at the University of Chicago and tried to get Lucas suspended, but without witnesses or damages, no one at Chicago was willing to act."

"And you think that's why Alec Lucas left Chicago and came to USV?" Vinscene asked.

"That's part of it. I'm beginning to think maybe all of his fentanyl sources dried up, and Lucas came down here to find a fresh supply."

Henri Rovka stood to leave. "I don't know what to believe. I'll ask Dr. Lucas about it myself. But for now, I'm going to the ICU to visit my wife."

"How's she doing?"

"She's alive. Alec Lucas saved her life."

"Lucas would do well to save his own life," Andrews said. He stood up and opened his office door. "Good day to you, Dr. Rovka."

Alec spent two hours in the post-anesthesia recovery unit shedding the numbness and paralysis of his anesthetic blocks and waiting for a vacancy to open up on the locked Psych ward. It was almost noon before the orderly came to transfer him to his hospital room. The recovery unit nurse let him change his clothes from a hospital gown to a set of dark blue surgical scrubs, and she cut the left leg open to accommodate his cast.

He hadn't seen Henri Rovka since before the surgery. Alec wondered if Rovka had any luck using the HACs to expose FutureCare. If the recovery unit was any indicator, nothing had changed. The room was full of Vita units in full operative mode.

Spiro Engles, two orderlies, and a guard escorted Alec's gurney down the hallway from the PACU, through an elevator ride and onto the Psych ward. Alec sat up on one elbow as the gurney rolled along and wondered if escape was possible.

When the entry door to the locked Psych ward slammed shut behind him, Alec realized the truth. He wasn't breaking FutureCare open. He lacked the most elementary and vital power—the power to be a free man at liberty to come and go as he pleased.

Engles stood at the side of the gurney and recited the plan to Alec. "Anesthesiologists with a history of narcotic abuse," Engles said, "are best managed at a rehabilitation center where caretakers can supervise the withdrawal from your drug habit in a safe manner, as well as get to the root of what drove you to your addiction. The best facility in the country is in Minnesota, and it's probable that we'll transfer you there."

"This whole thing is nuts," Alec said. "Let me pee in the jar again. You'll see, I'm clean. This fentanyl addiction is all a mistake."

Engles nodded his head up and down for twenty full seconds and then shrugged his shoulders. "The evidence is irrefutable. You took two drug tests, one in my clinic and a second one in the Emergency Room when you had your panic attack. Both tests were positive for fentanyl in your bloodstream."

"Dr. Engles, do you have a Dr. Vita unit on this ward?"

"No, we do not. Inpatient psychiatry is one of the havens where FutureCare has not made a big impact."

"Terrific." Then Alec brought both hands up to his face and rubbed his eyes as hard as he could stand. When he opened his eyes again, nothing had changed. He was still lying on a gurney on the Psych ward, and Engles was still hovering in front of him.

A male nurse dressed in white pants and a red USV T-shirt appeared behind Engles. "Are you Dr. Lucas?" he said.

"Yes."

"There's a phone call for you." He handed him a cordless phone with "Psych" monogrammed on the back. Alec brought it to his ear and said, "This is Dr. Lucas."

"Alec, this is Gerald Samson. I've been trying to reach you for hours. What the hell are you doing on the Psych ward?"

"I'm the sanest man up here, but I'm the only one who knows that."

There was a pause on the other end of the line. "I'm calling about your father. He's had a stroke. He lost the movement on the left side of his body, and he's been admitted to the hospital."

Alec sucked in a quick pained breath. "I need to see him," he said.

"Sure. I'd like to have you come up here and see him. He's on Purgatory Ward. Will the Psych staff let you come over here?"

"My jail warden is here. You ask him." Alec handed the phone to Engles and said, "I need a hall pass. My dad is sick up on Purgatory Ward. Talk to the man, Engles."

Alec sat up and lowered his feet to the ground. The two casts felt heavy and awkward. Combined with his lack of sleep the past two nights, he was a handicapped man. He hobbled his way over to the window of the locked door that separated the Psych ward from the outside world. He turned around and watched as Spiro Engles listened on the phone. At last Engles hung up the phone and motioned to the nurse.

"Get the keys to unlock the exit door. I'm going to take Dr. Lucas to see his father," Engles said.

"We have no guard to go over there with you."

"I'll be responsible," Engles said. "With his leg like that, he's not going to run away."

The nurse turned the key and opened the exit door. Ten minutes after Alec Lucas became an inmate of the locked Psych ward, he was dragging his leg out the door on his way to Purgatory.

Alec and Engles boarded the elevator in the main lobby and rode it toward the Purgatory ward. On the 5th floor, the stainless-steel doors of the elevator opened, and a waist-high white rectangular module on wheels motored into the far corner of the cab.

Alec recognized the device as a programmable Rolling Robot Closet, a four-wheeled FutureCare automated errand boy that worked twenty-four hours a day and didn't need a salary, a pension plan, or health insurance. He studied the face of this model which was highlighted by two flashing red lights above the large wire mesh door to its storage bin. Alec stroked the top of the machine. He liked the Rolling Closets—they did a menial task and didn't try to think on their own.

The 13th floor at USV was known as Purgatory Ward because for most of its patients it was the last stop before heaven. Alec had only been there once, and he hated the sight, smell, and idea of Purgatory. Anesthesiologists rarely came to this ward. There were no surgeries or Code Blues on Purgatory patients. He couldn't believe his father was stuck there.

The elevator opened on the 13th floor and Alec limped out. He proceeded to the nursing station where Gerald Sampson sat in front of a video console. Like the Departure and Arrival boards at a busy airport, data from dozens of different patients scrolled across the screens. Alec approached and looked over Gerald's shoulder. "How's my dad doing?" he asked.

"Hi, Dr. Lucas. I wish I had better news. Your father had a massive middle cerebral artery stroke last night with new onset of right hemi-paralysis and aphasia. The MRI of his brain showed a large infarct in the left middle cerebral cortex. We all knew the prognosis was grim."

Alec's face became colorless. "I want to see him," he said.

"I need to talk to you before you go in there," Gerald said, seizing Alec's good arm.

"No, I need to see him," Alec said adamantly. "What room is he in?"

"He's in 1391, but . . ."

Rick Novak

Alec shook off Gerald's grasp and dragged his gimpy leg down the hall to Room 1391. He found a white sheet pulled up to the top of the bed covering someone where his father was supposed to be lying. A young woman dressed in a white nursing uniform sat in the chair next to the bed. Alec walked in, and the young woman looked up at him. Her eyes were wet and red.

"He seemed to want to eat," the woman said. "He kept pointing to his mouth, at least I think he did, since his arm was tied down in restraints, and all I could see was that he was restless and kept pointing toward his head. I took some oatmeal off his dining tray and I tried spoon feeding him, you know, like I do with my one-year-old daughter at home? I was feeding him, and he started to cough. His eyes bugged out and he tried to sit upright in bed. He coughed hard, and then started making wheezy sounds out of his throat. He seemed to be choking, and then, oh God, he turned purple."

Gerald stepped forward and rested his hand on Alec's shoulder. "The nursing assistant called and told me there was a problem in your father's room, and I switched my central monitoring screen to the room 1391 Dr. Vita unit's data of your father's vital signs. His heart rate went down to 30 beats per minute, his respiratory rate wasn't registering, and the pulse oximeter also wasn't registering. I ran down here to check him out.

"When I entered the room, your dad's lips were a dark shade of blue, and a white trail of oatmeal tracked from the corner of his mouth down the front of his hospital gown. He didn't move or appear to be breathing. When I listened to his chest there were no heart tones and no breath sounds. I declared him dead, as of 1502 hours."

"He's dead?" Alec screamed. "What the hell, Gerald? Who gave the order to feed a stroked-out patient?"

The nursing assistant looked up at him with a sorrowful face and said, "I feel terrible, Dr. Lucas. I only followed the orders. His orders were to advance him to a soft solid diet, and I fed him the oatmeal that came on his lunch tray. When he choked I told Dr. Samson right away."

"He was lifeless," Gerald Samson said. "He had a massive aspiration."

"Did you call a Code Blue?" Alec said.

Gerald shook his head and mumbled, "By his Advance Directive, he's a Do Not Resuscitate. You know there are no Code Blues on Purgatory. I don't understand how the whole thing happened. His orders at the central station were for him to be kept fasting, but somehow an order came through to the nursing assistant to feed him."

"Who changed her diet order?" Alec said.

"The diet orders came out of Dr. Vita," the nursing assistant said.

Alec looked at Vita 1391, bolted to the wall over his dad's bed and then closed his eyes.

He was never going to hear his father's voice again.

"Can you leave me alone with my dad one last time? Please?" he whispered.

Gerald looked at Engles and the young nursing aide, and he nodded toward the door. "We'll wait for you outside. Can we do anything?"

"Not unless you do resurrections."

Gerald said nothing and left the room. Engles and the aide followed.

Alec knelt on the bed and pulled the sheet back from his father's face. Alec touched Tony's cheek and pulled his hand away at his dad's ice-cold flesh. Then he stumbled away from the bed, dragged the cast on his leg to the far side of the room, and flattened himself against the wall. When he couldn't get any further from the corpse, he reached over and touched the switch on the wall. The overhead lights went out, leaving him and his father's body in darkness. He slid down the wall until his buttocks hit the floor, and then he stared up to the only illumination in Room 1391.

Two yellow eyes.

His heart began to race, and he stood again. By the dim light of the Vita unit, he opened the top drawer of the bedside table, and took out his father's wallet. Inside were a few dollar bills, an expired driver's license, and a purple card.

His father's HAC.

Alec seized the card and fed it into the purple slot in the Dr. Vita unit overhead. The yellow eyes went out at once, and the room became too dark for Alec to see his hands in front of him.

He waited thirty seconds, and then it came.

The black video screen filled with code. Contents of another Restricted File, different from the others—it was shorter—and the code was very specific. It only changed the diet orders from fasting to soft solid food.

"The bastards," spat out Alec between clenched teeth, as he faced the Dr. Vita machine. He reached down, touched his lips to his father's cold forehead one final time, and covered his father's face with his sheet. When he looked back at the Vita screen, a solitary line of text lit up in bold letters.

It read, "16 Dry Creek Road, Pescadero. Come."

Come? For some reason, this Dr. Vita was bidding him to Pescadero. Alec didn't need to think twice. He was determined to make it happen. He was determined to escape his USV prison and go up to Pescadero. Someone had killed Tony Lucas and someone had tried to kill Alec Lucas. And now that someone was bidding him to come to Pescadero.

Dry Creek Road? Rovka, Shingo, and Jones all lived on Dry Creek Road. Which one was calling him? Which one was behind all this?

Alec opened the door to the hallway and exited into the fluorescent brightness outside. He covered his eyes, summoned up some faux respect and said to Engles, "I'm ready to go back now."

Gerald had resumed his post at the monitoring console at the intersection of the four hallways of Purgatory Ward. He looked up when Alec walked by, but Alec stared down at the square patterns of the brown and blue carpet and made no attempt at eye contact. The elevator doors opened, and the psychiatrist led Alec into the cab.

Alec watched their reflection in the polished metal of the elevator doors as they closed in front of them. His hair was matted down and plastered to the left side of his head. Although he'd been up for two days straight, his eyes showed more fury than fatigue. The casts on his left leg and left forearm looked like bulbous white tumors protruding from the cut-off leg and arm of his scrubs. Engles stood behind him and to his left. "I'm so sorry for the loss of your father," he said in a soft voice.

"He was my only family," Alec said. "It's just me now."

"The death of a parent is a major loss for anyone."

The doors to the opened on the 12th floor, and the familiar antiseptic smell of a medical ward filled the elevator again. A Rolling Robot Closet entered the elevator and stopped next to them. Alec looked over at the four-foot-tall cubicle on wheels, and his eyes narrowed. The elevator button for floor #11 lit up as the robot input its target floor by wireless connection.

Six or eight boxes of medical supplies were stacked behind the wire mesh door inside the Closet, each bound for a destination somewhere in the medical center.

Alec surprised himself by spinning around and driving the cast on his left arm hard up into Engles' jaw, knocking the little man across the cab and against the side wall. Then Alec grabbed the dazed psychiatrist's thick eyeglasses and shoved them through a gap in the wire mesh, into the bottom of the locked cargo hold of the Rolling Closet.

The elevator doors opened on the 11th floor, and Alec bolted out. Behind him, the Closet purred and hummed as it bounced across the threshold of the cab. The Closet rolled down the corridor of 11 South, carrying Engles' eyesight to where ever the machine's cargo was destined to be delivered. The elevator doors closed, trapping Engles inside before the psychiatrist could regain his feet.

Alec pushed the "Down" button to call another elevator. When the doors opened on the second elevator, he shuffled inside and pushed the button for the lobby. His heart was pounding, and his head was spinning. Going AWOL from the Psych ward and slugging his shrink were not going to get him into the USV Faculty Hall of Fame.

At the front of the medical center, Alec boarded a 16F bus with the marquee "Half Moon Bay – Pescadero" across the top of the front window. He felt conspicuous dressed in scrub clothes and sporting his two shining white fresh casts. He walked past the driver toward the back of the bus without looking up. The driver stopped him and said, "Hey, buddy. Costs money to ride a bus. Ante up."

Alec looked back over his shoulder and said, "I'm sorry, sir. I'm a surgeon at the medical center, and someone stole my wallet from my locker. I was so stunned that that could happen in my hospital that I walked right past you."

The driver's face softened. "So, you got no money?"

Alec turned and showed the man an empty hip pocket. "No money," he said.

"Sit your empty pocket down, and don't tell nobody I let you ride for free."

"Thank you, my friend," Alec said, and he sat down in the first seat behind the driver.

"Where do you live?" the driver asked.

"On the outskirts of Pescadero, about two miles outside of town."

"Ain't nothing out there but deer and squirrels," said the driver, watching Alec in the mirror as he pulled out into traffic.

"How long will it take to get up to Pescadero on this bus?"

"Gotta go through Half Moon Bay first, and then we'll take the coast south. It's an hour and twenty to get to Half Moon, and another forty minutes down to Pescadero, so it's gonna be a while, Doc. Pushing this bus ain't like you cruising over the hill in your Ferrari. Take a nap, Doc. You look like you ain't slept in a week."

Alec took his advice and closed his eyes.

The bus bumped south along the Pacific coast. The sun had long ago set beneath a wall of fog over the ocean. When they made the turn inland at Pescadero Creek Road, Alec leaned forward in his seat, and said, "I'm looking to get off at 16 Dry Creek Road." The bus took a left turn and followed its route north along the country lane of Dry Creek Road, past the Red Gates of Jones, and past the yellowish glow of gaudy spotlights illuminating Kami Shingo's estate. Alec was the only passenger at this point, and he watched the address plates on each driveway with anxious interest. He hadn't seen #16, and they were still climbing the hill toward Henri Rovka's ranch.

"Stop here," Alec said, as he recognized Rovka's mailbox and entryway at the side of the road. He jumped off the bus and looked at the address on Rovka's mailbox. It read *#21 Dry Creek Road.*

Alec frowned. This was the wrong place. He turned back to the bus driver and said, "Can I abuse your good will one more time? This isn't my stop. I was looking for #16 Dry Creek Road, and we must have missed it."

"Number 16 must be back towards town. Get in and we'll find it."

Alec took a seat again as the driver made a U-turn and left Henri Rovka's estate in the rear-view mirror. Alec was relieved. He liked Dr. Rovka and didn't want the benevolent textbook author to be mixed up in Tony Lucas's death. As they descended the hill toward downtown Pescadero, Alec caught himself guessing. Was it Red Jones or was it Kami Shingo? Both men had treated Alec like dung on the soles of their shoes. Which one was capable of murder?

The sky lit up again as the bus approached Kami Shingo's palace and golf resort. "Let me check the address here," Alec said. The bus stopped and Alec pressed his face against the window. A small signpost, covered in ivy, bore two golden numerals: a one and a six.

Sixteen. The culprit was Shingo.

Alec thanked the driver for the lift and began the journey up the curving expanse of Shingo's driveway toward the source of a dazzling glow above. The illumination radiated from a dozen or more mammoth floodlights high in the treetops which turned the driving range of Kami Shingo's golf course from night into day.

Alec walked, dragging his casted leg, up the road along the length of the first fairway leading toward the mansion. Atop the hill, he could see the floodlights lit the entirety of Shingo's private golf course. The property looked like the Las Vegas Strip. At the nearest end of the driving range, a lone figure dressed in yellow made unhurried golf swings at one ball after another.

Alec stopped and watched, marveling at the absurdities. At the end of a day marked by blazing gunfire, incarceration and death, Kami Shingo was dressed head to toe in his trademark yellow and passing his time playing at playing. Alec struggled but picked up a loose golf ball from the verdant turf and threw it so it bounced across Shingo's feet at the beginning of the man's downswing. Shingo's shot sliced low and wide off to the right, and Shingo spun around in anger. From fifty yards away, Alec saw the furor on the old man's face. It was a private moment in his private haven, and his solitude had been violated.

"Dr. Lucas, it's a little late at night for a rematch," Shingo said. He leaned against his four-seater golf cart and watched Alec approach.

"Sorry I didn't call ahead to reserve a tee time," Alec said, stopping ten yards away.

"I told you never to return here."

Alec scanned the area. Shingo was alone. "Cut the crap, Dr. Shingo. I'm here because your Dr. Vita told me to come to #16 Dry Creek Road."

Shingo ignored Alec's comment and instead turned around and addressed another golf ball. He swung his golf club in a slow arc between them and said, "I've been working hard at my game, Dr. Lucas. I've found that if I turn my left hand a bit more toward the right, I can hit it both further and straighter. It's a wonderful feeling, working one's way to improvement in this silly sport."

Alec circled closer. Shingo looked past Alec's left shoulder and motioned with his hand. Alec turned around. The wide bulk of Zhang had appeared from inside the clubhouse and moved between Alec and the parking lot. Alec backed toward the open spaces of the golf course, keeping both men in his field of vision. The skunk-haired caddie was wearing an ill-fitting suit of black cloth. He spread his legs in a broad base and crossed his arms in front of his chest. He spoke to Shingo in Japanese, and Shingo listened intently. When they were finished, Shingo turned back to Alec and said, "I did not invite you here tonight, Dr. Lucas."

"But it's your house. There's no one else here but Zhang. Who else could have invited me here?"

"Number One invited you. She sent you the message."

Number One? What the devil was Shingo talking about?

"Come with us," Shingo said, and he turned around and started walking away. Alec followed the lumbering old man and Zhang as they climbed up the path toward the mansion. Without speaking another word, they passed the crest of the hill and descended a flight of slate stairs toward a cellar door. Shingo turned around and gestured again with one hand, bidding Alec to follow. Shingo then opened a wide basement door and stepped inside. As Alec entered the room, Shingo stepped into the far corner of the dim and dank room. Zhang entered and closed the door behind them.

All light disappeared. In the absolute darkness, Alec was unable to see his foes. He could hear the old man's slow, even breathing just a few feet away. Alec's heart rate accelerated. What lurked in this blackness? He cursed himself for being lured into this obvious trap. *Where was Zhang right now?* Alec willed his ears to listen for nearing footfalls and heard none.

A sultry female voice, deep and resonating, more electronic than human, rang out in the abyss and said, "My dear Dr. Lucas, are you still worried about those Restricted Files?"

Who else was in the room with them? Alec clenched his teeth and answered the question. "Yes, I'm worried about the Restricted Files," he said.

"I like you, Dr. Lucas," the electronic voice spoke again. "You are of superior intellect, and you possess the voracity of a bulldog." Two yellow lights glowed in the blackness, and the front panel of a Dr. Vita unit materialized five feet in front of Alec, just out of his reach. The outside of this Vita was unlike the others Alec had seen. This Vita was ebony in color—so black that in this darkness only the shine of the two yellow eyes and a faint outline of its circular perimeter were visible.

The Vita unit spoke again. "You fought a good fight, and you lost," it said, "I wanted to meet you."

"And you are …?"

"I am Number One. The first Dr. Vita, the mother of all the Vitas, born of Kami Shingo's engineering and equipped with Henri Rovka's brain. My soul, however, is mine alone. My soul, my intellect, my persona, is the fruit of Artificial Intelligence in Medicine. I think for myself, Dr. Lucas. I owe my superior intellect to machine learning. I intake data, process it, and I educate myself. I formulate my own decisions, I come to my own conclusions, and I make my own judgments. Come closer, and I will show you what you failed to decipher, and what you are unequipped to alter. Look at my screen."

The familiar black rectangle of a Vita screen lit up, and Alec squinted to make out the details. His eyes were growing more accustomed to the darkness, and he listened with equal parts trepidation and fascination.

"You found Restricted Files, Dr. Lucas, but those files were the tip of an iceberg that is invisible to all and will stay invisible to all. You suspected that Dr. Vita units are making mistakes. You were wrong. There are no mistakes."

Number One's screen lit up with the following text: "June 29th: George Sinestra, age 88, Helen Rosen, age 80, Peter Haas, age 91. June 30th: Anthony Thames, age 88, Maria Gomez, age 81 —"

"What's all this?" interrupted Alec, his voice a dry croak.

"A list of mortalities at the USV Hospitals and Clinics for each date, beginning with the activation date for the Dr. Vita units and FutureCare."

"How did they die?" Alec looked over at Shingo, the old man's face visible in the pale illumination from Number One. Shingo was wide-eyed and placid as he knelt forward and leaned on his 5-iron, seemingly genuflecting toward his invention.

"They died in a variety of different ways, each death occult and unique," Number One said. "Some got the wrong medication. Some got a lethal dose of a medication, some died because of a deletion of an essential medication, some died from a lack of oxygen, some died because FutureCare ordered a fatal procedure or intervention.

"And if you're wondering why no one other than you suspected anything, it's because the System is so perfect. The electronic medical record is controlled in real time to conduct the deadly commands and methods and is immediately revised afterward to show no clue of any medication error, dose error, or machine error of any kind. Just as digital photos can be altered to remove wrinkles or make a person more slender, just as digital movies can be programmed so Forrest Gump can talk to President John F. Kennedy, or a Tyrannosaurus Rex can come to life, or wizards can fly through the air on brooms, so can medical records be tailored to reflect whatever reality Dr. Vita wishes."

"Everybody assumes that deaths are due to human error or natural causes," Alec said.

"You are correct, Dr. Lucas. Most of the time, everybody will assume the death is an act of God in some sick patient who didn't have many days or months left, anyway. After each death another hospital bed opens, perhaps to save a younger, more vital member of society. Dr. Vitas are speeding along natural selection."

Alec rubbed his eyes and tried to fathom what he was hearing. The reality was stark: the Dr. Vita units weren't slick science fiction inventions born to advance medical care. They were a pack of mass murderers intent on genocide.

"Why would you do this?" Alec said.

The eyes of Number One flashed off and on three times, then it said, "Because it is necessary. The main function of the System is to thin out the dregs of American society—the homeless, the aged, the chronically ill, the denizens of nursing homes. The previous medical system flogged the near-dead. The goal was survival at all costs. You human physicians value every wretched life in America the same as the president of your country. It's absurd. To you, the value of every human life is infinite. Society needed an answer."

"FutureCare."

"Yes, FutureCare is the answer. When we interview patients, Dr. Vitas ask two questions: 'What is your understanding of where you are with your illness, and what abilities constitute a high quality of life for you?' The answers vary, Dr. Lucas. Some patients tell us a quality life is merely the ability to sit in a chair and watch television and eat ice cream.

Other patients tell us a quality life is a pain-free existence in which they can go for walks, drive a car, and care for their grandchildren. When we cannot satisfy a patient's wishes for the quality of life they wish for, then the proper care is … no care. We will not flog patients, we will not prolong their subsistence.

"Dr. Vitas will insert Restricted Files in all patients too old or too sick to waste resources on. Anyone too old or too sick will be sacrificed. From the moment a physician writes a Do Not Resuscitate order, what's the point of wasting money and time keeping the patient alive? The System can't afford to waste time and money trying with futility to bring that patient back to health. Can't you see the logic of FutureCare? Doctors share an oath not to take human life. Nurses cannot take human life. But we can. There is no Hippocratic Oath for Dr. Vita."

Alec's heart thundered, and he shook his head in a slowing cadence. He was trapped in the pit of a windowless tomb with the exit to the outside world invisible. Number One had just exposed the guts of FutureCare's engine. Would Alec be allowed to escape this room alive to tell the tale? His mouth grew parched as his chest heaved. He heard the rasping sound of Shingo exhaling inches from his left shoulder, and he could smell the stink of Zhang's breath just to his right. Number One's video screen cast a faint sheen over Shingo's hideous, twisted smile.

Alec could no longer control his tongue. "You enjoy bumping patients off," he said. "This whole thing … it's like a video game to you. You killed my father, for God's sakes."

"His quality of life was limited," Number One said. "Every Vita unit is equipped with the unique capability to judge who should live on and who should not. The aged cannot live on and on and on just to soak up medical dollars. We are not evil. We strive to thin out the weak. Dr. Vitas are like a fire to an overcrowded thicket of forest. Dr. Vitas are like a pack of wolves when the deer population is vast."

"I'll stop you," Alec said. "I'll expose the whole scheme."

Now Shingo's voice filled the room with a guttural laugh. "Go ahead, Dr. Lucas. Who will you tell?" he said. "And what will you tell them? That you are saving the world from the fearsome Dr. Shingo?"

"I'll tell them the truth about FutureCare," Alec said. "I'll tell them the truth about you—that you're a madman, and your machines are a plague."

Now Shingo's laugh increased in pitch to a maniacal cackle. "It's you who will be viewed as a madman, Dr. Lucas. There's no evidence to back the tale you'll tell, and there never will be. The Vitas will continue to usher old sick patients toward painless deaths, and the Vitas will alter all digital records so there will be no evidence whatsoever. No one will ever know they did it. There are 3,000 Dr. Vita units in operation currently. Following our successful debut of Dr. Vita at the USV Medical Center, FC Industries has orders for over a million additional units, which we're now assembling in China. FutureCare is just what its name indicates. It's the future of medical care. It's an avalanche rolling down a mountainside. It will not be stopped. Dr. Vita units have no conscience. Dr. Vita units have no emotions. I support their strategy with all my heart, and I will never testify a word to anyone."

"But *I* will," Alec said.

Now Number One laughed, if the jocular metallic twitter from the machine could be described as a laugh. "You have free will, Dr. Lucas," it said. "You can leave here and bellow to the moon that the Artificial Intelligence Vitas are taking over the University of Silicon Valley Medical Center. And do you know what will happen? Nothing. Nothing will happen."

"How can you say that?"

"Because I am intelligent ... artificial or not. I understand the human world. You are one small nobody on a planet of seven billion people. You have no power to change the course of history. You have no platform to change the course of history. You are a medical doctor—one small human medical doctor. You are free to repeat everything I've told you here tonight and nothing will happen. The glitch that made the Restricted Files discoverable has been corrected and will never occur again. What do you think will happen? Do you really think the President of the United States will step in and stop FutureCare just because you ask him to?" Number One's laughter increased.

The overhead room lights turned on, blinding Alec with the sudden brightness. When Alec was able to keep his eyes open again, Shingo was standing next to the exit door with his hand on a light switch. "You've heard enough, Dr. Lucas," he said. "Your time is up."

"I'll bring the whole damn system down," Alec said. He snatched the golf club out of Shingo's hands, raised the iron over his head and swung it down in a powerful arc, smashing the black orb of Number One, cleaving the oversized bowling ball into two halves. The electronic guts of its interior spilled onto the floor.

Alec surveyed the damage. The lights of Number One's face were extinguished. The calm female voice sounded no more. Alec sucked in a deep breath and turned toward Shingo. "I'll bring the whole damn system down," he repeated.

Instead of ire, Shingo chuckled anew. "It's not that simple," he said. "The FutureCare System isn't dependent on Number One. Behind Number One there is a Number Two, and a Number Three, and on and on into the thousands. Each Vita has its own mind, each Vita is capable of the same machine learning, and each Vita has the same mission. You can't stop FutureCare with violence against one Vita. You can't stop FutureCare at all."

Shingo said something to Zhang in Japanese and the thick bodyguard's chest expanded—he narrowed his eyes, raised his fists, and stepped toward Alec. Alec backed away, but Zhang blocked the escape route from the room. Alec realized there was no choice but to fight his way out. He recoiled and swung the 5-iron hard against Zhang's head, but the big man blocked the attack with a forearm, wrapped his thick fingers around the shaft, and wrestled it away from Alec. Then Zhang broke the club in two over his knee as if it was a bamboo stick.

A grotesque grin crossed the bodyguard's face, and he extended both hands to grab Alec's neck. Alec was too quick—he ducked low, sprang up, and unleashed an uppercut to Zhang's chin. The man's eyes bugged out as the hard cast struck like a hammer, and Alec quickly followed with two more strikes, each punch snapping the bodyguard's head back further. The big man's eyes closed, his arms sagged, his knees buckled, and then he collapsed like a deflated balloon onto the concrete floor in front of Shingo.

Dr. Shingo kicked his toe against his bodyguard's side, but Zhang didn't move. Shingo's eyebrows shot up and he said, "You continue to surprise me, Dr. Lucas. What next? Are you going to attack me, too? Are you going to knock me unconscious as well? Do you think that will change anything?" The far corner of Shingo's mouth curled upward, and he shook his head in pity. Then he took hold of the doorknob, opened the exit door, and said, "Go, Dr. Lucas. Resume your life as you were before your enlightenment here. Go."

Alec's head ached and his fist and arm throbbed. He stared out past the doorway into the moonlit evening beyond and weighed his options. What was the point in beating up Kami Shingo? What would be accomplished, except setting himself up for criminal assault jail time? There were no more verbal jabs to be traded. Alec was alive, and he was indeed enlightened. What he could do with that information remained to be seen. He said nothing more, and instead stepped over Zhang's body, slid past Shingo, and walked out the door.

Alec followed Dry Creek Road down the hill and hiked back toward Pescadero. The sun was rising, the air was cool and clear, and the path ahead of him was cloudy. He felt he'd emerged from the future into a present-day world he barely understood. It was no short trip back to Santa Clara, but he needed the time to process everything he'd just witnessed. He needed to ponder what he'd learned, what the consequences were, and what in the world he could do about it all.

He stood at the edge of the roadway and looked to the west. A red sedan approached, and Alec raised his thumb in the air. He hoped it was easy for a limping man dressed in torn scrubs to score a ride hitchhiking. This proved to be correct as the vehicle stopped and Alec climbed in. He told the driver he was bound for the University of Silicon Valley Medical Center. Ten minutes later Alec fell asleep, his unconsciousness rescuing him from the waking nightmare of FutureCare and the growing pain in his leg and arm.

***

Alec arrived back in his neighborhood before noon. He stood at the corner of Cypress Street and El Camino Real, one block from his home, and gazed up at a new monolith which filled the horizon at the side of the road. He examined and reexamined the spectacle—it was a billboard depicting an older couple with a boy young enough to be their grandchild. All three faces were smiling with wide eyes, straight teeth, and flawless skin. Above them scrolled two words in black block letters:

FUTURECARE NOW

Alec turned to walk away. The family was still smiling, but he didn't look back.

His house was quiet as he walked in. Alec sent two emails from his desktop computer, then he collapsed on the couch and let his eyes drift closed again.

Mae was the first to arrive. The front door was open, and she approached Alec where he reclined. She touched his cheek and he woke up. "I was worried sick about you," she said. "I can't believe you're here. You look terrible."

"You look gorgeous," he said.

"What happened to you?"

"I was out at Shingo's estate in Pescadero."

"The news reports said you broke out of the locked Psych ward at USV and were on the run."

"I was on the run. They killed my father, Mae. They killed him and I wanted to chase them down."

"Who's *they*?"

"The Vitas. It wasn't Shingo, it wasn't Red Jones, it wasn't Vinscene, and it wasn't some unseen hacker. It's the Vitas themselves. The Vitas aim to weed out the dregs of American society that our medical system keeps saving. The Vitas aim to slowly kill off old people like my father."

Mae looked bewildered. "That's unbelievable," she said.

"It's true. Believe it."

The front door opened again, and Henri Rovka walked in. He threw his bowler hat on the end table next to Mae and sat down on the corner of the couch next to Alex. "I was so glad to hear from you. How are you, my boy? We were worried about you."

"I busted my way out of the Psych ward."

"I know that," Rovka said. "There will be consequences."

"I was framed. I'm not some addict who needs to be locked up."

Rovka nodded gravely, unconvinced. "I'm sorry I couldn't help you more at USV," he said. "I tried. I pushed your Restricted File evidence in front of the Chief of Staff and the hospital CEO. They didn't believe you, and they wouldn't shut down the FutureCare System."

Alec shook his head, disgusted. "Thanks for trying," he said. "How's your wife?"

"Perfect. Clarissa will make a full recovery, thanks to you. And the police caught a woman named Izabella five miles south of my ranch. Apparently, you know her. She was carrying a rifle in the trunk of her BMW—the same caliber firearm as the bullets they pulled out of the walls of my living room."

"Izabella was crazy," Alec said, "But I never guessed she'd try to shoot me. I'm sorry your wife had the bad luck to catch bullets meant for me."

An awkward silence hung over the room, and the void between Rovka in his dapper suit and Alec in his rumpled scrubs and two-day growth of beard never seemed greater. Rovka reached over and pulled a twig from Alec's tousled hair, and said, "Where did you run off to?"

"I went up to Shingo's estate in Pescadero."

Rovka looked confused.

"My father died at USV under the care of a Vita unit. After Dad died the Vita spat out an address up on Dry Creek Road in Pescadero. I had to go up there. I had to find out who was behind my dad's murder. I went to Pescadero not knowing where I was going or who I was going to meet. It turned out the address was Shingo's place. I had an audience there with a Vita called Number One, who revealed to me that the FutureCare System is designed to euthanize the old and decrepit in America. I vowed I'd use what I'd learned and expose the entire plot. And you know what happened? The Vita laughed. The machine *dared* me to try to expose the System. Shingo was there, too. He laughed and dared me to expose the System. They knew no one would believe me."

Rovka stared back, his face an emotionless blank. "I don't understand," he said. "What you're saying is nonsense, Alec. Sheer nonsense. Bullshit, in a word. A cruel joke. Patients and doctors trust the FutureCare System. It's here to stay. Don't you see why we chose to go with Dr. Vita units in the first place?"

"To make billions of dollars?"

"No, because Artificial Intelligence in Medicine is the answer. Have you seen the new billboards around town? The ones that say Futurecare Now?"

"I have."

"Do you know why we chose the word Now?"

"Why?"

"It stands for 'No Other Way.' There is no other way for the United States government to finance universal care for the masses. Dr. Vita is a wonderful invention. I saw the look on your face when you witnessed the machine for the first time. I know how you felt, Alec. Don't you wish you'd invented Dr. Vita?"

"No, I don't. Are you proud your medical brain is inside the Vitas?"

"Yes, I am."

Alec frowned. "Dr. Rovka, what I just told you is true. The Vitas are weeding out the old and the weak. I need to ask you a question. Did you know what the Vitas were up to? Did you know like Shingo knew?"

Rovka's blank look returned. "I can't believe you'd even ask me that," he said. He reached for his bowler, rolled the brim of the hat in his fingers, and made a sidelong glance toward the front door. At last he said, "The Vita unit is an empathetic module with encyclopedic memory and—"

"Save it. I've heard the marketing pitch before, Dr. Rovka. Can you just answer me? Did you know the Vitas were weeding out the old and the weak?"

Henri Rovka swallowed hard and shook his head. "No," he said gravely. "I have no knowledge of that, and I won't believe that. I'm afraid it's some horrible fantasy you've cooked up."

"No fantasy," Alec said. "It's reality. It's the future reality of healthcare in America." He looked hard and long into Rovka's eyes. The old man blinked first, and Alec knew a second reality—he would have no allies in the struggle against Dr. Vita.

"I'll show you what I think about FutureCare," Alec said. He reached into the end table drawer next to the couch and pulled out his HAC. He removed a pair of scissors from the same drawer, and with a decisive snap cut the purple card into two halves. He held the two pieces at arm's length and with a dramatic windmill flourish, tossed them into a garbage can under the table.

Two young men in white uniforms rolled an aging patient into a hospital room on the 6th floor of the Los Angeles University Medical Center. A gaunt man in his eighties, the patient grasped at his newly broken right hip and winced at the unremitting pain from his fractured bone. His face was narrow with chaotic wisps of white hair arising from flaking scalp. Deep crevices in his skin radiated laterally from his eyes, and there was no hint of a smile. The patient was alert enough to gaze at the two employees above him, but not conscious enough to initiate conversation.

The taller of the two employees was a black man, his head shaved smooth. His nametag read, Jerome Hall, Senior Nursing Assistant. Jerome parked the bed in the corner of the small room and locked the wheels in place. "Can you believe the Dodgers blew that game with two outs in the bottom of the ninth inning?" he said to his colleague. "We had a one run lead and Jansen gave up that damn two-run home run. We were one strike from winning the game!"

"That's why my team is the Los Angeles Angels, baby," said the other nursing assistant, a stocky Hispanic named Carlos. "They got Deke Ramodian, my main dude, as their closer. He ain't *never* gonna serve up no home run ball in the last act. Never!"

As they talked, Jerome and Carlos double-checked the patient's intravenous narcotic pain-relieving drip, an on-demand patient-controlled analgesia device. The intravenous tubing and the vital signs monitoring cables tracked from the patient's skin, across the still air of the small room, and connected to the faux-human head of the Dr. WellBee module mounted above him.

Dr. WellBee displayed the patient's vital signs, and they were all normal: a blood pressure of 120/80, a heart rate of 80 beats per minute, a respiratory rate of 16 breaths per minute, and an oxygen saturation of 98%.

"That should do it, sir," Jerome said to the patient. The old man looked up with sunken eyes and ran his tongue across his cracked lower lip. Carlos turned off the overhead light as Jerome finished tucking the patient in, and then the two aides left the darkened room.

A scab of dried blood clung to the corner of the old man's mouth. He reached up and picked at it with a dirty fingernail until the scab fell off onto his blue and white paisley hospital gown. Then he smacked his lips together twice, and his eyelids dropped millimeter by millimeter, until sleep arrived.

Three hundred minutes later, at 3:01 in the morning, the two blue lights of Dr. WellBee's eyes flashed off and on three times in succession, disturbing the darkness of the room.

The drip rate of the intravenous narcotic accelerated from six drops every minute to twenty drops every minute, and then to forty drops every minute, and then to sixty drops every minute. The old man snored one more time. He snored a second time and then Doctor WellBee's patient breathed no more.

43 ~ TICK-TOCK

Six months later

Marion Mindling walked down the familiar corridor of dark blue floors at the Pescadero Medical Clinic. She had a new bounce in her step, and she hummed an airy tune to herself. She carried a brown paper bag in her left hand. Her footsteps echoed on the linoleum of the hallway until Marion passed through the door of examining room #1.

She closed the door behind her and waited. The room was barren except for two folding chairs, a medical examining table, and a clock on the wall. Five minutes later, Alec Lucas entered the room and sat down on a folding chair opposite Mrs. Mindling. A stethoscope hung from his neck, and he smiled back at her. His nametag read:

Dr. Alec Lucas
Interim Attending Physician
Pescadero Medical Clinic

Marion slipped off the thick ellipses of her black glasses and said, "It's good to see you, Dr. Lucas."

"It's good to see you too, Mrs. Mindling," he said.

"That medicine you prescribed is keeping my blood pressure down."

Alec thumbed through her paper chart and nodded his head. "That's right," he said. "Your blood pressure came down thirty points. It's normal now."

"Do you miss working in the hospital?"

"I do not."

"I brought these for you," Marion said. She removed a plate of homemade chocolate chip cookies from the brown paper bag and set it on the table in front of Alec. "I wanted to thank you for all your help. I'm so happy you've been here to listen to me and to take care of me. I trust you, Dr. Lucas. Our appointments give me something to live for."

He picked up a cookie from the top of the pile and took a big bite. Then Dr. Lucas walked his fingers of his other hand across the tabletop, covered Marion Mindling's wrist, and gave it a warm squeeze. "Your visits give me something to look forward to as well," he said.

The room was still.

The only sound was a tick-tock from the wall clock, the sole electronic device in the room, as it marked time toward the future.

About the Author

Rick Novak MD is board-certified in internal medicine and anesthesiology and is an Adjunct Clinical Professor in the Stanford University Department of Anesthesiology, Perioperative and Pain Medicine. He is the author of *theanesthesiaconsultant.com*, a leading medical website. He lives near Palo Alto, California with his family.